NEW YORK REVIEW BOOKS
CLASSICS

CW01263940

TIME OF SILENCE

LUIS MARTÍN-SANTOS (1924–1964) was an innovative anti-realist writer as well as an eminent neuropsychiatrist and anti-Franco militant. After graduating with a degree in medicine from Salamanca University, he moved to Madrid in 1947, where he specialized in psychiatry and became involved in the city's literary culture. In 1952 he was appointed the director of San Sebastián's psychiatric hospital, and a year later he was awarded a doctorate for his thesis, "Dilthey, Jaspers, and the Understanding of the Mentally Ill." He joined the clandestine PSOE (Spanish Socialist Workers' Party) in 1957, becoming a member of its executive committee in 1958, an affiliation that led to his imprisonment in 1958, 1959, and 1962. *Time of Silence* was published in a heavily censored form in 1962 and was an immediate success. At the time of his death following a car accident in January 1964, Martín-Santos left behind a large body of unpublished stories, plays, and novels, including the unfinished sequel to *Time of Silence*, *Time of Destruction* (published posthumously in 1977). His short-story collaboration with Juan Benet, *El amanecer podrido* (The Putrefied Dawn), was published in 2020, and in 2024 the Spanish publisher Galaxia Gutenberg embarked on the publication of his Complete Works.

PETER BUSH has translated, among other books, Josep Pla's *The Gray Notebook*, which was awarded the 2014 Ramon Llull Prize for Literary Translation; Ramón del Valle-Inclán's *Tyrant Banderas*; and Joan Sales's linked novels, *Uncertain Glory* and *Winds of the Night* (all available as NYRB Classics). He lives in Bristol, England.

TIME OF SILENCE

LUIS MARTÍN-SANTOS

Translated from the Spanish by

PETER BUSH

NEW YORK REVIEW BOOKS

nyrb

New York

THIS IS A NEW YORK REVIEW BOOK
PUBLISHED BY THE NEW YORK REVIEW OF BOOKS
207 East 32nd Street, New York, NY 10016
www.nyrb.com

Published in the Spanish language as *Tiempo de silencio.*
This translation published by arrangement with Galaxia Gutenberg, S.L., Barcelona
First published as a New York Review Books Classic in 2025

This publication is supported in part by a grant from Acción Cultural Española (AC/E), a state agency.

A catalog record for this book is available from the Library of Congress.

ISBN 979-8-89623-003-8
Available as an electronic book; ISBN 979-8-89623-004-5

The authorized representative in the EU for product safety and compliance is eucomply OÜ, Pärnu mnt 139b-14, 11317 Tallinn, Estonia, hello@eucompliancepartner.com, +33 757690241.

Printed in the United States of America on acid-free paper.
10 9 8 7 6 5 4 3 2 1

I HEARD the telephone ring. I picked it up. I didn't catch what was being said. I put the receiver down. I said: "Amador." He walked over his thick lips and grabbed the phone. I was looking through the microscope and the preparation didn't seem to have worked. I took another look: "It's clearly cancerous." But with the mitosis, the blue stain was fading. "You know, Amador, these bulbs can fuse too." But no, he'd trampled on the cable. "Plug it in!" He's on the phone. Amador so fat and smiley. He speaks slowly and looks my way. "We're out. We're out of them." No more mice! The bearded man in the photo opposite me, who'd seen it all and freed the Iberian people from its inferiority complex in matters scientific, sharp eyed and motionless, presiding over a dearth of guinea pigs. His smile, so understanding, casting that complex aside—understands—the lack of cash. A miserably poor people. Who could ever again aspire to the Nordic award, to the tall king's smile, to enthronement, to the sage's passage across the arid peninsula hoping brains and rivers will bear fruit? Abnormal mitoses, clotted on the slide, immobile—when they are movement itself—Amador, immobile at first, putting the phone down, smiling, looking at me, saying: "That's the end of that!" But with his afternoon-snack smile, his broad smile. "Your lips are so blubbery, Amador." The MNA strain that was so promising. The phone rings again. I ignore it. "Why are you laughing, Amador? What are you laughing at?" Yes, I know, no more mice. Never ever, despite the man in the photo[1] and the rivers disappearing into the sea.[2] We might construct dams to stop the flow of water. But what about the free-ranging mind? The source of invention. The explorer of living reality with a sharp nose and slim scalpel who penetrates all that stirs and discovers something never before witnessed by non-Iberian eyes. As if it were a bullfight. As if there were no difference between a guinea pig and a bull, as if we could continue despite our desperate plight, despite the lack of cash. That cancerous strain bought with funds granted by the mint. Transported from its native Illinois. Now no more. Amador is smiling because someone's talking to him on the phone. How can we ever progress, if as well as being so dim-witted, we have peninsular man's gaunt features, and a brain mass diminished by a monotonous diet of vetch, beans, chickpea pulses, poor in protein. Only bacon, bacon and hash, for men like Amador, who laugh although they are sad, knowing that the last mouse of the MNA strain is gone, telling us that no researcher will ever be presented the chalice by the tall king, the laurel, the flaming torch to run with and brandish before the concert of nations and proclaim the unsuspected grandeur this people earns in the battle against that languid mitosis that grows and destroys, here as much as in its native Illinois, the glowing flesh of not-quite-menopausal women, whose periodically flowing blood is no longer life but deception, and more deception. *Betrogene.*[3] Death defeated. "Wait, pick up the black receiver, tell the minister responsible, tell him, dear Amador, that our research is surely worth a little mouse." Stop laughing and, above all, stop dribbling out of the corner of your mouth, it makes people question your background and intellect. "We ate rats during the war. I find them tastier than cats. I'm up to here with cats. We've caught so many cats. The three of us, Lucio, Snarler, and yours truly." Protein for a famished people, whose mitoses (normal in their case, but deficient), at the moment when motoneurons migrate towards the cortex, falter and perish because of that lack of early substance, perhaps their number is reduced, perhaps they're poorly situated and sourced, perhaps they're short of the necessary connections. And that's why we're unable to discover the causes of destructive neoplasia. Amador looks at me. He sees my absurd face. It makes him laugh. In the binocular, not electron, microscope, because there's no cash I tot up the monstrous nuclei, and now wearing his gray-brown beret and white coat, Amador goes into the back room, where three skinny dogs are howling, dogs that only pee once in a while and stink so terribly. Eager to finish off the dogs as he finished off the strain, Amador is hanging on an order I don't give, I simply look and listen, waiting to hear whatever he'll come up with to save my skin. "Snarler's got some," says Amador. Wrong. All mice aren't carcinogenic. All mice aren't from the native Illinois strain, skillfully selected from sixteen thousand strains in luminous laboratories with shiny glass walls, and air-conditioning specially installed for a better quality of mousey life. Skillfully selected from families of autopsied mice where they discover the tiny tumor in the groin containing the mysteriously self-generating death that doesn't destroy only mice but also blonds from the Midwest brimming with protein from when their mothers of Swedish or Saxon origins gestated them and from their subsequent lactation and schooling. Although beautiful, languid maybe, but never oligophrenic, with the correct migration of neuroblasts to an orderly arrangement of flesh and complex lipids around the electronic brain they now use to tot up mitoses in those transparent palaces. Here that isolated strain is now extinguished by a lack of vitamins, after the pitiful funds from the mint ran out. Mice transported from their native Illinois—male and female—with a separation of the sexes to avoid endless, anarchic copulations. A properly regulated generation of pregnancies. In purpose-built crates, by air, and at considerable cost in foreign currency. And now they are no more, they kept dying quicker than they reproduced—quicker than they reproduced!—and Amador laughs and says: "Snarler's got some." Snarler visited us in this place stinking of howling dogs that don't piss. As they don't piss, a prey to their violent emotional burden, the dogs eliminate their essences via their sweat. As they sweat only through the soles of their feet, the dogs also eliminate their smell through their breath, tongues hanging out to help it on its way. When the dogs are operated on and given polyvinyl or polystyrene femurs, they suffer so much we are grateful that no wilting, noncancerous, sex-deprived Anglo-Saxon virgins are around to pass on their spiteful rancor to the Animal Protection Society. Otherwise there'd never be any research here since the most basic elements are unavailable. And the likelihood of repeating the gauche gesture of the bearded man before the tall king would be completely nonexistent—as now—as well as ludicrously absurd, at once unanticipated and grotesque. And no longer as giants instead of windmills, but as phantoms instead of desires. Because who cares about dogs? Who could care less about a dog's pain, when its mother couldn't give a fig? It's very true that nothing will come from this research into polyvinyl, since specialists in gleaming laboratories in all civilized countries throughout the world have already proved that a dog's vital tissues won't tolerate polyvinyl. But who knows what a dog from this neck of the woods can tolerate, a dog that doesn't piss, a dog Amador stuffs with dry bread dunked in water? There's no comparison, and that's why Snarler may have remnants of the strain. Reproductions only Amador knows about may have come to pass, weird crossbreeding with female mice or females of similar or almost identical species. This may give rise to the inception of another, yet more important discovery, as a result of which the Swedish king may bend over us, speaking in Latin or macaronic English with an accent quite different from a Midwestern blond's and give to Amador—to our very own Amador, sporting striped pajamas since he can't stretch to a tuxedo—the unique, most coveted of prizes. Snarler will be there with his new strain conceived after profound cogitation, after calculating coefficients, performing crossovers, and establishing gene maps. After implanting chromomeres in salivary glands and reimplanting them in the ever so crucial glands through which life is transmitted. Amador knows that Snarler possesses the MNA strain. The import from Illinois can't have been completely lost. After being transported in a four-engine or perhaps a twin-engine jet, specially insured, a premium paid, and examined and granted a certificate by the US border veterinary service, it was then carried by Snarler in an empty egg carton to his very own hovel, where his two daughters—one sixteen, the other eighteen, neither a blond, neither gestated with an adequate diet in their mother's Toledan womb—are also breeding strains. As a result of which there is a distinct possibility that the cancer may reside not in the inner groin but in the armpit. That it's not ectodermal but mesodermal in origin. And that it may not only be fatal to male and female mice, but was randomly transmitted in the course of a negligent breeding process to the two non-blond girls from Toledo, who, what with inexpert medical care and lack of an opportune operation because of an erroneous diagnosis, may perish, leading to an autopsy authorized by their alarmed father—his face stricken with terror at his own possible infection—which may lead to the discovery in their swollen armpits and groins, pregnant despite their virgin state, of large tumorous growths, secreting toxins that paralyze their ailing brains and inside which—miraculously!—despite the seemingly hereditary nature of the Illinois strain, is a virus that is recognizable even through the ineffectual binocular microscopes we enjoy thanks to that old bearded gentleman, a virus from which we obtained, by cultivating it repeatedly within the ovary of an undernourished girl from Toledo whose mother was protein deficient when she was carrying her, a vaccine that can be successfully applied to the human species. "Your Majesty, honorable members of the Academy, ladies and gentlemen: the beginning of our experiments, as in the case of that erudite Englishman whose eye was caught by bactericide fungi, was a chance thing..." Amador says the stolen strain is indeed the good one from Illinois and Snarler took samples of both sexes with the exclusive intention of maintaining genetic purity and thus selling these specimens back to the laboratory when its own supply died off, for—without any statistical data—he'd noticed that their death rate was higher than their birth rate. "But can't you understand he's a thief, that we can't buy back from a thief what he stole from us and that it's quite out of the question for the Institution to agree to buy back at an exorbitant price what was stolen from it or what descends from stolen goods (and, by the way, what guarantees do we have?), given that we live in a state of law where such things exist as police, judges, and the ability of the free citizen to inform?" "There's no proof," says Amador. "There's no proof that they are stolen." Yes, there is. The microscope's identification of the spontaneous appearance of tumors in the groin. This strain alone among all those existing on the peninsula possesses that miraculous, lethal property. It alone serves the aims of the research. It alone spontaneously generated the phenomenon that drives human families to despair and individuals to suffer physical pain and the progressive cannibalizing of their own living flesh till death do us part. Amador hasn't a clue how the genetic process—used in this way—has been able to achieve a result totally opposed to what the early pioneers of this science would have desired (the creation of perfect humanity, the eradication of all inherited diseases), in other words the creation of a race of mice in which the execrable is a given, the execrable presence that preoccupies humanity after average-sized microorganisms have become extinct. But he feels quite overawed by the wonderful resources through which science has been established and as a result of which—an unexpected but important side product—researchers can marry and live in apartments built by the state and even he, Amador, can survive on miserable handouts from these researchers to supplement the pittance that is his wage. "Basically it's a good thing. If not, we'd have to stop. His daughters look after them. If not, they'd be dead by now and not breeding as they do, one litter after another. The hovel's crawling with them." But how come they don't die on them? What powers do these undernourished girls from Toledo wield to enable the mice to survive and breed? What makes them die here in the laboratory? Although it doesn't gleam and isn't air-conditioned, it surely has conditions more like those of its counterpart in Illinois, more suitable than Snarler's hovel. Maybe the constant howling—quasi-human howls because surgery is so humane—of the dogs with polyvinyl femurs irritated the nervous system of the MNAs and accelerated their premature death (premature even for carcinogenic mice) or at least their distinct lack of interest in procreation, thus they forget that precious combination for the total eradication of cancer: their constant spawning and spreading of cancer. Or rather, maybe Snarler's daughters possess such a passion to bond, such mammary insights, such an ability to reproduce that the fluids they create suffice to reignite the desire to reproduce and the ceaseless flow of flawed offspring. I look through the microscope and feel hate. The blue light lights up the preparation again and the motionless mitoses, coagulated by formol, still appear to be voracious. "Don't leave, Amador, I've not finished yet." "If you say so." "You're duty bound to stay with me or with any other researcher until we leave, until the research is finished." "If you say so." "Don't tell me you believe in this legal-working-day nonsense?" "No, sir." "Do I perhaps work a legal working day?" "No, sir." "I'm still looking for the mitoses." "You don't say." "Until I drop. Listen," I say. "Go on," he says. "Why don't you tell Snarler to bring his mice here and I'll see if they belong to our strain, and perhaps I will buy them from him or perhaps I will accuse him of thieving." "They're the real deal." "Tell him to come, right away." "He won't." "Why not?" "Because of the potential accusation of theft; the deputy-director fired him before. It's not the first time. It was cats last time. When they put little wires in their heads and they forgot them and he went and sold them back, and students went to insert their little wires and found the rusty old ones. I know mitoses make it worse, because they die on you whatever you do. But cats resist like wild animals, although they do get a little stressed. They bit Snarler and almost gouged his daughter's eye out. But they resist." "All right, tell him to come." "He won't. Half-Cock thinks he went to the Americas. If he sees him again, he'll destroy him. He's never been back since he said he was emigrating." "So how did he get my mice?" "*I* gave him a pair. Of course I did. If not, how would he ever have known they were the real deal?" "You don't say." "Besides, at the time, we had loads. They were dying like rats by the day. It's when the dogs with the shot of polyvinyl were so perky." "Don Óscar will give you a tip, I suppose." "Naturally." "Hey," I say. "Out with it," he says. "Tomorrow we'll drop by his hovel." "He'll love that!"

There are cities that are so out on a limb, so lacking in historical substance, so harried by arbitrary governors, constructed on a whim in deserts, so sparsely populated by a perceptibly unbroken line of families, so far from a sea or a river, so flamboyant in the way they distribute their wretched poverty, so favored by a splendid sky that almost makes one forget all their defects, so naively self-satisfied like fifteen-year-old girls, so globally resourced to enhance the prestige of a dynasty, so endowed with treasures—conversely—that those not created in their day can be forgotten, so coldly conceived but so desirous of enduring into the future, so lacking in true nobility, so packed with preening braggarts, so heroic at times, though nobody knows quite why, unless it's in an elemental, physical way like the young peasant crossing a river in a single leap,[4] so intoxicated with themselves though the liquor they're drunk on isn't at all intoxicating, so unexpectedly dominant in other eras over foreign capitals boasting two cathedrals, various collegiate churches, and haunted castles—a haunted castle at least for every century—so incapable of speaking their own language with the correct, flat intonation it's given by towns 125 miles to its north, so surprised by the arrival of gold that could be converted into stone but is perhaps transformed into carriages and teams of horses with gold-on-black livery, so lacking in a genuine Jewish quarter, so full of men who are solemn when important and affable when unimportant, their backs so turned on everything natural—at least until elsewhere they invented the electric train and ski lift—so rent by ecclesiastical courts delivering their victims to the secular arm, so seldom visited by genuine members of the Nordic race, so overrun by obtuse theologians and so short on first-rate mystics, so full of composers of popular ditties and authors of drawing-room dramas, romantic dramas, cloak-and-dagger dramas, barroom dramas, point-of-honor dramas, kidnapped beauties dramas, cheap and sleazy dramas, French salon dramas, but commedia dell'arte they are not, so crisscrossed by double-decker omnibuses pouring out smoke, the blacker the better, over pavements where people wear gabardines on cold, sunny days, and that don't have a cathedral.

In the presence of these cities, one must suspend judgment until one day, until suddenly—or perhaps gradually, though it beggars belief—it assumes a shape we intuit is present but can't see, until that substance now dragging itself along the ground takes on a solid form, until those who now laugh learn sadly to stare their miserable fate in the face and abandon the grandiose round or elliptical reinforced concrete buildings and retire to the privacy of their own homes.

Until that day comes, still suspending judgment, we will merely visit gloomy taverns where the glass eyes of a stuffed bull peer out over rows of bottles, and walk late into the night down the Calle del Nuncio or the Calle de la Bola where we stumble upon the savaged roots of what might have been a completely different city, we watch simpleminded soldiers stroll around a big square on Sundays while birds commit suicide one by one in the huge empty belly of a horse,[5] we pursue in the night the hurried steps of a small, nervous woman apparently intent on going somewhere, we embrace drunkards who've resigned from reality, we contemplate the gallant attitude of a policeman when a woman walks by who is taller than he is, we ask a taxi driver with yellow feline eyes how it's possible to defraud a fabric emporium, we go to a dance hall until the giant green-uniformed bouncer recognizes us and with a friendly grin lets us in without a ticket, we spend the whole afternoon in a café without the waitress giving us a single smile, we pretend to drink and drink very little, we pretend to talk and say nothing, we pretend to go to the movies but go to the room in the boardinghouse with a red eiderdown, we visit the art museum with an English girl and realize we don't know where to find any of the paintings that she knows except for *Las Meninas*, we invent a new literary style and promote it over several evenings in a café until we become completely part of the scene, we begin friendships that won't accompany us to the grave and loves that won't see the night out, we drop in on a student hop where girls enter gratis, we calculate how many cigarette lighters a dwarf sells on a street corner, we find out how many metro tickets a woman sells in a metro entrance as she suckles a child on a winter's morning, we guess what economic law enables matchstick sellers to sell cigarettes singly and with the proceeds have enough to feed their lovers, we wonder who had the lunatic brain wave of throwing blind folk on the streets even on days when huge snowflakes fall and on nights when only those going to premieres venture out, we try to imagine—for Christ's sake—how all these people survived in what they themselves call—and they'll know why—the hungry years.[6]

In this way we grasp how a man is the image of a city, and a city, a man's exposed entrails, how a man finds in his city his focus as an individual and his raison d'être, and the manifold hindrances and insuperable obstacles that prevent him from being himself, how a man and a city have connections that can't be explained by the people he loves, nor by the people the man causes to suffer, nor by the people he exploits who bustle around him placing bits of food in his mouth, stretching pieces of cloth over his body, putting leather artifacts on his feet, running professional caresses over his skin, mixing sophisticated drinks before his eyes behind a gleaming bar counter. We also grasp how the city thinks with its thousand-headed brain scattered in a thousand bodies though united by the same will to power thanks to which sellers of spliffs, crooks by convent back doors, chancers profiting from easy lays, owners of carousels not powered by electricity, apprentice toreros solemnly contracted for bullfights in towns in the surrounding desert, parking valets, club ball boys, and infinite shoeshines are encompassed by a radiant sphere that's not Le Corbusier but radiant in its own right, with no need for architectural backup, radiant because of the sun's brilliance and the luminescence from an order that's so harmoniously and graciously upheld that the annual percentage of common criminals is in constant decline according to the most reliable statistics, that this man is never lost because that's why the city exists (so he is never lost), so he can suffer or die but never be lost in this city, whose every corner is a practiced people finder, where this man can never be lost even though he wanted to be because a thousand, ten thousand, a hundred thousand pairs of eyes survey and classify him, recognize and embrace him, identify and save him, allow him to find himself when he thought he was totally lost in his natural milieu: in prison, in an orphanage, at the police station, in the lunatic asylum, in the intensive care unit, so that this individual—in this place—is a hick no more, you look like a hick no more, man, though anyone would think you *are* a hick and it would have been much better if you'd never left your village, because, man, a village hick is what you are.

Life can be hard, but sometimes village folk have such lovely firm flesh and walk or gesture or split their sides so well when nothing calls for laughter, or shudder sensuously, simply because it's sunny and the air is clean. That deceptive beauty of youth seeming to hide the existence of real problems, that appeal of childhood, that tumescence of nineteen-year-olds, that potential sparkle in people's eyes when they've been suffering fifteen or twenty years of poverty, shortages, and hard grind can be confusing and make it seem things aren't so bad when everything is really bad. There is beauty made of gracefulness rather than good looks, made of agile quick-footedness, where what may appear mere vivacity already verges on rapacity and a hypnotic stare can be mistaken for the eagerness of desire rather than any lack of satisfaction.

"My husband might have left me something more but left only his memory, which I find utterly delightful, his big mustache and dark eyes, his playful, bellicose stance that never allowed me a moment's peace, because being so ready for it he enjoyed flirting with a bit of skirt, although I prefer to think they drooled after him, since I can't imagine him chasing after a single one; truth is he always had his arms round one of them, especially when he was in uniform for he always liked to spend his pay on vaunting his beauty and charms. As well as my memory of his fine figure and my daughter—because I find she's so like him with his fine figure and almost his gallant manner, and unhappily even her dark fluff reminds me of his mustache—he left me his state pension, the one granted to those who fall on the field of battle, and a medal that, added to the 325 and a half pesetas, is still very little for two women living alone. There were also a few Chinese figurines he brought back from the Philippines campaign,[7] when he was so young and didn't win any medals because of pure envy. And thankfully he gave me my baby girl before he went off to those islands because on his return he was useless for inseminating, though not—thank God—for making love, only for making me pregnant again, because I'd like to have had three or four more, but being so manly and so lustful he met up with a Tagalog and was convinced she was young, pure, and clean, but the dirty bitch went and infected him and she went the whole hog, didn't wash or take any precautions, until he was fouled up and his ducts blocked and although he did what he could, and the frigate's naval doctor, a good friend of his, tried to cure him, like others who'd accompanied him and caught the pestilence because of their manly deeds with other Tagalog girls, there was nothing to be done, and I was left alone with my Carmencita who was twenty-eight when he was killed fighting the Moors, when *that* disaster came to pass.[8] Apart from the little figures and the unhappy condition he brought back from the Philippines, five fans and some silk shawls, one painted with birds of paradise, the second with exotic flowers, and the third with the large face of an indigenous woman, and it's very rare they have that third image, but that was precisely why he brought it back for me, because he was always drawn to what's rare and weird. I think he was always flat broke and there was no way you could put a brake on him, he was always in the casino, always drinking over the limit, always strutting his stuff, flaunting his good looks, and ability to outdo everyone in almost everything, at least with women from what I personally could gauge and it's quite likely that he exercised his talents more outside our home than inside, where I was legit always spellbound, mouth open and waiting for it. I never got over losing him, nor did my poor daughter, who could never enter society for lack of someone to introduce her, and at the time of her catastrophe, she was left on the shelf without a father or big brother to oblige her brute of a boyfriend to face his responsibilities although—truth be told—I was almost happy he walked out on her because he was impossible and would have made her unhappy and dragged her as low as you can go. I even imagined him pimping her, profiting from my daughter's sexy figure and the attractiveness she inherited from her father, which, in her, though rather manly—if not butch—simply had to be a powerful lure for all the men who saw her at the time; that was followed by the hard years of total debasement when anything went, even civil-only marriages and divorce, and then the hungry years, I'm convinced he'd have pimped my daughter and put her in bed with man after man, because she too—and how, with the temperament she'd inherited from her father—found it hard to stay quietly at home, and I understand him imagining there are men like my hubby who are so attractive to women that my poor love of a daughter can't resist them precisely because of the temperament gifted to her by her father and yours truly, who's not exactly made of stone either, thanks be to God. The truth is we have managed better, I do believe, on our own, with the occasional help, than if we'd had to cater to that parasite, the father of my granddaughter, and I can't figure out how she turned out so lovely being the daughter of that father, who wasn't at all one of those pleasant, strong, and full-on men but who behaved like a mollycoddled ragdoll of a man with the mannerisms of a torero or, at the very best, a Gypsy dancer, and as far I was concerned, I wasn't at all sure he wasn't a tad limp wristed, but perhaps my comparatively manly daughter let herself be seduced, perhaps because she was the opposite of her father, who scared the living daylights out of her as a child because she sometimes saw how he beat me, and saw that I, strong as I am, could only give in since he was one hell of a man who completely lorded it over me and had what he willed of me. So my daughter preferred a half man she could keep a tight grip on or turn inside out when she'd decided that was what was needed, and even so he saw off her maidenhead—rather soiled by that stage—and brought into the world my beautiful granddaughter, nineteen years old by now, who makes me swoon whenever I see her, because I've always been so partial to beauty and can't resist her, especially since she's my blood, and she's a knockout. Because one has to admit the father's effeminate ways suit the girl well. She's turned out more polished than my own daughter, so made in the image of my husband, with her dark fluff and brawny arms, hot tempered, attractive but so ungainly when compared to my granddaughter, with her delicate, gentle charms, willowy waist, and titivating totter. Apart from the 325 pesetas and 50 centimos, and my daughter and my granddaughter's potential, the Philippine junk, shawls, and four mahogany dining room chairs, the big wardrobe with a mirror, and the late Empire–style double bed, my hubby left me nothing, so we had no choice but to set up a boardinghouse, taking advantage of a large empty apartment on a low rent, well located in a side street off the Calle del Progreso, which, although near houses of ill repute, wasn't shabby enough to be mistaken for one, and, on the contrary, I was able to encourage some real gentlemen to come and reside there. I had no money to buy furniture and cover costs, so I had to go out and call on all my husband's comrades, those who hadn't fallen in the tragedy, because plenty of poor souls did, but they'd found a way to avoid going, and they were the ones who could help me most since they soon put themselves in my dead hubby's shoes and imagined seeing their own wives in black and my mournful mien on their faces; although I couldn't tell if it would have made such a great impression because I don't know many marriages so together as mine. *He* was a real man, he was always ready for whatever was coming; he held me in high esteem and knew a legit wife will always do what the thousand filthy bitches won't do, even if he couldn't keep his hands off them when he was hundreds of miles away on those islands. But, in the end, I had to remove my veil to persuade them, although only a few had money, for most got by on a weekly pittance, and I showed my noble, tear-filled face, I'd painted my eyes with a little bluish liner and used a lot of face powder so I looked extra white and pallid since, unfortunately, I've always had a good color, and my husband always thought that was a good thing and spoke to my temperament, though it doesn't mean that many other men, in thrall to the whims of fashion, didn't prefer anemic, chlorotic types who drank vinegar and, even if they didn't, could be pale faced because their blood's so thin. I took my daughter on these visits, in a little girl's short skirt that revealed her thighs, although she was rather old by this point; those gents looked at her rather embarrassed, not because they desired her, their desires dampened by the grief of the moment and the demise of their excellent colleague, but because they understood she *was* desirable and that, if I ever fell into dire poverty, she might be fodder for lechers, and so they felt more compassionate, and besides the shekels on behalf of their good friend which helped establish the boardinghouse, some promised to be actual clients when they were posted to the capital, which they often were, so that initially we never lacked lodgers, for it is *very* hard when you're starting off. Naturally, many of them paid very little, what they could spare or borrow, something like half of half a week's wage, ridiculous amounts for a residence I wanted to give a touch of luxury, so that the clientele might be in step with the social standing I then enjoyed as a war hero's widow, although that standing gradually faded and was sunk forever by my daughter's misfortune, so our boardinghouse also went down in the world, at the same time as the furniture and drapes, lace curtains and carpets, and various embellishments I'd initially bought now looked past it. And as our clientele went downhill, the presence of the torero-dancer-sweetie I mentioned frightened off the two married couples who worked for the Ministry of the Interior and who had been, till then, the principal cornerstones of my respectability. They were two childless couples and I'd shown the wives the photos in my husband's souvenir album, always skipping the pages with the Tagalog girls he'd also gifted me because he was a joker and said that would show me which side his volcanic passions tilted and how their breasts were as drooping and pointed as he'd said they were. But my strength of character weakened, I was rather too upbeat at the success my boardinghouse had enjoyed at its outset and at the ease with which, as a proud hero's widow, I'd been able to persuade those gentlemen to send the money needed to fill some of the holes created by my mismanagement. That was when I went overboard and hit the Rhum Negrita, and as my immoderate imbibing of such liquors increased, I dropped my guard and the wanton boyfriend popped by more often, believing that not only were my daughter's white thighs hidden in my house but a good haul of doubloons from overseas were too. Obviously he was wrong about that, but he almost started to beguile me on those ill-fated days, when every single afternoon I was so happily drunk on the liquor that brought consolation for the tragic, definitive collapse of my womanhood; my periods were petering out and I took that very badly—a morale-shattering blow—and sought deluded bliss in liquor and even took a shine to that young fellow who knew how to manipulate me, charming me with his feminine wiles and bringing me a bottle knowing full well that, because of my weakened character and the hard times I was going through, his meals would be catered for (at the time I didn't want to think his bedsheets were as well), but I found it alarming how my desire was replicated in my luscious, vivacious, beloved daughter, because she was almost a mirror image of myself: I saw my dying beauty live on in her. We no longer wore black as in the days when we went in search of money to refurbish the apartment and I'd had to dress my lovely girl as an adult, she who still didn't have as much as a hair on her lip (as she has now), and to lend an air of respectability to her nighttime excursions, I willingly accompanied that invert to various places where I wouldn't have allowed him to go alone with my daughter. They were taverns of ill repute, with private rooms, where it was such fun to get tipsy and glimpse the life men lead, the life my husband had no doubt led. That's how I discovered the delights of nights on the binge, ostensibly chaperoning my daughter, though my chaperoning did no good. Some of the friends whom the invert brought along and introduced me to when I'd succumbed to Rhum Negrita—although I wasn't totally plastered—dared to pinch me and say how white my flesh was, which sent a shiver down my spine like when my late hubby creeped stealthily in late at night, got into bed, and bit me on the shoulder, almost before I'd woken up, dreaming I was a tender Tagalog girl being eaten alive by a cannibal. One day I was stupid enough to show the wives of those civil servants the tits of the Tagalog girls and say: 'You can see they're not a patch on me and yet, although I'm better endowed, my deceased . . . ,' which shocked them so much that they decided to leave the boardinghouse after unleashing a righteous sermon, and they were even more shocked when muted moans were heard from my daughter's bedroom and she appeared in the doorway in her shift saying: 'Mama, I've had a terrible attack of nerves, I had a horrible dream,' although it was really nothing to shock anyone, merely the effect of wind or hysterical giddiness caused by the girl's unsatisfied femininity that I, like a fool, left unattended. The invert's friends were of a piece with him, semi-female too, and small, much smaller than me, and they spoke with an Andalusian accent and clapped their hands really well, which is what my girl and I most admired in them, since apart from that they had no culture or conversation, but what was most valued in that tavern world was the ability to clap, a skill that brings lots of fun to the party, and which my daughter soon picked up while I was a hopeless case. It was a pleasant time for me, against the odds, although I vaguely felt that my boardinghouse was going to the dogs, my daughter too, but thanks to those distractions I succeeded in forgetting the desire I felt for the ghost of my husband and even the tragedy of ceasing to be a woman, which always terrified and bewildered me, because how are you supposed to adapt to that new existence, or bear all the ills in life without proper relief or consolation? And I decided only Rhum Negrita could supply that, or some harder liquor I found that my stomach could cope with. Once I'd taken the change on board and stiffened my will, I knew you could put up with anything, and I don't drink now and am a rather boring old fusspot, which, though it's foul for me, may help my nineteen-year-old cutie pie, whom I'm not prepared to see do the same fool things I allowed my own daughter to do when I fell victim to the ups and downs of the change, bouts of stupefying madness, when you can't see things straight and really believe the moment that door shuts, everything's at an end and life isn't worth the candle. My poor daughter should have realized her mother wasn't well, but she had nothing else to hold on to, so the invert of a dancer, when he saw that the doubloons from overseas were a mirage, that the boardinghouse had emptied out and my daughter's belly was getting bigger by the day, cleared off, leaving us in the depths of despair. But I immediately decided that the best thing about his departure was that he hadn't pimped my daughter, which at the time the poor dear seemed resigned to. I told her straight what she owed her wretched mother who'd sacrificed so much for her and how it was better to devote her time to bringing up her beautiful baby girl, and I pointed out the delights of her home-cum-boardinghouse, which, although worse for wear because the tasteless, out-of-fashion trappings I'd purchased were looking shabby, still offered the essential items for the nourishment, repose, and care of honest citizens. Then another class of clientele began to knock on my door and, coming as they did after we'd painted the town red, my daughter and I strove to adapt to them; we now were both in the category of widows, so my daughter had to wear black again, which suited her down to the ground, and as an unofficial widow she began to notch up successes that were broadcast less widely, pursued more discreetly, and brought better economic rewards and also gave her the satisfaction of knowing she was contributing to the education and amusement of her jewel of a daughter who, as I said previously, outdoes us both with the female traits she inherited from her indulgent rake of a fruitcake father, and when we see how she possesses our presence and beauty, plus the added value of his effeminate attributes, our mouths water and we don't know which saint to turn to to ensure that this masterpiece begotten by our sinful ways doesn't depart the straight and narrow, but that the delightful blossoming bud she is now ripens successfully into the most delicious fruit she quite frankly deserves to be."

With such high hopes the two work colleagues set out to the legendary shantytown and Snarler's rabbit-breeding and mice-focused fields! Such close friends, researcher and youngster, ploughed through the Madrid hordes oblivious to the social difference in their respective backgrounds, indifferent to all gaps in culture that might hamper their conversation, unaware of the strange reactions provoked in those who noticed their different attires and airs! Because they were both united by a common goal and interest—although for different reasons—in the possible existence of genuine descendants of the select stock of mice, hereditary carriers of cancers developed spontaneously in the groin leading to the animals' inexorable death, though not before, on attaining the age of reproduction, they'd given birth to multiple little beasts equipped with features analogous to those of humankind—despite their different dimensions—endowed like us with livers, pancreases, suprarenal capsules and Winslow's ligaments, which could then be motive for serial scientific hypotheses and maybe for unexpected discoveries as to the causes of the supreme illness.

It was a beautiful morning, quite like so many mornings in Madrid when the sky's barefaced candor tries to blot out the outrageous scars on the earth. Streets just washed by municipal workers, gleaming granite brought from distant mountains and hewn into square slabs by armies of tireless stonemasons, then laid via an intricate technique with the help of water, sand, and an iron bar (later, when the trade went into decline, with a slosh of liquid cement between the cracks), and thronged by crowds of individuals plying various trades, everyone poorly dressed and most unshaven. Pedestrians clothed in nondescript hues from pale purple and yellowish brown to greenish gray, so dingy and lackluster in this city, dull outfits that can't simply be down to the poverty of these denizens—and the subsequent slow, scrimping renewal of their wardrobes—but must also relate to the purifying impact of the chemical makeup of air, particularly rich in ozone, and the physical nature of the unusually bright light persisting for so many hours it's beyond the pale for individuals who are not black. Indeed, citizens of standing should wear cotton made in Manchester, ruby red, turquoise blue, and daffodil yellow, long sleeved, with large gouache designs to highlight the buxom forms of local women and, in stark contrast, the waxen complexions of men. Don Pedro was thinking along these lines without communicating his reflections to Amador, who may very well have been unable to rise to the challenge of considering such chromatic-geographical laws but would simply have preferred to suggest they imbibe any of the suitably refreshing liquids on offer in any of the numerous bars invitingly opening their doors as they crossed that urban landscape.

However, such an idea still seemed off the scientist's radar and Amador decided to defer the suggestion until he saw an opportune moment, as when sweat stealthily streamed down the academic's forehead or breathless gasps replaced his as yet inaudible breathing.

The crowds—at odds with the proverbial idea of their lethargy and indolence—jostled and hurried beneath the wanton sky. They were going down Calle de Atocha, from the heights of Antón Martín, from beyond which Amador had gone to find his beloved researcher and boss and drag him from the welcoming chiaroscuro of his boardinghouse, a dismal den where he daily immersed himself with graveyard good cheer and arose every morning with all the pain of birthing. Amador nevertheless did see vague if unmistakable signs of the affectionate-visceral protection his researcher boss received in that house. A white hand, at the end of a white arm, cautiously maneuvered a brush over his shoulders. Full lips on affable faces muttered advice as to punctuality, the sun's pernicious impact on the shantytown, the suitability of certain tramlines, the various parasites nimbly hopping hosts. A musical voice, from afar, hummed a fashionable ditty the researcher seemed to hear with an uplifted smile, of which, for the moment at least—Amador deduced—the loftiest level of his mind was unaware.

"Did you bring the cage?" said Don Pedro, scrutinizing the bundle Amador was carrying under the previous day's newspaper in order to avoid spotlighting evidence of the existence of the progeny of the supposedly surviving mice they were going to requisition today, which his haste rather than his lack of care had prevented from being completely obliterated, as he—genuinely—believed he had fulfilled his duty, and added: "Come on!" while Amador answered belatedly: "Yes," without remarking on the pointlessness of his reply, since what other oblong object of that size and light weight could he have placed under his arm on that morning that was still on the hot side?

Women were also going up and down the slope, at the bottom of which was the small Glorieta with the usual hodgepodge of buses, trams, red-striped taxis, handcarts, peddlers, traffic police, beggars, and general public lingering with a hidden design that probably had nothing to do with the arrival of a train in the adjacent station, nor with their unlikely visit to the not very distant Museum of Art, nor with the eruption of armies of patients and nurses from the imposing pile of one of the neighboring hospitals. Don Pedro noticed none of these women and still seemed to be relishing his memory of the white arm and the lilting voice not belonging to the same individual, but both of the female sex, both recently bereft, and both were all for Amador. Confident as he was of his sex after proving himself consistent in a thousand battles fought on fields of feather from immemorial adolescent years (if that age can be described as adolescence for boys of his class), neither his garb, even more nondescript than that of most passersby at that workaday hour, nor the peculiar item he was carrying—even when its mysterious contents clearly upped his ante in terms of erotic fascination—nor his evidently subaltern status, nor even his servile deference towards his self-absorbed colleague, nor the scant appeal of his features after three days of hirsute increment prevented him from essaying knowing glances and approving comments at every desirable young woman walking past, some of whom, to judge by their appearance, occupied an economic, professional, and even amorous class superior to his own. Don Pedro took no notice of his assistant's peripatetic activities and, having finally given up on his unconscious relishing of the unknown treasures he'd left behind in his dismal den, he began to anticipate the pleasure of the moment when he met the coveted objects of his experiments, imagining the possible consequences of the degeneration the MNA strain must have suffered, caused as much by the almost inevitable random crossbreeding (rather than a strictly eugenic incestuous one) as by an environment far too removed from their original source in Illinois and the almost unimaginably haphazard diet with which Snarler managed to keep the wonderful little beasties alive—if, that is, he actually had. The composition of this diet was the outcome of an exponential function at an unverified level and an indefinite set of variables among which one could indicate, albeit merely on a temporary basis: the cash earnings of Snarler and the various members of his family, the assumption (as probable or not) in the said Snarler's mind of a hypothetical livestock sale, the relative hunger at mealtimes of Snarler and his wife, the tender loving care (perhaps dependent on their earthy adorers' more or less viscous attentions) of their now menstruating offspring, the seasonal flora of the area inhabited by the family, and an essential component, the qualitative composition of the trash thrown into the nearby dumping ground (a mere two miles from their hovel) by the carts of a trash-collecting family cooperative that had agreed one day to let Snarler extract fodder from the heap. A degenerate breed of carcinogenic mice surviving miraculously thanks to the New Deal decreed by F. D. Snarler for an era of critical shortages—mice that lived on when their peers had failed to survive in the regulated context of the laboratory—had to be a very impressive breed indeed. Live matter is so adaptable! Always fresh surprises to illuminate those who know how to see! Oh how many different breeds of starling, now transformed into subspecies, may populate the fragmented forests of an archipelago! Oh the barely conceivable, barely imaginable, tenderly cherished possibility that one—one would be enough—of the pubescent girls from Toledo might have contracted, through cohabiting in the hovel, a cancer of the groin or armpit entirely unusual at her age, and never before seen in the human species, that would—finally!—be evidence of the potential viral transmission that assumed hereditary proportions only because the gametic cells (inoculated *ab ovo* before life, prior to reproduction, prior to the appearance of alarming swellings in the parents), endowed with unlimited latent immortality, took a leap across the abyss between generations and contained their full plasma—with their death-carrying elements—in that liminal origin, within the egg of the new being!

But, for the moment, the descent of the slope in Atocha was pleasant enough; only ugly men and attractive, though dirty, women were visible to the young sage, and no image of genuine mice came to irritate the sensitive gelatin of his eyes. They walked on and Amador cursed the direction of a promenade that reduced the likelihood of his pensive companion tiring and of their entering one of the taverns down below, which, by the packed, promiscuous Glorieta, spew out a frankly intoxicating aroma, representing for contemporary stomachs what the medieval philter did for love, of squid fried in olive oil reheated from the previous day, if not from three or five days previous. Thanks to the potency of the fry-up and the rich calories the boiling oil generates, the volatile esters from the squid's ongoing putrefaction are totally absorbed (being such thermolabile compounds), and the matter, thus transformed, can be ingested without danger and with evident relish.

As they walked down the boulevard they passed on both sides open doorways and ready-made merchandise on the shelves in shop windows selling a thousand different items. Everything you could ever want, from motley heaps of ladies' white, pink, purple underwear cheaply manufactured and pressed against the glass, the great scam of bargain offers, and even square-headed nails, plastic glasses, luridly colored plates, and gifts like a cheap gray china huntress, a brass Don Quixote next to a silvery Sancho Panza screwed onto a lump of black glass, a leather-lined pen pusher's inkpot with heat-molded designs, a glass paperweight with mother-of-pearl seashells, a photo frame made from slivers of glass with its very own Ava Gardner, and, to top the lot, a set of seven red saucepans ingeniously arranged from big to small. Other, more seemingly perilous, shops were pharmacies and drugstores where every insecticide (slowly turning yellow) known to man was on sale, as well as huge numbers of ointments and cough syrups from a thousand laboratories, some of which were set up in the back of the shops in contravention of every manufacturing regulation laid down by pharmaceutical science. Above some of these pharmacies, shrouding old wrought-iron balconies from long before foundries hiked their prices, were large white billboards splashed with letters big as slippers that read: PHIMOSIS, SYPHILIS, VENEREAL, INEXPENSIVE CONSULTANCY. At the sight of these flourishing examples of the industrial exploitation of science in whose development he was playing his part, Don Pedro didn't react squeamishly but was nobly of the opinion that this projection onto the lower echelons and ignorant masses of such sublime principles was in itself a desirable act. For how else could one cater to the ordinary men walking these streets, who obviously had no access to the vast caring bodies within the social security system, to be a beneficiary of which one had to demonstrate an official record of a specific work position, and whose burden of pride stopped them from visiting free consultancies for illnesses that aren't the product of narrow, impoverished lives but of an excess of energy, vitality, lust, and even, occasionally, of filthy lucre? No: fifteen-peseta consultancies were a good idea, and permanganate washes in the penicillin era were a good idea too, since at the end of the day, by prolonging the cure, they enhance the emotions aroused in manly chests by those endorsements of a newfound eroticism, painful crosses that, not without their touch of heroism, dignify the lowest, if not the most laudable, functions of human nature.

Quite oblivious to this current of humanistic-demonic thought and the hygiene needs in our intimate life, Amador continued his descent, one step behind his natural master, with the squarish bundle at his side, unappreciative of the wealth of commerce and well-being passing him by, his attention still riveted by the bars in the small square coming ever closer and by a possible—if unlikely—refreshing halt at one of them. He justified himself by considering that Don Pedro hadn't had to walk down that slope after climbing it, Don Pedro hadn't had to rise early to catch the metro from the distant Tetuán de las Victorias to the Institute for mucky research, Don Pedro hadn't had to foot it to the boardinghouse after collecting the cage. Although the researcher proved his instinctive democratic support for the people by personally making the effort to go to Snarler's hovel, he would have given even more striking proof by grasping the urgent need for a beverage felt by Amador, who had been scurrying on his behalf for the past few hours.

"Hey, are those the hovels?" asked Don Pedro, pointing to some whitewashed undersized buildings, with one or two black orifices, from one of which a hazy column of gray smoke rose up, the other being covered by burlap sacking gathered up at one side, at the entrance to which sat an old woman on a low chair.

"Them?" replied Amador. "No, they are *houses*."

They then continued walking in silence along a stretch of roadway where barely visible remnants of tar blotched the expanse of open fields, where the grass that had grown in spring has already withered.

Amador added: "When they left the village, I told him he'd never find a place to live. And he was already saddled with a wife and two daughters. But he was desperate. And ever since the war, when he was with me, he'd felt nostalgic about the place. I mean, he felt its pull. Madrid *is* moreish. Even for people not from here. I am, I was born in Madrid. In Tetuán de las Victorias. Before there was any football.[9] And he insisted on coming. Even though I'd warned him not to, that life is very hard, that if life in the village is difficult, here you also have to make a go of it, he was too old to start a trade, and they only want young guys. That, without a trade, he'd be scrabbling around his entire life, that he'd never find anything decent. I warned him time and again. But he'd got that bee in his bonnet because he was here in the war. And, you know, he crashed here. Everything fell on my shoulders. Because seeing as we might be cousins, or not, and your mother went into labor on the same day as mine, as your mother came to Madrid, mine was in service in a doctor's house and they'd both come; in short, I suddenly found the whole family on my back, as they say. Naturally. I don't stand on ceremony and I always tell it like it is, which is what I did. Because they suddenly set up in my kitchen with a mattress he'd brought from the village and they slept there, all cheek to cheek. The girls were like my fingers, their little legs so thin they made you wince. But I refused to go soft. I know life is hard, but I'd told him no way, you can't stay here. I don't know why he thought I was going to sublet to him. But how was I ever going to sublet to a friend, for that's a surefire way to fall out with friends and end up daggers drawn. Because of him, not me. I like him, but I know he's stubborn, a real ass. He's an animal. And always has a knife on him. And that's when I found him work in the laboratory to get him off my back, because he's a no-hoper and would never have found a job to pay his way."

"He got work in the laboratory?"

"No. But I arranged it so he got beasties, from wherever. I mean he was useless, he couldn't do a blind thing. He hadn't worked in the village either. He's a tough guy, but hands-off when it comes to work. If you can't work, at least you must have your wits about you to find some. But not him. I can't think how he didn't starve to death back there. Of course, he started to look alive. I think his wife's father had a tidy sum; all he did was squander it. And then he started, we've got to come, we've got to come, until came they did. His wife, a little martyr. As for his daughters, they've perked up a bit."

"So what did he do in the laboratory?"

"What I said. He got us beasties. The subjects of our experimentation, as the late Don Manolo used to say. He went to the pound and bought unclaimed dogs, before they were claimed. Or did a deal so the guy in the pound didn't return them to people without means and then make a few pesetas that way. You can always rely more on what the Institute pays and the tips some doctors give out. Don Manolo was never known to tip but he taught him a lot. And so he learned to hunt dogs himself so he could forget the pound. He raked it in on two fronts. Then there were the first-year scholarship holders, who want to finish their theses in two months, and who paid him top dollar for dogs when he pretended there were no more dogs left on this earth, and kept hold of them until prices soared, like shopkeepers do, while in his hovel the dogs ate all the bread, the little girls cried and that was so cute. Cats are harder, but he learned in the end. He's quick at that kind of thing. He was a poacher in the village, whenever he went out with a gun, and God knows where he got it, because he never had money to buy one. He loves catching a cat here, a dog there. He liked collecting snails in the Tagus Valley, where there are lots. Not like this blasted countryside that doesn't give us a single snail."

"So why didn't *you* see to getting dogs?"

"I did until he turned up. But if I hadn't found him something, they'd still be holed up in my kitchen with their mattress and belongings. Besides, I have a regular wage and why would I want more, no need to be greedy. Naturally I charge him."

"How so?"

"Well, so much per beastie. For each dog or cat he sells me, I get a slice, since I set him up. He wasn't going to get that scot-free. He's very grateful and pays up willingly, because I wouldn't think twice about getting rid of him and finding someone else. Though frankly I'm not really tempted, after all, we're family and he can be real moody and I don't like that knife he carries everywhere. No. I see eye to eye with him. Ever since we were together in the war. He went awry when he started doing what he shouldn't, you know, the dogs abandoned by those doing their theses, soon as they'd finished with them, in a flash when they get two or three results, they say they have thirty or forty findings and write what's expected of them, even stuff they've never seen, and they forget they've left wires in a cat's head or colored tubes in a dog's guts, and off they go to make their fortunes. The worst was that he forgot too, and when he sold a wired-up cat to a newcomer, his honeypot fell apart. He saw straightaway I'd have to lay all the blame on him. But Half-Cock insisted he be booted out of the Institute forever and that's a real pain because now I have to go and find the beasties myself and we have to switch their cages in the middle of the street, or in the Retiro, when nobody is around, which is a risky business, especially with cats you can never work out."

"Hey, where does he breed the mice? Do they all live on top of each other? Do his girls play with the mice?"

"His girls are at an age when they want to play with something else."

"But might they be infected?"

"How the hell do I know?"

"I'd like to know if they might have been infected."

"You'll see for yourself. The fact is the poor never get infected. They're immunized by the filth they live in."

Some nights, Pedro subjected himself to the after-dinner ritual of table talk. The three women in the household were so nice to him. It no longer felt like a boardinghouse. It had turned into a family that was both protective and oppressive. The wily old dowager had gradually gathered together a group of permanent, single, middle-aged long-term lodgers who withdrew to their rooms as soon as they'd eaten their desserts. There was a tall, sad fellow, a commercial rep for medicaments. A bald gentleman, an accountant or senior bank employee. Another, a retired military man. The widow always ensured she had at least one retired military man in her boardinghouse in memory of her late husband. The room for the retired military man was furnished with a degree of barrack-room austerity and over a white marble fireplace that was never lit was hung—as a form of decoration—two Malayan *krises* crossed over two pots the deceased had also bequeathed, out of one of which stuck the staff of a tiny Spanish flag made of pink and topaz crepe. Then there was a childless couple who said very little. Both wore black, both were little and pale, rather wrinkled, both pairs of white hands straightening the tablecloth and clearing the crumbs while they waited for their oranges. This couple lived in the worst room in the boardinghouse, an interior room with an iron column in its midst. The wife had made a sheath of dark material to cover the column's lower half. That way "it's not so cold," she explained timidly.

Pedro was obviously the favorite, the spoilt boy. His youth singled him out. The feminine trio was too sensitive to that objective fact—*young man*—for him to be, at any time during his stay, mistaken for any other species of human being.

The first generation was a solemn, stalwart, enterprising, almost boisterous old woman, if such an epithet can be applied to an aging legitimist monarchist. The first generation maintained a fine figure and despite her age she gave out the orders. She was a shrewd judge of men. She could also melt into a smile. She used brassieres that clearly silhouetted her bust and a corset that perfectly molded her waist. She held herself erect and, unlike her daughter, though so strong, she didn't have a trace of fluff on her upper lip.

The second generation was seriously overshadowed by her imposing mother and awareness of where she'd come from. Subdued or defeated, despite her equally imposing physique, she had the character of a cat, of a make-believe, affectionate animal. She'd spent her life playing the role of the spoilt child, the small child, the tricked child, one who does her mother's bidding. This role didn't spring directly from her manly nature or sturdily boned frame, but had been forced upon her by a more domineering mother. And she still resisted the effort needed to make readjustments she should have made long, long ago. She put on the charms of someone ten years younger, in clothes already ten years out of fashion.

The third generation was nothing like her elders, except in her language, catchphrases and vocabulary she had of necessity picked up from them in nineteen years under the same roof. The third generation had innately everything her mother had pretended to deploy throughout her life. Life in such a feminine atmosphere (despite her elders' bursts of energy and purposeful pantomiming) had gradually blessed her with a mixture of tenderness, candor, and impressionability that always threatened to brim over. She was very beautiful. As a result of her mother's affectation she also moved, spoke, and behaved as if she were verging on a luscious, pubescent fourteen rather than an already far too carnal, rounded nineteen. That meant—for example—that she could amble along the apartment's passages or be in the vicinity of a seated man's eyes as if she were totally unaware of the existence of her breasts. Or that, when her hips collided with the jamb of a door, she'd stop in shock as if her body were precociously endowed with that futile fullness. Was there anything in her mind that corresponded to that affected unawareness of her body? Maybe there was, and that enigma wasn't the least of what lured Pedro into the trap that the Trimurti of disparate deities had set for him.

In the eyes of all three he embodied the envoy with the magic touch who would transform the fortunes of the entire family, giving it a new direction and meaning. The granddaughter saw in him the angel of the Annunciation wielding his resplendent sword; just as the daughter saw a rather tardy epiphany looming before the fruit of her womb and the dowager perhaps hoped his helping hand would bring her own glorious transfiguration at the top of a mount. The trio were ready to trigger the conflagration with varying degrees of cynical premeditation.

On some nights Pedro subjected himself to the after-dinner ritual of table talk that took place in the drawing-cum-living room after the maid had cleared the tables and replaced the chilly atmosphere of a third-rate hotel with the warmer, if no less bland and tawdry, one of a modest middle-class drawing room living on past family glories.

The three goddesses perched on three different podiums. There were two leather-lined armchairs, remnants of a set the widow had acquired with the donations from the war hero's comrades. These two armchairs were home to old, good-quality English springs that were completely beat-up though still comfortable. The dowager sat on one. The other was for Pedro, even when he sometimes insisted that the insipid second generation ought to occupy it in recognition of her age and sex. But out of respect for grandmother and their guest the second generation sat stiff-backed on an ordinary dining room chair, for hours on end if required, although she tried to appear relaxed, crossing her legs or fanning herself with a newspaper or even allowing herself to lightly retouch her lips in the presence of strangers or even—I jest not—struggling to smoke a cigarette (that wasn't black) that Pedro hastened to light. As suited her energetic, flirtatious character that was full of promise, the youngster sat in a rocking chair. And not only did she sit on this item of furniture that was about to disappear from a world in which combustion engines and jet planes supply more perfect ways of enjoying the voluptuous pleasures of motion, she rocked nonstop, allowing anyone who watched with a keen eye to register the smooth movements powered by the delightful muscular contractions of her fine calves. The girl threw herself back, letting her hair fall over the chair's low, curved back, and her tresses—more abundant than the two women's had ever been—cascaded down in waves the golden reflections from which glowed throughout the drawing-cum-dining room, lending a visual fragrance that dazed them and allowed them to sit in silence and time to slip by. Pedro wasn't the only one to contemplate that flow of molten gold that kept descending on and retreating from his hands, both mothers also looked on with equally possessive stares. They too relished with virile sensuality substance that delivered a firm promise, flooding the drab atmosphere of the drawing-cum-dining room, transforming the stink from barely digested meals and recently peeled oranges into the scent—similar but so different—of a Parisian banquet with demimondaines and fruit transported from the exuberantly fertile tropics.

They talked, however conscious that the words the foursome exchanged in conversation meant nothing—communication was sustained by postures and gestures, by inflections and glances, by smiles and sudden silences. Because the young girl's beauty would strike them so violently that—mid-sentence with no reason to apologize—Pedro simply fell silent; which was a signal for the two mothers to also admire her figure, the alabaster white of her neck, or the stretching of a leg from which a leather-lined mule had just fallen, or for them to be surprised by how the girl's skirt had eased a little more upwards than usual to reveal a small expanse of smooth thigh yet to be deformed by fat.

If a lodger happened to enter the drawing-cum-dining room to collect a forgotten item (a lighter, a letter, a pink ribbon), or if the sturdy maid returned to place in the dresser napkins she'd mistakenly taken into the kitchen, the three goddesses would tremble in rage and the dowager's dark eyes would glower at the intruder's contemptible face; the young woman would halt the gentle rocking of her chair and the second generation hide her cigarette and swiftly uncross her legs. Even Pedro, the only fortunate spectator those three vulgar, demoralized women deigned worthy of that display of their concealed divinity, also felt the spell had been broken. And he felt obliged to shift in his seat, to stir himself and half open the newspaper as if he were fully intending to read it, until the intruder finally disappeared.

"You're so young," said the old lady, "you've never had to go to war. But don't think for one minute that's such a good thing. I find it rather sad. Men return from war more manly. The girl's grandfather taught me that."

"Unhappily," smiled Pedro, "I'm the peaceful sort. The fights that interest me are those of viruses against antibodies."

Kabbalistic words he deployed as the victim of the unreal atmosphere of those exchanges. But his words weren't misplaced. For although not one of that trio understood his remarks, they welcomed them with a cheerful smile as living proof of the higher sphere the young gentleman inhabited, something they already suspected, were even familiar with, but which became emphatically obvious when he exhibited a depth of a knowledge they didn't share but were no less quick to applaud.

"They've stopped dancing the Charleston and the one-step," said the second generation. "Today's youngsters prefer a more languid form of dancing. At least that's what I've heard."

"I must admit, madam, that I don't dance. I'm so clumsy I fall over my own feet. I stumble and tread on the toes of the unfortunate girl who's come my way. Of course, I've almost never danced. Only at the occasional wedding."

Hearing that word, the youngster blushed—as corresponded to her nineteen years and her state of enchantment.

"I can't believe that. You've only danced at weddings? You must have occasionally gone to a cabaret or a tea dance. Young people of your age used to adore tea dances. At the time of the war in Africa they were fundraisers presided over by the infantas. When I was young, I went to several, and they had interludes to collect money, and couples danced the Charleston wonderfully well. Of course, times have changed."

"Don't act old, Dora," protested the elder mother. "I mean, if *you* are old, what does that make me? You like to humiliate me by acting older. Would you believe people used to think we were sisters?"

Pedro was no less horrified that Dora might have gone to teas organized by infantas than that her mother might have gone along purporting to be her sister. The deceit behind these statements together with his lack of awareness of the real dives Dora visited with her mother when she was first dishonored—which made him imagine them to be much worse—didn't spark in Pedro any urge to mock or scorn, but conscious that those conversations were a real work of art, he was convinced a profound truth lay in their words (a truth fashioned by ardent desire, not by elusive, changeable facts) and joined in by inventing other statements of a similar stripe.

"I remember my mother telling me about those charity tea dances for the Red Cross. Perhaps you may even have met her"—immediately correcting himself, thus scaling an even higher peak of perfection—"although it's quite true, now I think about it, that can't be, because she was much older. She'd have been among the elderly ladies seated there admiring you dance."

When she heard that, Dora preened and crossed her legs higher. Her legs were her best feature, and her propensity to sit on a high chair was thanks not just to modesty but also a vague upsurge of narcissism that been rarely satisfied in the last twelve years. But remembering what was the real (silent) focus of that encounter, she continued: "But I've never been a good dancer. My daughter's the talented one. My back's always been a bit too stiff. You should take her to a club one day," immediately regretting a risqué suggestion that threw too much light on the nature of the fiction being so finely elaborated there.

"You cannot permit," the old woman interjected, "a child of her age to visit such places."

"I mentioned it because Don Pedro is so serious. Although I can quite see he'd be bored by a little girl."

"Not at all, madam. I'm sorry I can't dance. But if you want to give me some lessons, when I've made sufficient progress, I'd be most honored to take you and your daughter to wherever you might want to go."

"That's completely insane! You are simply being a polite gentleman," retorted the dowager, mortally pained by the idea of her two descendants setting off to a dance floor without participating in the fun herself, though she recognized how grotesque her presence would have been on such an expedition.

The young girl nervously followed the thread of words, blushing, then rocking faster, slowing down, then smiling wanly, exhibiting yet again her perfect figure with shameless abandon.

As the evening progressed, the sense of intimacy deepened. Markers of the passing of time—a last slamming of the kitchen door, the click of the light switch in the passage, the commercial rep's switching off of his wireless whose buzz reached them through the walls—

heightened the solitude encircling their after-dinner chat. In these last seconds an extended silence fell on the four actors in that drama. In this silence the three women's hidden assumptions became more perceptible to Pedro, as if the three Fates were whispering about the meaning informing the threads of their lives. As the rocking chair started to swing after a short pause, Pedro heard the first generation: "Do it," the second generation: "As far as I'm concerned . . . ," and the third generation: "I like you."

And he felt slightly nervous as he yielded slowly to temptation.

There were the hovels! Like Moses many centuries ago on a higher mount, Amador had climbed up onto a small mound at the end of the disintegrated road and was solemnly pointing, as a smile exploded on his gloriously thick lips, to the little valley hidden between two lofty piles, one of rubble, one of trash, from the old, long-raided municipal dump (from which searches by locals had extracted all valuable or edible matter they could profit from) where the proud citadels of poverty flourished cheek by jowl. That finite flatland seemed to be packed with oneiric constructions fabricated from wood from orange and condensed milk boxes, sheets of metal from oil or tar drums, unevenly cut, undulating uralite, the occasional odd tile, twisted poles from faraway forests, pieces of blanket once used by the army of occupation, granite rocks smoothed and rounded to reinforce foundations a Quaternary glacier had brought to the moraines of the steppes, air bricks stolen from building sites and transported in raincoat pockets, mudbricks in which thin straw does for mud what iron rods do for reinforced concrete, rounded pieces of vessels broken in the ruins of liturgical taverns, wicker circles that were once hats, Empire-style headboards from which the brass fittings had already been removed in the Rastro, fragments of bullring barriers still stained the color of rust or blood, and yellow, black-lettered tins of American Aid cheese, all congealed by human skin, sweat, and tears.

Heavy drapes in the windows of those unlikely mansions, Bohemian glass pendant lamps that shook in the wind, expensive clothes from a crammed laundry basket weighing down washing lines in backyards, fridges (gleaming ivory white) crouching behind army blanket doors, and thick pile carpets softening the sound of footsteps would come as no surprise to Pedro, who was well aware of the foibles of human nature and the lunatic way in which people who should carefully manage their meager means foolishly blew their money. It was quite reasonable, then, to find herds of squealing pigs nourished on thirdhand fodder in bathrooms, and a daughter of the family lurking there in a posh household maid's headgear because she was unfit to work even as a whore, or a stout matriarch wearing a red silk nightgown and expensive oriental babouches, her chubby white fingers displaying a meaningless wedding ring, just as some women living in the neighborhood, rather than spending their time usefully sewing and mending, sat on canisters and wantonly played cards with the same clear conscience as honest laborers on a Sunday afternoon in a bar, or albums of Nestlé picture cards in the hands of scrofulous ragamuffins already smelly at their tender age and ignorant of any moral scruples, sexually active married couples sharing the same big bed with grown-up children to whom all is revealed, a cornucopia of images of smarmy-smiling saints listening undeterred to a magnificent, grandiloquent litany of manly swearing, a soup tureen made in Limoges brimful under the bed like a potty.

Despite such easily corrected contrasts the entire residential area was so beautiful! What a wonderful display of Iberian man's ability to improvise, create, and construct! What a tangible demonstration of the life-giving spiritual values—so envied by other nations—that enabled this harmonious city to arise from nothing, from trash. Such a moving spectacle, a source of noble pride for their compatriots, that little valley swamped by the proliferating, babbling stuff of life, all glitter and color, which left nothing to be desired and indeed surpassed the perfect creations—so boring and lacking in charm—of the most intelligent species: ants, diligent bees, and North American beavers! How it revealed the verve of a civilization that knows how to exhibit its creative powers, whether it be with scant raw materials on the central mesa or with the rich abundance of jungles across the oceans! Because if it *is* beautiful—something which other, seemingly superior nations have achieved only by dint of organization, hard work, wealth, and (why not say it?) the sheer boredom spawned by their pale-faced countries—then a shantytown like that just has to be an inspiration for artists and a field of study for sociologists. Why go to the antipodean isle of Tasmania to study human customs? As if we couldn't see on our very doorstep men who speak our language solving life's eternal problems with breathtaking originality. As if the taboo of incest weren't more audaciously violated on these primitive nuptial couches than on any paradise island's beds of leaves? As if the elemental institutions of these groupings weren't as remarkable and complex as those of peoples yet to transcend the tribal stage. As if the invention of the boomerang hadn't been so dramatically outdone, even made to look ridiculous, by the manifold ingenious devices—which we have no time to describe—thanks to which these folk survive and breed. As if it hadn't been demonstrated that the temperature inside an Inuit igloo in January is several Fahrenheit degrees warmer than in hovels in the slums of Madrid. As if it was news to us that the average age for loss of virginity is lower in these hovels than on the hills where central African tribes practice such complicated and grotesque rites of initiation. As if the steatopygic fat of Hottentot women weren't perfectly counterbalanced by the gradual lipodystrophies of our Mediterranean females. As if belief in a Supreme Being weren't matched here by a more positive, reverential fear of the equally omnipresent forces of public order. As if, sir, man weren't the same everywhere: always so inferior in the sharpness of his instincts to the most brutish of animals and so endlessly superior to the idea that philosophers spin of him.

Amador's fleshy lips didn't lose their smile while Don Pedro meandered engrossed in his contemplation of the hovels. There, in some hidden hollow, inferior to man and controlled by him, mice of carcinogenic stock continued to eat the diet invented by Snarler and to reproduce despite vitamin deficiencies and jailbird neuroses and that small zone of investigable life sunk in the rough seas of odorous suffering moved him in quite new ways. He doubted his calling; perhaps it wasn't only cancer that deformed human faces and gave them the swollen, bestial features of the ghosts that surface in our dreams, and that we naively imagine don't exist.

"What did she reckon? That I'd go soft an' provide for the kid? 'He's yours, he's yours,' she kept sayin'. As if I didn't know she's bin with others. Even if it was mine. So what? I'd known for ages she'd bin with others. 'I'm yours, an' he's yours,' she said. That was her tack after I knifed Pretty-face. Pretty-face couldn't have cared less. Everybody was scared of him. Me too if I wasn't carryin' my knife. He knew she was with me an' he started touchin' her boobs right in my face. That slut lookin' scaredy and lookin' at me. She knew I wasn't carryin' my blade. Fuck the twat of that slut's mother. An' on she went, 'He's yours, he's yours.' I know he's mine. An' so fuckin' what? I'm not goin' all soft and providin' for the kid. The slut should have watched out. What did she reckon? That was her tack because I'd poked Pretty-face. Why did the slut screw around? 'I didn't, I didn't, only with you.' But when I first did her, someone had already paid her a visit and I said to mysel', 'Hey, Dynamite, somethin' fishy here.' But I didn't say nothin' because I was still sugarin' her up. But it *was* fishy. 'No way, no way,' she kept sayin'. As if I was gonna swallow that. Pretty-face touchin' her up in my face an' she lovin' makin' me jealous. The fool. I went up to my hovel an' came back with my blade. An' I looked before I went in an' she wasn't stuck agin' him now. She only let people touch her up when I was around, the fool. Nobody dared stand up to him. They didn't carry knives or didn't know how to handle one. My blade gives me more balls than the toughest tough. An' he spat in my face: 'She's crazy for my prick.' I can't stand these types that talk all dirty as if talkin' that way nobody was gonna poke them. As if! An' seein' I was sayin' nothin' and layin' off: 'Give Dynamite a slug.' I can't stand people callin' me Dynamite except on my say-so. But shush, me keepin' low an' she lookin' at me as if to say I was a fag. And he, 'If you don' wan' no slug, soda water.' An' he brings a siphon an' squirts it in my snout an' I drink it. Lookin' him in the mug. An' him laughin' his head off, 'You can goggle all you like.' An' he mutterin' to himsel', 'No spunk. No spunk anymore.' I'd sugared her up but now she was starin' at me as if I was a fag. I shit on your mother's twat, you slut. Then when you could see her belly growin', she kept givin' me the eye and rubbin' in it. Pretty-face splittin' his sides. Still talkin' dirty. An' all of them a load of chickens starin' at him. Her brother lettin' her be touched up right in front of himsel'. But when I went for my blade, she backed off. You could see she were soft on me. She only let him when I could see... But I just laughed because that's just like them. They egg you on. As if when a woman's soft on you, you're gonna say amen Jesus to everythin'. When I'd got my blade, I just waited until he came towards me so cocky. He was totally plastered an' reckoned the world was his oyster. What I didn't forgive was him callin' me Dynamite. I shit on his daddy's grave. I knifed him in the back an' he collapsed in the mud. An' you should have heard him... that if the Virgin of the Pillar of Zaragoza and Alicante... an' the one on high who is three in one. A mass of blood an' mud. I beat it. I cleaned the blade an' put it under the mattress. The cops came an' questioned me. 'Out with it, Dynamite.' An' one whack after another. But I, 'You must be jokin'.' 'We found your blade. Let's look at your paws. It's got your prints on it.' But I knew that was a lie. So I got done an' was put inside. A short sentence for possession. But there was no proof of the other stuff. That was goodbye to Pretty-face. An' that was when she believed. I got out an' she was waitin' all meek an' mild to throw herself around my neck. Her belly swelled up like anythin'. 'Get lost.' 'It's yours.' 'Get lost.' 'It's yours.' 'You've bin with other guys.' 'I ain't.' 'Somebody got there before me. You put blood on the sheets. Get lost.' I gave her rope while I was in the slammer. She'd visit an' prod. What was I supposed to say? Sure. That I'd knifed him for her. She kept on. Tell me where I'll get the dough. But they're like that. I kept encouragin' her. But when I got out she wanted more an' it weren't gonna happen. I fancied Snarler's other daughter. That gal was a looker. An' the other kept on,

'It's yours.' An' even sent her kid brother after me. The one who didn't lift a finger when Pretty-face was all over her in front of him. 'You git, remember Pretty-face.' 'My sister's a good girl. You put a bun in her oven.' 'Look, you git, she'd been with other guys.' 'You did it.' 'Remember Pretty-face.' An' she got worse an' worse. As if bawlin' me out got you anywhere. An' starts shoutin' at me in the street. An' took me before a judge to make me keep my promise. 'There's no proof.' 'You've been seen with her.' 'There've bin others before me. There's no proof.' The judge was up to here, and me, even more so. An' her belly growin'. An' she won't leave me in peace. 'Leave me alone, you slut, or I'll give you somethin' to remember.' One night, instead of shoutin', she throws herself on me in the dark. 'You love me. You love me.' She was cryin'. I couldn't keep my hands off her. Even with that belly on her. I mean she thought that was it, the fuckin' slut. An' came back for more the day after. But I wasn't havin' it this time. An' she followed me in the mornin' and evenin'. An' I lost my tether. I punched her an' flattened her nose. An' now she was about to bring forth. That made me hate her even more. I flattened her face. I hit her too hard for a woman. But I'd had it up to here. In the end back to court. The fuzz knew but had no proof. Another six months inside. Just as well. In the meantime she gave birth. She didn't come back for more. An' I feelin' so good. I'd told Florita, Snarler's other girl, that I fancied her. When I came out, she didn't give me a glance. She went all over with the kid. A baby can be so like its father! He's a spittin' image. But there's no proof. The nasty piece of work leaves it with her sister an' goes on the street with her broken nose. She could have bin a real goldmine. But I've always liked bein' the real deal for women. When they're smitten, they're like that. That's what women are for. An' I was thinkin' how I'd never get enough of Florita's tits. Soon as I got out. An' her father turns up. Snarler can be moody an' knows how to handle a knife. Those crazy guys from La Mancha. An' she's underage too. I don't want no trouble. I beat it. But I'm mad for her. She's not like her sister. She's afraid of me. I get my fill now an' then. If Snarler catches me. I don't want no trouble. But I'm not gonna leave that chick. I don't dare take her out. A feel now an' then but no more. As I don't drink. I have a coffee and I'm better. I play dominos or cards. I make out. I work a bit. An' go dancin' in afternoon hops. I've always liked to jitterbug. An' I pick up the odd gal. But it's that Florita who's on my mind. An' the feels I've had have left me wantin' more. An' nobody had better go near her or he'll feel my blade badly. No more Pretty-faces out there."

And having contemplated the remarkable spectacle of the forbidden city with the curved spikes on its roofs to ward off flying demons, Amador and Don Pedro descended from the surrounding hills and, gingerly teetering their way between a variety of obstacles, barking dogs, naked children, mountains of dung, cans full of rainwater, they reached the front door to the Snarler residence. The worthy owner was there, his back turned to them, busy sorting on his hovel's floor a series of motley—presumably valuable—objects he must have extracted from the trash heap he'd rented some months ago. But the moment he was alerted by a throaty rasp from Amador's fleshy mouth, he straightened quite gracelessly, and an expression of real surprise spread over his face, furrowed by time and toil and twitching tempestuously from the nervous tic to which he owed his nickname.

"What a pleasure to see you in this neck of the woods, Don Pedro! Long time no see! Why didn't you warn me?" He aimed his question at his friend and quasi-relative. "Come in and make yourself at home."

He acted like a good bourgeois, doing the honors by his peers, ushering them into the silent, dusty gloom of the room, where velvet-lined seating awaited the worthy weight of the bodies of those individuals who, endowed with a status equal to the house owners', can take their seats and engage for lengthy periods of time in conversations that—albeit boring and vapid—never fail to comfort all participants by indirectly confirming their membership of the very same honorable social estate. So Snarler suggested Don Pedro sit on a kind of bed made from boxes and covered by a dingy gray blanket in the absence of any sheets. Then gracing his face with the courteous expression inherited over the centuries by peasants from the Toledan countryside and imbuing his naturally brusque voice with a mellifluous lilt, he finally articulated with an effort: "I'm sure you'd like a drink."

After which, forgetting for a second his decision to soften awhile the harsh tone of his voice, he shouted: "Flora, Florita! Bring us some lemonade right away! The doctor's here."

A series of short, muffled noises issued from the area of the hovel hidden from the entrance by a reddish curtain of indefinable cloth. Despite Don Pedro's protests and Amador's sardonic laughter, Snarler insisted on accelerating the pace of events by sticking his woolly head behind this dividing curtain and half bellowing various unintelligible orders. He later emerged adopting a more sociable stance with an array of facial expressions (striving to restrain his irrepressible tic), softening his tone and even trying to modify his physical profile with a half-hearted attempt to hunch his shoulders while simultaneously rounding his back.

Amador had sat down on one of the objects that Snarler had been sorting, a rusty pot with a hole. But in that position his back was turned to the door and increased the gloom in the hovel, prompting their host to say: "Come on, Amador. Move aside. Can't you see you're blocking the light for the doctor?"

By this time Snarler's offspring had showed up to pay her respects through the drapes veiling the rest of his real estate, and smiling with a titter that revealed the thick red line of her top gums over small white teeth in the middle of her round face, she proffered a half-filled glass of water into which lemon juice had been squeezed, to judge by the pip floating there like a small blimp.

"Give it to the doctor, Florita! Help him cool down!"

"Here you are, sir," Florita ventured with a slight blush, her flustered eyes meeting Don Pedro's equally embarrassed gaze.

He didn't dare scrutinize any part of the hovel's interior, even though his curiosity was urging him to do so, for fear he'd offend those gifted with such pathetic riches, but at the same time he understood that the owner's self-respect required him to say something flattering, however unlikely and absurd that might seem.

"This lemonade is really refreshing," he said finally.

"They send me these lemons from our village," Snarler lied with the authority of a landowner managing distant minions, "and I might add, they're the best."

"Would you like another glass?" said Florita.

Don Pedro was quick to refuse, while Amador said overfamiliarly: "Bring me a glass, honey."

"Honey wasn't made for the mouth of an ass" was the girl's sparky response, which showed that, just like her father, she was able, though younger in years, to invent two identities and use them appropriately, according to the status of the person she was speaking to.

"Give him one!" ordered her father, more conscious than she of the economic ties guaranteeing the subsistence of his honorable family, ties that linked him to a member of the Institute's staff, to whom, conversely, he owed unspecified favors and who'd been a wartime comrade, something both tried to bury in silence, but which neither had forgotten.

"Don't be so cheeky to Uncle Amador," he added, performing this new kind of tribute to someone less sophisticated socially speaking, but perhaps, in the last instance, more intrinsically vital.

With that, blocking the light from the hovel's doorway again, a stout, almost circular woman's body made an entrance, draped in that blackish cloth which over time turns partly gray-brown, partly greenish, like the color of horsefly wings or an old soutane.

"You must forgive her, doctor, sir," said Snarler, "but this is my wife and the poor thing doesn't know how to comport herself. Do excuse her, she's literate. Hey, Ricarda, this is the doctor who is honoring us with his presence."

"May your shadow never grow shorter," said Ricarda.

She held up one of the skirts that covered her like the concentric layers of an onion, and which contained indescribable matter that, Amador deduced, was fodder for the mice. That substance gave him the opportunity to broach the reason for their visit, momentarily suspending the round of polite chitchat.

"Fine, to get down to why we're here," he said, "because Don Pedro doesn't have time to waste on nonsense."

"Fire away, doctor, sir."

"What the doctor wants to know," specified Amador, "is whether or not he should put you in prison."

"What's that?" shouted an alarmed Snarler, while the no less alarmed Don Pedro shook his head and right hand (now free of the bitter lemonade) in disbelief and said: "Not at all. On the contrary, I wanted to thank you if you've managed to look after them and succeeded in breeding them."

"A-ah, the mice," said Snarler, subsiding.

"The dear little mice," laughed Florita, forgetting her role as the bashful, blushing maid. "You bet those rascals breed, and how. They make me sweat and even nibble me."

Saying which, she unbuttoned the top part of her dress, revealing to all present her cleavage and two or three small red marks that could very well have been caused by the sharp teeth of mice in heat.

"It was all down to the cold," explained Snarler, that well of wisdom, reassuming his more solemn stance and relaxing his face. "I'm sure they keep them in incubators in the Americas. Not like us here in temperate climes."

Amador looked at him sarcastically and almost laughed, but Snarler, ignoring the impact his old comrade in arms caused with scraps of learning whose sources were a mystery, continued: "Everybody knows that heat gives life. Like in the ditties about King David. Two young girls kept him warm, or he'd have died. And it's the same with ponds and reservoirs. You only need the sun to blister down for the mud to come to life with worms and creepy-crawlies. You only need to see old folks leaning on walls in winter. What would become of them without that three o'clock sun? There'd be no old folk left. That's what happened to them mice. How could they ever get in heat if they weren't warm enough to keep alive? That's why they swelled up with lumps like testicles, if you'll forgive my French; when they died and you burnt the midnight oil studying why, it was simply the cold."

Don Pedro listened in astonishment to this etiological theory of spontaneous cancer brought on by the cold; he was fascinated by the possible prophylactic outcomes Snarler had deduced, useful not only in keeping the mice alive, but also in ensuring they reproduced.

"What will you come out with next, Father? You and your explanations! Nobody can shut you up. My father should have been a preacher or a dentist. Yet people say he's a clod. He's cloddish by nature, but not when it comes to know-how."

"Shut up, you silly!" he protested modestly. "The truth is if you give mice the heat they need, they'll breed, and I see you knew where to come to find them. I've got them here, yes, doctor, sir, the children of children I won't call grandchildren, because I don't reckon animals are much into families. And even the children's children's children."

"In other words, the great-grandchildren," laughed Amador, applauded by Florita, who'd forgotten her timidity from the second she showed her cleavage and the bite marks that enshrined her as a martyr to science.

"Father was behind it all. But me and my sister had to put up with the mice's nasty habits."

"Shush, girl. And don't say any more unless you're asked. Look how quiet your mother is and how she doesn't interfere, and she had to deal with those same nasty habits."

In effect, Snarler's roly-poly consort, who, unlike her husband, was gifted with a smooth, motionless face, listened as if that conversation she was hearing were a symphony performance. It was clear that, though she didn't understand one scrap of what was being said, she enjoyed the sounds uttered by all present. In order to be less in the way she'd sat on the floor, and her white, round, ankleless legs peeked out from under her multiple-layered skirts, while she still held on firmly to the miraculous mouse feed in her lap.

"Might I ask how you gave them that natural heat?" asked Don Pedro, after minutes of disbelief at what he was hearing.

"You can ask, but I won't tell you out of respect."

"All right," butted in Amador. "You can tell me later. Let's have a look at these great-grandchildren and find out if they're bastards or not. Because if they are, we're not at all interested. They have to be brother with sister or at most daughter with father."

"And that's what they are," Snarler declared roundly.

But that was that. Snarler refused to show them his setup. He promised to bring the offspring at the agreed time and place, but he didn't want them venturing farther into his den. Don Pedro was now too curious to agree to leave after he'd drunk all his lemonade. He wanted to get to the bottom of that mouse-breeding enterprise of both mice and women in conditions so different from those believed to be tolerable. The smells issuing from behind the reddish curtain into the hovel's most densely inhabited area, the presence at his feet of the wife's mute, inert mass, the Toledan girl's bites comprised, alongside Snarler's scientific-reasoning mindset, a tout ensemble that he couldn't easily walk out on, that he wanted to get to know, although behind this endeavor there was as much straight curiosity as genuine interest, as much a need to procure mice for his research as a desperate desire to observe humankind in its most impure iteration.

The breeding ground for the carcinogenic race was to be found in the inner realm of Snarler's hovel. Each mouse was kept in a rusty wire birdcage. These cages had been obtained from the mounds of scrap metal and repaired in rough-and-ready manner by Snarler himself, helped by his younger, nimble-fingered daughter. They hung on the walls of the bedroom. His wife poured the feed she'd brought in her skirts into their white, glazed feeding bowls. The small space was made of boards somewhat warped by damp, but basically smooth. The gaps between the boards had been filled by rags to form a watertight area. The cages were hung artistically in triangular formations, enabling a harmonious distribution of negative space, light and shadow, as in an art gallery whose stinking rich owner has bought more paintings than he can accommodate. There was a large square mattress on the floor of this smallish room. The bodies of Snarler and his consort entered from one side and their nubile daughters' more svelte forms from the other. A cousin now doing his military service used to sleep in the outer chamber on the small mattress where Don Pedro had perched. But the four of them continued to sleep on the big mattress for several reasons: Because the four bodies raised the temperature in the hermetically sealed room (the less they felt the cold, the better the mice thrived, according to Snarler's theory). Because they'd got used to the arrangement. Because Snarler liked to hit against one of his daughters' legs during the night. Because that way he could keep an eye on them, and knew where they were the whole night, that most perilous of times for young girls. Because they required fewer sheets and blankets that way, as for the moment they'd pawned the ones used by the conscripted cousin. Because the smell of bodies—once you got used to it—is comforting rather than off-putting. Because Snarler, without knowing what the word meant, felt like a biblical patriarch to whom all those women belonged. Because Snarler's consort was quite scared of him and couldn't deal with his outbursts of rage without the equivocal help of his daughters' silent presence. Because the last stage in mousey procreation consists in getting the exotic breed of mice to be in heat. Because Snarler had placed the mice in three small plastic bags and hung them between the breasts of the three women in his household. Because he believed that with the help of this human heat the in-heat was generated twice as easily: because it was heat and was female heat. Because he didn't want the ripening process of the mice's vaginal mucus to be interrupted by his girls sleeping in the outer chamber, where inadequately plugged spaces between boards and the paucity of nocturnal promiscuity meant heat levels decreased. When the mouse was finally in heat, Snarler took it carefully from the little plastic bag where it had spent several nights and placed it in the nuptial cage to introduce the powerful stud, who was always so eager to copulate, especially when stimulated by a sniff of estrus. This copulatory cage was covered in burlap reinforced by wadding and seed fiber suitable for nest building but Snarler removed the pregnant females from it outside the loving hour, as if he believed the sight of such riches for the embellishment of future homes might be an added aphrodisiac. Once the period of gestation had begun, they never again enjoyed such wadding and seed fibers, for it would have made breeding costs extortionate, and they had to be content with a little commonplace straw in their aerial mansions. Once born, the mice of either sex heralded their presence with the subtle chirps of little nightingales, while their mothers were capable of giving birth—unlike the human species—in reverent silence before the mysteries of nature they themselves were enacting. After this prim, proper, often nighttime confinement, the morning of Snarler's tribe was cheered by youthful mewling and the girls laughed in their bed, wrapped in their sleeveless, dirty-white nightshirts, shouting: "Father, the one at the top has given birth," "Father, and so has mine, the one that nibbled me." "Father, I told you she wasn't properly covered, the slut's indecent, fartin' and guzzlin' nonstop, and then she refused Manolo who's very sad," "Who did that nunnish nun think she was!" If Snarler had drunk too much the night before, he took no notice of his daughters' cries and grunted and stuck his head back under the blanket while his tubby consort was already working outside or had departed to the trash pile they'd contracted.

Days passed cheerfully in that household. Only piffling banks of clouds partially darkened the almost always pink sky. In the morning, gentleman farmer Snarler Smith visited his breeding grounds, where the wombs of his pedigree mares, refined by the cleverest of endogamic exchanges, brought forth the longed-for thoroughbred fruit. He barked out abrupt orders that his trained staff effortlessly understood and executed on the spot. Holding a glass of hard liquor, he clicked his tongue as he felt the firewater burn the roof of his mouth. High leather boots stamped sonorously on timber floors. Then he conversed with local dignitaries on the boundaries of his estate. A pastor who cared for the souls of his flock, he spoke of his community's spiritual state. "I think there's going to be fireworks over the evictions." An ardent applier of poultices, pooh-poohing half-baked midwives who presumed to embrace science, he explained: "As long as those girls keep drinking that quack Blasa's water hoping to abort, they'll become chlorotic or tubercular, and everything will turn foul colored in their guts. Anything that's not proper surgical is a waste of time and they'll end up in the disinsecting unit." A shantytown self-made man profiting from the sale of food in minimal doses, he'd say that the purchase of sugar in ten-cent lots only encouraged the vice of wanting to drink coffee at all hours of the day, while now you even find people who are disgusted by sweet potatoes and want only real spuds, one vice after another, as if we were a wealthy country. They could get by perfectly on saccharine and sweet potatoes, which, as well as being nourishing, save on sugar, but now people think they have a right to everything. Architect-surveyor-contractor of hovels, cheerfully ignorant of municipal regulations and diktats, he built as few now can, obeying the free-flowing will of his artistic instincts in accordance with the materials at his disposal. "I'll turn that room into a grand place, with a fireplace and all, for three thousand reales. But that's no good because when it rains there'll be puddles. There won't be no puddle if I give you a roof gutter to take away the rain! But it's a no-go, they don't want no puddles in their house. But it only rains here once in a while. What's the point of you saving, I ask myself, if you carry on living like bugs. Hey, that's poverty for you!" Snarler had town-planning concerns. "We could have a little square there where the kids can play. We could add one of those smooth rocks and even a geranium." "No, you can't touch those rocks, I've reserved 'em in case they decide to use 'em and, let me repeat, they're mine. Nobody's gonna take 'em from me."

As well as the developed land, Snarler had other building land, surrounded on all sides by a would-be park or garden. A common-law right asserting free range had led to burgeoning properties on the land of a speculator from the other city who was still arguing over the price per square foot with the real estate company that would one day show up with bulldozer and trucks and underline the temporary nature of these under-par investments, sales, rents, evictions, and house exchanges, in the same way as tribal ownership and the usufruct of indigenous peoples' hunting grounds conflicted with new economic realities when true civilization finally arrived. But here, in a kind of paradoxical reverse march, these old rights rested on the vestiges (never abandoned, simply never applied) of old common law. As if in a rehearsal of what existence might be like the day after an actual atomic war, when the remnants of humanity, resistant by random good fortune to radiation, established themselves amid the ruins of the large contaminated city and began to live by making the most of materials that were now useless. In this way, that community's inhabitants could see in the distance constructions going up—a different world of which they were at once excrescences and parasites. A vital duality prevented them from being integrated as collaborators or serfs in that great enterprise. They could only survive on what the city throws out: trash, detritus, charity, San Vincent de Paul sermons, rubble, empty food cans, unskilled laborers' minimum wages, the savings made by ever-loyal daughters in service. Nonetheless, daily they must head for that other reality (like indigenous peoples off to happy hunting grounds) and station themselves at strategic points on the stairs to the metro to reap minimal spoils, from produce spurned by markets, the offerings of soup kitchens, or profiteering from cigarette lighters.

Well-established, a frontier veteran, a town dignitary, respected by his peers, a counselor, Citizen Snarler, from the heights of his fruitful livestock farm, looked down on those newcomers who—clad in rags, front and back—spilled out of filthy third-class trucks from the distant land of hunger. With contemptuous swagger he identified on the faces of these "Koreans"[10] the stigma of shame and inferior races. He intuitively understood those men would never be capable—as he had been—of achieving the worthy status of a free-market entrepreneur who signs contracts with an upstanding legal-scientific institution in the neighboring city yet to be destroyed by the bomb. He predicted with a quick glance at their faces that sooner or later those subhumans would end up as dead meat, meager fodder for worms, via any one of the abstruse ways of starving to death (tuberculosis, scrofula, lathyrism, spitting blood, a progressive tremble in the heels, a stab to the stomach, collapsing from inanition, etc., etc., etc.); or they'd end up being fed at the expense of whichever state survived the bomb in high-rise red blocks with serried ranks of small, identical windows that could be seen in the distance; or they'd end up being humiliatingly dispatched to the land of hunger whence they had come and which—you bet—was absolutely bombproof.

That gentleman passed his days happily enough, relishing his comfortable status, warmed in bed by several bodies, consoled by alcoholic intake, confident in the certainty that he'd achieved all that thanks to insights that allowed him to perfect his methods of capture and breeding and his deft choice of pasturage and pulses, he was so intelligent, though unlettered, and helped by his select contacts and protectors from that other world, who sometimes even descended on his house as if they were family, Amador and even the doctor who'd spoken to him as an equal, without presumption or mention of the tangible differences and deep abysses that sundered existences located on different sides of the color barrier.

Less blessed than in other countries, these co-citizens of the Snarler community and Snarler himself, together with the great and the good of the Republic, couldn't attribute their belonging to this or that world of the two (at least) that constitute the superimposed strata of the social reality of all cities, all nations, all continents to the (ever-so-comfortingly fortuitous) accident of skin color and relative proportions of muscle and sinew fiber of the calves corresponding to individuals of two well-defined biological races. Here, a degree of narrowness of the forehead (which perhaps, if seen positively, could be extended) wasn't reason enough to consider oneself as other. Black prince and dignitary, Snarler showed off his pearl-gray topper and red waistcoat—with a rooster's feather proudly slotted into a buttonhole—amid the black men with protruding bellies and poor black women with swaying hips hard put to support even a loincloth. When he summoned his black peers (if not in toppers, at least in bowlers) to play cards and sip drinks in local watering holes—while run-of-the-mill folk had to choose between raw sweet potatoes for dessert or boiled and salted sweet potatoes for starters—they were convinced that the world was as good as it gets, although they, the blacks, noteworthy stockbreeders, miners, traders, and dealers in ivory and ebony to distant potentates, still enjoyed the blessed gift of a black skin, unlike those beings from the stars, Martians or Venusians, who, according to data from their black science, must be white, blond, with dazzlingly blue eyes. And the idea that the world was as good as it gets was reconfirmed even more dramatically to Snarler when, at nightfall, he left the palatial watering hole, feeling a cozy warmth in the pit of his stomach, and, upon reaching his stately pile, checked that the three bodies were sweating on the mattress, and simply or silently entered that gratifying space where his physical pleasure accelerated, or—if he so preferred—administered a round of slaps to his sleepy-eyed flock, once more asserting his seigneurial status. And if he, at that lovely moment when one falls asleep, heard his yearlings chirp, then Snarler slept not only happy, obscenely happy, but even displayed an elegantly ecstatic smile on thick lips tempered by time, the strictures of a war, and two declarations of peace that he'd blissfully put behind him.

As it was Saturday night, Pedro ate more quickly. In the dining room he sat behind the wrinkled married couple and between two small tables occupied by two single men. The pollock eating its tail appeared on his plate, so perfect in itself and so emblematic that Pedro couldn't stop smiling when he saw it. By eating that pollock he entered into deeper communion with boardinghouse existence and joined the tables of true martyrs to a life without comfort who'd gradually molded the essence of a country that isn't European. The homely ouroboros seemed to smile ironically. It wasn't biting its tail with real gusto, but nibbling delicately, just enough for it not to escape and exhibit itself as a full-length ignoble ocean fish, not yet completely rotten, a string of dark blotches on its white flesh signaling the onset of putrefaction. The lemon juice he squeezed out to fend off what might be less than sacrosanct reminded him of the bitter lemonade he'd drunk days ago. He shook his head and attacked the cold orange. Guests exchanged pointless remarks. The maid moved more hastily than on other days, mindful of her night out. Pedro said goodbye. He turned his back on his nightly table talk with three infatuated generations. He went down the passage to his room, and as he made his way to the front door, the dowager emerged to say goodbye and recommend that he button up to the neck even if it wasn't winter yet and advise against staying out too late even if tomorrow was Sunday.

Pedro tripped down the three flights of shadowy stairs lit by anemic light bulbs. The old wooden steps smelled of dust, and some creaked. A loving couple hugged in one corner of the next landing down—the maid from the downstairs apartment and a soldier in civvies from her village. He walked into the small street. He strode past a tavern displaying a bull's head. He came to the Plaza de Tirso de Molina. A few guys looking like pimps stood in the entrance to a low dive awaiting their first customers. He continued along a nigh-on-flat side street. Most of the down-market shops on the street were in darkness. Only the odd one was consuming kilowatts. In one higgledy-piggledy store, secondhand coffee-making machines jostled against old tables and wicker chairs. He reached the corner of Antón Martín with its metro entrance and brighter lights. Two taxis were parked there; another was slowly making a U-turn. Some ugly, garish women openly solicited on sidewalks or drank coffee in dubious dives with lots of fake gilt. Street sellers of diverse stripes hawked their goods despite the lateness of the hour. He walked on. A Gypsy voice rang out from a cheap tavern with live music, maybe rehearsing for later on, because no customers were in sight. A biting breeze blew from the east. To avoid it he left the Atocha slope that was so open to the elements and engaged with more twisting, sheltered side streets to the left. They were practically empty. He meandered slowly down to the big hotel district. Cervantes had lived thereabouts—or was it Lope?—or maybe both. Yes; around there, on streets that had so unadulteratedly preserved their provincial aspect, like cysts in the big city. Cervantes, Cervantes. Can he really have lived in a town like this, in a city like this, in such drab, ordinary streets, he, a man who possessed that vision of humankind, that belief in freedom, that disillusioned melancholy so removed from heroics or braggadocio, fanaticism or blind certainty? Can he have breathed this excessively clean air and been aware, as his writing indicates, of the reality of a society where he was forced to collect taxes, kill Turks, lose a hand, seek favors, inhabit prisons, and write a book whose sole aim was to make people laugh? Why would a man whose sunken shoulders carried a level head with the utmost melancholy want to make people laugh? What was it he really intended? Renew the novel form, lay bare the mean souls of his fellow men, ridicule that monstrous country, earn money, lots of money, so as to be no longer as embittered as collecting taxes on goods can embitter a man? He's not one to be understood by the existence that shaped him. Like that other man—the gentleman painter—he was always at odds with his trade and maybe would have preferred to wield the pen only to flourish his signature on letters of exchange against Genoese banks. What did the man who best understood the men of his time want to tell us? What does it mean if the man who knew that madness is but nothingness, emptiness, a void, nonetheless maintained that man's ethical nature is located in madness?

Those are knotty questions. While Pedro gently trod the space where that disabled gent had gone before him, his own morbid rationalism spiraled around him.

First spiral: An ethics exists—of an understandable, commonplace nature—according to which it is good, sensible, and reasonable to read novels of chivalry and recognize that those books are full of fakery. The novels of chivalry attempt to impose on reality another, more beautiful world, but this world—alas—is fake.

Second spiral: Nevertheless, a man appears who tries to make what cannot be, come to be, against all the odds. He decides to believe. Evil—that was only virtual—becomes real for this man.

Third spiral: The man who acts in this way—despite acting so—is called *The Good Man* by his fellow citizens.

Fourth spiral: Belief in the reality of a good world doesn't stop him from perceiving the constant evil in the world down below. He still knows that this world is evil. His madness (give it a closer look) consists only in the belief in the possibility of improving it. When we reach this point, we can only laugh since it is so obvious—even to the dimmest—that not only is the world evil, but it can't be improved one jot. Let's laugh then.

Fifth spiral: But doubt arises whether laughter is enough, whether it isn't necessary to crucify the madman. Because what is particularly shocking about his madness is that he is trying to affirm and exemplify the same ethics that those who laugh at him claim to honor. If one stopped laughing for a moment and stared at him, one might be infected. Might he be a danger to society?

Sixth spiral: Yet there's no need to exaggerate. There's no need to take this conjecture to an extreme. We mustn't forget that the madman is exactly that, *a madman*. The author's final word is concealed in this act of "making" his hero mad. The impossibility of realizing goodness on this earth is but the impossibility a poor madman comes up against when he tries to do just that. All doors remain open. What Cervantes is shouting to the rooftops is that his madman wasn't really mad, he only did what he did in order to be able to laugh at the priest and the barber, for if he'd laughed at them without previously demonstrating that he was mad, they wouldn't have tolerated him and would have taken the necessary measures, setting up, say, their own little local inquisition, their own little rack and their own little almsgiving to help the poor of the parish. And the madman, manifestly non-mad, wouldn't have been given a wooden cage but a splendid linen straitjacket supplemented by twenty-two sessions of electric shock treatment.

But nobody knows who this man they call Don Miguel was who may have trod that quiet, clean, provincial street. He was never consumed by the raging madness that slumbered within him, he simply dreamed it, and by expelling the phantoms from his aching head, he avoided turning into the Messiah. Because he didn't want to be the Messiah. He wanted to earn money, collect taxes, marry off his daughter, obtain favors, render the powerful gentle and benign. The story of the madman and all his other marvelous stories weren't vital to him, but an amusing sideline, tiny painted puppets, spurious offspring he had to keep casting into the world (and this is the ultimate truth), as he didn't earn money, as he couldn't cover his debts, as he mis-married his daughter, as he failed to obtain favors, as he was even scorned and forgotten, on his deathbed unable to go mad.

He's now well on his way. He's crossed the fleeting, doleful, nocturnal city of closed churches and open taverns, of swinging electric lights and cars hurtling at top speed at that hour of night through the intersections of main roads as if driven by suicidal clear thinkers, drop coupés of a cold evening flaunting the blond tresses or mink stoles of classy chicks, expensive makes of silver-plated automobiles with smoked glass concealing the brutal, drunken faces of the powers that be, mighty vehicles cruising slowly like elegant whales, shimmying voluptuously after a woman who's just left the bar with the famous name and who's only waiting for the pitch black of night to thicken to make her choice, effortlessly aided by a remote-controlled door, vehicles hurtling like rockets towards a future of palpable pleasure. The heat from hotel doors hits him like bad breath from a nearby mouth, not that he notices, as he's so absorbed in his meandering meditation. But now he does, he stops and watches the passing cars and hears the special squeal of high-quality tires screeching over flagstones, when only a lonely car drives across the vast deserted square with its chariot fountain drawn by lions. And he walks on to the café,[11] where it's also hot, but with a heat unlike the grand hotels', which is from courtesan bodies; it's the gleeful heat of young people, a heat from rippling muscles.

The moment he enters, he knows he's made a mistake, that a visit to this café was precisely what didn't appeal to him, that he'd have preferred to continue summoning the ghosts of men who spilled their cancers on blank sheets of paper. But he's there now and the octopus's adhesive pull keeps him there. Its noisy gob starts to sing. Its soft, multiple visage rings the changes, gazes at him. He's said hello, he's all ears, tentacles inevitably cling to him. He's now joined a community to which, in spite of everything, he belongs and from which he can't easily detach himself. When he enters the city—in one of its most alert perceptions—has taken note of him: he exists.

Like playful, promiscuous wavelets in Ondarreta,[12] gathering their bodies at the liveliest moment of the tide in surprisingly limited areas, invading the vital spaces of all and sundry, uneasy but content, aspiring, despite the sparse territory, to maximum occupation of what's available, every individual eager to be welcomed and contribute, shamelessly revealing the threadbare nature, if not of meat reheated or stewed, of their theories, poems, or critical brilliance, that culture crowd spreads over the constricted beach, happier than any bathers, enjoying the rays of a distant solitary sun, exacting every possible ounce of intensity, each a sun unto himself and the rest of those roundabout, uninterruptedly admiring themselves, basking in heat akin to a solarium's when the ultraviolet rays penetrate to a depth of four hundred microns of skin and activate dormant provitamins, capillaries, and melanophores. But unlike that solar morphine that sweetly stupefies and invests humans with the inertness of matter, the nocturnal drug of the literary café triggers and ferments stimuli in hidden gray cells, ideas from which will one day stir the best of minds in lecture theaters, colleges, and seminars. Those small sparks of violet light a vigilant eye can trace on the temples of maestros on a Saturday night, who use such platforms to effortlessly introduce into the foreheads of garrulous, callous youth, a fertilization so vital for the onward march of the great chariot of culture, like pollen playfully blown by the wind, transported by the common bluebottle or, in the case of the Madagascan orchid, on the proboscis of a moth yet to be categorized but whose length augurs well, guaranteeing an outcome indispensable for the continuous evolution of the species. And not because each maestro (whom nobody recognizes as a maestro, by the way) tells each disciple (who never considers himself to be a disciple, by the way): "You must do this," "Learn from what I say," "Don't overdo the gerund," "Never write a literary work in which the sexual element is completely absent," "Observe the living reality of human nature in the boardinghouse where you modestly reside," drawling dogmatically, but because they pronounce judgments like: "He's a complete idiot," "He hasn't a clue how to write," "He hasn't read Hemingway," they create a collective topsoil, a loam on which they all unconsciously feed, and thus, never praising, always criticizing, contemptuously raising an eyebrow to mid-forehead, giving an approving pat on the back to the least gifted of their audience, talking about football, pinching a female philosophy student, admiring the black velvet dress and long tresses of a cheesy hanger-on, cracking a cruel joke about a lame painter dragging himself towards their table, magnifying their amorous prowess thanks to a crafty reiteration of phone calls, treating the waiter who's already penned seven plays with downright impertinence, wangling an invitation to a coffee and a digestif from an uninitiated provincial, chain-smoking, gabbling nonstop, and never listening, they all guarantee the historical and generational continuity of that void in the form of a poem or Garcilaso that goes by the name of Spanish literature.[13]

Pedro halted for a second at the edge of the beach to orient himself and find a small patch of empty sand where he could flex his mind and debate recent reading. Matías raised a distant arm. To reach him he must cross the sonorous chaos, the rhyming, the leftovers of all the deceased *ultraístas*,[14] the vacuous words of Ramón and his ghost still spawning *greguerías* in the queer actors' cottage,[15] the stuffy, pale-faced girls in black who, when it's fashionable to paint mouths, paint their eyes and, when it's fashionable to paint eyes, paint their lips blood red, the smoke from a hundred thousand and one cigarettes, the pedantry galore being spouted forth, the blackened nails, the stinginess holding back five pesetas for the nighttime cup of sugary coffee that gives them the right to stay in that shrine where honeyed wisdom spreads its stickiness over the marble tabletops.

He crossed the room as best he could, threading his way between sonorous bald pates and glowering eyes. Matías was keen to introduce him: "Hey, she's worth a try. She's read Proust," pointing out a bespectacled girl who, for a change, wasn't clad in black but a lemon-yellow jersey that clung to her curves.

"Really?" Pedro responded warmly.

"Look at her no more.[16] You'll embarrass her," said Matías. "Have a gin."

And, putting Pedro out of his mind, he immediately turned to the girl and explained yet again, even more brilliantly, exactly why the American novel was so important and why its most distinguished writers were so superior to démodé European fiction, which had run to the end of its literary cycle and didn't know how to move on, perhaps because awareness of the end of the said cycle and its inevitable collapse led to pure technical wizardry that was inane, and only chauvinist pedantry could make the mental retards in Gallic lycées and dumbheads in the wide world believe they were still producing great novels, which were only French cleverness with a smidgen of intensity, reality, and true greatness, at best exercises in calligraphy, sewing by anemic young girls in Swiss finishing schools, if not mere embroidery and cross-stitching. The young woman laughed and bulged her jersey.

Fortified by the gin, rushing to have his say, Pedro too—and why not?—joined the debate. Playing little aesthetic games. Waves that come and go. Tides in the mind. Pepínvidalides from Egypt.[17] Situations in which the logjam is absolute. Yes, it's self-evident, axiomatic. One must read *Ulysses*. All American fiction comes from *Ulysses* and the Civil War. The Deep South. It's hardly news. The American novel is superior, influences Europe. It originates there, there and nowhere else. And you, my love, you too. If you don't read, you'll go nowhere. You'll keep repeating the little European tale of Eugénie Grandet, and weep over the misfortunes of orphans forever and ever. Amen. So be it. *Ansiswateel*.[18]

Her yellow jersey seemed propelled by the drag from an irresistible undertow when a tall, bearded young man looked at her through round spectacles. She disappeared. She no longer existed. Red-painted mouth. Vaporized.

Unperturbed, they chattered on, interacting symbiotically, solidified into a single, sensitive substance. The city, the moment, the rigidity inherent in a specific situation, in specific pleasures, in unconsciously respected prohibitions, in sinfully parasitic lives in the dogmatic rejection of established dogma, in the aesthetically imprecise identification of norms, in a lack of purpose fought with manly violence—leading to nil outcomes—made them what they inescapably were (though they believed they were the fruit of their own endeavors). The gritty realism of their lives never coalesced into a style. Nothing came from any of that.

He ordered another gin and began to liven up. He'd also downed a black coffee. He felt strong minded and a prey to tenuous temptations.

The conversation had enthused him despite its spiraling vacuity. The image of Cervantes returned stupidly to his imagination like a repeated, meaningless tune. Cervantes in the midst of that smoke and chatter had no logic to it. And Matías's literary sentimentalizing nonsense only spelt out his lack of a guardian angel to help him take the fish by its gills. But Matías exuded a clammy heat that stuck him to his side for what seemed like an eternity. Was Matías already drunk? Probably not, at that midway point when both conversation and wit are still possible.

But, here you go, Matías was now introducing him, with no warning, to a German painter with a tricky surname whose cacophonic resonances recalled the name of a Swabian philosopher.[19] The German painter was tall and thin—consumptive—and came with a blond goatee. He had the weak eyes of a spoilt brat and seemed in need of protection. Ungainly and fearful, he looked at Pedro, who made an effort, insisted he sat down, and ordered him a hefty gin so he could drink it quickly, silently, and put himself in the mood. Matías seemed to have taken him under his wing because of his own humanist inclination, rather than the scant humanity emanating from the German, and was waxing grandiloquently about vague topics quite unrelated to painting, war, or the blitzed melancholy of a cancerous German mouse. But this knight of the sad countenance wanted to speak only about painting and tell them he'd be exhibiting at the Buchholz, emphasizing that his art was neo-expressionist and asking them in full flood, no beating about the bush, after downing ample amounts of gin, why they didn't immediately move on to his studio, where, poring over his pictures, they'd grasp that a German artist didn't need sensuousness to express the tortured pathos of a guilty and defeated people. "But first let's drink up," Matías protested.

"Bono," agreed the painter.

He was very impatient. It was absolutely necessary for his new acquaintances not to form an opinion about him solely on the basis of his physical appearance and imperfect hold on their language, which prevented him from communicating his ideas, but instead to acquaint themselves with his oeuvre and place him on the pedestal he (naturally) deserved. He immediately took out an inordinate wad of notes for that time and place and ordered the waiter-dramaturge to bring them fast and furious doses of that deadly alcohol. Which, nimbly delivered by the liquid maestro, ensured swift, consummate imbibing without anyone reacting in shock, except for the painter, who insisted on repeating the same smart conjuring trick a number of times at his own expense.

"Now this is here," he solemnly declared while raising his glass, "and now it isn't," when his glass was emptied. "It's passed inside my corpus."

Laughter wasn't the suitable response to this kind of humor by affirmation, but an immediate move to a universal application of the method was, and Matías kicked off, inspired by his guardian angel.

"This chair is down here," taking the one on which he'd been sitting, "and now it's up here," placing it on the black marble tabletop.

"But your corpus isn't where it was," the German protested, progeny of a race much better equipped for pure metaphysics.

"But it is," said Matías, clambering up and sitting down triumphantly to gestures of disgust accompanied by a touch of admiration from a literary crowd on a moderate or nil intake of alcohol.

Three waiters proceeded energetically towards the magisterial chair and Matías had to curb the temporal *durée* of his experiment that, on the other hand, seemed to leave nothing to be desired, spatially speaking. Down below were three or four strange, long-haired women in black velvet, and two or three actresses with mascara eyes smiled, concluding he was an idiot. This brief break in routine, achieved so cheaply, filled him with a sense of his own infallibility, quite like that of other occupants of portable chairs more laboriously earned in centuries past and in keeping with time-honored rituals stipulating chastity accompanied by the preservation of intact glands, which, to his mind, didn't seem less onerous at that point. On his descent, the still-not-mad painter continued applying the affirmative method to matters of great social import.

"This isn't paid for," he declared to the waiter with a smile. "And now everything is paid for," after handing him a document of payment to the bearer that exceeded by miles what they'd just consumed.

"Just a sec, sir, just a sec," said the waiter, pursuing them with Iberian integrity, as the threesome hastened into the murk outside, intoxicated by alcohol and the pride born of acts of freedom, ready to embark on the ship of expressionism and sail across the unruly ocean of the night.

"My corpus is now inside," declared Matías, "and my corpus is now outside the bar," after negotiating the revolving doors endowed with four wings, manufactured from gilded brass and red felt rather than feathers.

"Your corpus is no longer your corpus," retorted Pedro. "Your corpus now belongs to Bacchus."

Upon which the German, after the lapse of time necessary for him to comprehend, replied by exploding for the first time—though not the last—into Valhallian guffaws that echoed off trees, houses, and the Ministry, alarming a night watchman sitting on the street corner.

"That's very bono, very bono," he amicably allowed. "Would you like to be in my studio?" he followed up, doubts suddenly surging from a layer of his being lathered in alcohol and laughter.

"Bono. Let's be there," Matías concurred, imitating him.

And amid the painter's now gratuitous guffaws, they staggered through the night towards an attic on Calle Infantas where the thirsty offspring of his genius awaited.

They climbed the gloomy staircase, clutching each other to avoid stumbling, and the painter opened the door after various unsuccessful hits with a variety of keys. Finally inside, they were engulfed by the pitch black and a smell of fresh paint. More fiddling before the light finally came on, revealing countless canvases lining the walls of an extensive studio, every one a portrait of plump, rubicund womanhood.

"No, no, no!" exclaimed the neo-expressionist painter. "Not mine. Nothing mine. Another's work," while Matías bowed reverentially before a canvas he'd randomly selected, as if calculating the value of that flesh by its weight.

"Noteworthy," Matías declared. "It's got magma."

"Please," the German insisted. "Mine is another," pointing to a door hidden behind the large easels.

The studio's owner and Bono's artist-painter colleague seemed to be quite clear about his aesthetic ideal and reiterated it without an atom of shame or false modesty. The rubicund ladies smiled stereotypically on their toasty faces and placed their limbs in the most varied poses according to the banal recipes of the art of combination. Naturally, the presence of two bodies rather than one on each canvas would have permitted combinations and permutations ad nauseam, but even without what would have been quite a sleight of hand, the artist had managed to use these basic ingredients to give an approximate idea of the infinite.

"*Jubilatio in carne feminae*," chimed Matías.

"*Pulcritudo vastissima semper derramata*," followed up Pedro.

"Please. Not mine."

"Not yours, but very bono."

"Not bono! Me loathe. This isn't artistic. It says nothing. Not being expressionist. German art different."

"The number of nudes he paints indicates the levels reached in the repression of a people," Pedro opined abstrusely, thinking of his own repressions. It was gratifying to remain in that vast greenhouse of opulent peonies rather than step into a would-be masturbatory Dachau.

As if telepathically in tune, Matías exclaimed: "I've never been so reminded of the gas chambers."

"Not chamber. Shocking!" the artist protested and yet again he applied his logical, affirmative method: "Me no painted pictures here. Me painted pictures there," flapping his long arms and pointing across the carnal space of that ample studio.

"Before they sent them into the chamber, they stripped all women and gave them a soap and towel to make them think they were going to take a shower. But they were skinnier."

"Terrifying image of death, don't disturb my inner repose," recited Pedro.[20] "Me not dead there and then. Me alive here and now."

"I say that my paintings are there."

"They aren't holding bars of soap. It would be more hygienic."

The outraged German rushed towards his artistic cubbyhole, disappeared from sight through a narrow doorway. A little later, they heard a scream and a highly unmetaphysical curse; because of his sense of cleansing, he only worked at break of day and, lacking any electrical elements, could offer no widescale exhibition of his own product. He emerged soon after, a blotch of wet green paint on one sleeve, holding in his other hand the painting he'd led them to that spot to view, far from the Saturday night jamboree. They'd now been isolated from night's giddy pace and elemental-germinal energy pullulating down neighboring streets past a cuboid form of space partly occupied by deeply sleeping neighbors, and from deep inside their alcoholic haze they resolved to call to account their pioneering friend. As an overarching explanation of that night, the dizziness, the gas chambers, the nausea in the presence of nudes and himself, the latter held aloft his favorite painting, its paint still not dry.

It was a really bad painting. The theatrical ruins of a blitzed city were represented in lighter brown with sporadic touches of hellish red against a darker brown backdrop. Stones were stacked too high on both sides of an urban gorge not entirely blocked by rubble. The thrust of the composition was a big crowd of seemingly human beings, more ant-like than anything, and much smaller than usual. These beings made up a kind of vast river bubbling down towards the foreground of the picture. The disorderly gesticulating within that filthy insectivore world was apparently an attempt to express collective despair in which the suffering of infinite pain was accompanied by awareness of the rigorous justice they deserved. The fecaloid nature of the painting and vermicular character of its protagonists were no obstacle to it being contemplated, as fervently as a mother (but not a father) gazes at her newly born child, by the barely syntactic drunkard, a good payer, declamatory wit, and Saturday-night wizard who'd judged it necessary to drag them away from their wallowing in an infinite ennui of pink skin to view what was an unpleasant contrast.

"What did that guy just say?"

"Shocking..."

Such was the reaction of the two non-expressionist Iberians, non-builders of gas chambers (though maybe they had bellowed behind barriers around a bullring until the horn had finally penetrated Manolete's femoral triangle), non-organizers of pogroms (though maybe in their genes, several centuries ago, they'd turned inquisitional racks, worn stoles or hoods), what else could be on their minds?

"Bono. Been here, seen it," said Matías.

"Do you think it's bono?" asked the German, ever oblivious to the things of this world.

"Very bono."

"Bono."

"But what is it about? The failure of European civilization or the need to lose a stale virginity you'd preserve by dint of little treats and nocturnal losses?" asked Matías, sticking to his theories about the origins of works of art.

"Excuse me?"

"It hasn't got magma."

"What be magma? Plis."

Matías surveyed the length and breadth of the studio, bright electric bulbs and couch at one end, where the model for the pink ladies no doubt posed as the German's colleague continued his exploration of the positional potential of human bodies in three-dimensional space.

"You want me to explain?"

"Yes, plis! Do explain."

"A would-be painterly painter, you didn't paint these works that are here. You painted the work that is there. If you, rather than painting the work that is there, had painted the works that are here, you wouldn't have painted the work that is there. Rather than showing us the work that is there, you'd be showing your friends the works that are here. Knowing you hadn't painted the work you have there, you wouldn't have brought us here, but, forgetting what you want to paint, which you ought not to have painted in that way, you'd have brought us to the works that are there, and we wouldn't have come here... Get my drift?"

The German said nothing. Then repeated timidly: "But what be magma?"

"Magma be everything. Magma the pregnant reality of matter that sticks. Magma the protean form of vitality coming into being. Magma the smutty stickiness of sperm. Magma rock forged in its primitive state, before it fractures into stones. Magma the Jews when they are still in their ghettoes indefinitely reproducing..."

"I be Jew."

"What?"

"Yes, by an Israelite mother."

But then Pedro stooped forward as if suddenly he were greatly interested in the ant-like people descending the channel between the ruins. Could Matías have got it wrong? Might that not be in fact the essential magma? 'Twas ever thus. The man who appears on a Saturday at the right moment and says the right words and intuits how to touch the fibers of your heart and spark human warmth just has to declare, when the time is ripe, that he is a Jew or a Mason, or was once a Jesuit.

"Come on! Let's depart this shrine to art! Let's abandon this vessel marooned in the roofs of night! The storm will blast apart its worm-eaten timbers! Man the lifeboats. Man the lifeboats, everyone! I badly need a drink!" and Matías the sudden shrinking violet cast not one last glance at the tempting petal-like females, leapt down the stairs, followed at a prudent distance by Pedro and the captain of the leaking ship, who, as befits his worthy profession's code of honor, was the last to abandon ship, though not before he'd first studied the rushing waters sadly, yet pensively, wondering hopefully if he might not plug the breach with tar and burlap.

The street welcomed them with a soothing, crisper breath of air and a certainty that the night and all its potential were still there for the taking, despite the insectile humanity and neo-expressionist daubing by Central European nations who haven't a clue about that thing we call life. The cold air wafting into their faces immediately restored

Pedro's alertness to his freedom, Matías's individual alertness to his omniscience (which he'd almost lost for a moment), and the strength of will they'd both recovered in order to pursue their drunken bender to its logical end and slow-burning apotheosis. They strode into a small bar on the same street, a notice on its door invitingly declaring: LARGE GLASS OF COGNAC 0.50, not out of any enthusiasm to speculate by investing such a tiny amount on a high-octane dose, but driven by a true researcher's investigative impulse to gauge in his own throat what dreadful drink might be available at such a knockdown price. At a glance the amber liquid did indeed resemble what we think of as Spanish cognac, and the snifter's shape was normal enough, but the rest of its organoleptic properties destroyed any pretense to similarity. Initial intakes powerfully raised the alcoholic ceilings of their minds and brought a recalcitrant, regurgitant aftertaste to their palates, burying any residual gin or Veterano, and would have soon soured the night of stomachs less proofed by heroic spirit. Vapors generated by the snifter's ingested contents exploded in a round of belches that stank of sapling wood, in a constant viscous repetition significantly underlining the dangers night held in store for its aficionados.

But how comforting to be reassured by this bevvy concocted from cola and shoe polish, eau-de-vie and stewed mulch that they were up for anything, absolutely anything on this wildest of nights! After they'd knocked back that poison, the German painter disappeared, swallowed up by an aspirating-propellant gas chamber blowing down the main axis of Calle Infantas; he mumbled a couple of meaningless "bonos," tried unsuccessfully to embrace them, smiled yet again, gazed at a woman cantering towards the next brightly lit bar, and was swept away by a chariot of fire.

Next to vanish was the bar with its zinc counter, drinkers' stolid faces, and nighttime barman's brawny arms and rolled-up sleeves. The entire, barely existent phantasmagoria went into reverse and plunged down a newly created abyss. Forewarned by these sudden transfigurations of a possible ascent to their personal Mount Tabor, they hung on to each other's shoulders, despite their differing heights, and stalwartly tried to resist the worst of the storm. Soaked by inevitable, repeated gulps from the balloon, holding on to the mutual cord bonding them to humanity, having put a proper distance between those pink paintings and their present reality, they now felt caulked and ready for a hazardous crossing. True enough, taxis with menacing green horns lurked nearby, piercing the night with their klaxons; true enough, flabby, dark-haired women loitered in dark *mouton doré* coats, lips a garnet red; true enough, luminous neon signs outside several establishments were legible through a clouded consciousness; true enough, they harbored a foggy notion that after an indeterminate period of time and exhausting various, as yet unforeseen pleasures, they'd return to the warmth of their usual nocturnal abodes, where they'd be aroused from their repose by unimaginable blasts—comparable only to the angelic trumpets on the Final Day of Judgment—and hauled back to a quotidian reality where they occupied slots like screws or metal cogs in machines that juddered but never entirely halted; but despite all the hustle constituting their real, if fractured, universe, they stayed immersed in another, lower existence where edges were blunt rather than sharp, where friendship expressed itself not in intellectual interpenetration but as animal heat on shoulders supporting a center of gravity with a dangerous tendency to lurch vertically from a limited base circumscribed by two invisible, bony tripods, on left foot and right, uneasily guided by nerve endings that were responding less positively than normal.

But even the worst of moments is only that: a moment. Human nature is so very limited! Although at any given time an individual may seem to escape his own being in an athletic leap or a ballerina's pirouette, in ecstasy placing himself in direct contact with the deity, or in mere glorious inebriation that brings pure, timeless euphoria, such glimmers of eternity reveal themselves as fragile and ephemeral. A leaping athlete accepts his muscular thighs won't prevent his knees from flexing as he lands, a pirouetting ballerina finishes up in her partner's strong and gentle arms, a mystical ecstasy akin to bliss surging from the nether regions is proof of faint powers of sublimation and alcoholic inebriation that isn't self-contained but ushers in vomiting and groaning.

So their worst moment and its burden of eternity passed, and thanks to several unsweetened double espressos and a bracing exposure to the cold breeze in the street, they began to feel less need of that reciprocal anti-gravitational support. As soon as they'd seen off the nausea brought on by rotgut firewater, the need to totter off to the next street of San Marcos became self-evident. Their resilient stomachs withstood the blow below the belt, they'd not vomited, their fingers weren't shaking, their faces *were* greenish but they'd not had a close-up of the ground, and they now found themselves seated on red plush in a small drinking haunt with a nickel-plated bar where a jukebox repeated time and again the same Andalusian song, a saccharine cante hondo, as the old needle scraped black ebonite. Further inside sat a paunchy female peanut seller and a handicapped, though not blind, old man who peered at them from behind dark spectacles. The neighborhood night watchman was leaning on the bar, swaddled by his usual farthingale of sashes and scarves. Several tables behind, a woman was relaxing, the nocturnal sort, but, unfortunately, quite sad and chaste. Above her, at a higher level, several other old men—maybe ushers from the adjacent movie house—were silently sipping milky coffee. The lavatory door squeaked open and shut, its rusty mirrors barely reflecting the light from a few yellow bulbs. That building was a survivor from a bygone era, yet to be transformed into a cafeteria, whose melancholy depths were too overwhelming to be tolerated for long. The night watchman's beady eyes squinted their way, and the men who'd chivied the jukebox into once more delivering the same whining song were a couple of pimps in black who quietly tapped their heels to the rhythm and said nothing, looking at each other, laughing, barely clapping their hands, taking care in the course of the night to ensure their white scarves remained neat and tidy between their jacket collars and the overlong, greasy ringlets on the napes of their necks.

"And that young man will still be out gallivanting on the tiles, like a loser, just like my late hubby, when he's really something else and just what our little girl needs. I think that silly Dora has already sown the seed, and suggested rather too obviously that her little girl is a stunner, a juicy morsel for a man who's savored so little. An experienced man would know what to appreciate, but this poor critter—basically a critter I think I love like my own son—doesn't know how. He thinks of her as a little girl and the moment he feels pressured he'll be off like a shot to another boardinghouse and someone else. And our little girl will be left rocking on her chair, or at best she'll land one of those pathetic commercial reps or no-hope pen pushers who've got nothing going for them. As if our child were meant for them. I'd prefer she did what her mother did, which may be infra dig, but at least it's not pathetic. But wait a sec, let's not fear the worst. He'll bite. Sure he will. He's a touch head-in-the-clouds, like the intellectual, researcher, or whatever he is. He can't see the forest for the trees, and is green behind the ears and slow to recognize our girl's class. But the day he's smitten, he won't be able to help himself and will fall lock, stock, and barrel and comport himself like a true gentleman, because that's what he is and that's what's always rung bells for me. What you call the genuine item. Someone who does what a gentleman has to do, not like those other good-for-nothings and cocky so-and-sos. Not like the girl's butter-wouldn't-melt of a father, may God curse him. The fact is I go into a dither when he goes out. I can't sleep. At my age we don't sleep much, though we look good for our age. And when he goes out, I can only see him in cafés with those waitresses who come on to you, if they still exist, or, in private rooms, led on by bad friends, a man I'm sure hasn't the slightest idea how to clap his hands to the beat, surrounded by dirty sluts who'll do anything to lead him astray, turn him into someone else and open his eyes. Not that they aren't open, the little angel sees well enough, he's a biology student, after all, but he sometimes seems so innocent I'm shocked because I don't think any other man would have left her in the state she's in, like the day she left her mother's womb, he's not touched her even though I put him in the bedroom next to hers, and that fool Dora goes and says to him: 'You know she sleeps on her own,' men find these things out by themselves, you don't have to put it into words. He must be such a naive innocent abroad not to have dipped his stick. I don't think this manner of man existed in my time. He likes her, of course he does, that's obvious. You can see it in his eyes when he watches her rocking so temptingly, so flirtatiously, ogling so, though she's wet behind the ears too. I can't credit he can be so naive. But it's a fact they'll lead him off the straight and narrow. I'm almost scared the girl sleeps on her own, it puts her on a plate, and any of these men, like the commercial rep, could try it on and decide she's a *bocato di cardinale*, as my late hubby would say of this part of my thigh when he felt it because it's so white—and still is—and he'd pretended to nibble it. What a tease! What you call a real man! But I like this guy too. I like him, though I don't know how to set his urges racing, and because it really wouldn't be right, I reckon, to set up my grandchild as I set up my daughter, which I did to such advantage like that proper bawd, Celestina. Because when that fool of a dancer jilted her like he did, if it hadn't been for me and my skill as a go-between, which don't bring a blush to my cheeks, because at the end of the day God made the world the way it is, I'd have found her in the same pickle a few months later, because I've never known anyone so incapable of putting herself in the spotlight, as that joker would say, the Frenchman who was such a man-about-town and wanted to put the spotlight on her in Paris, in *la douce France*, so much so that if I hadn't intervened with my wits about me, I'd have lost my daughter and all hope of any spotlight. But no way, I'm my mother's daughter after all, and by that time I could work my tail off because the change was a thing of the past and I was fine and knew the café-cabarets like the back of my hand, except that the best place to sell secondhand goods is one's own home in a decent, respectable household where everyone thinks she's virtue betrayed and talks so sweetly and feels tempted to mention marriage, though in the end nothing's doing because it's obvious that would be the last straw. But here I am worrying because he's gone out on a Saturday night. On a Saturday. As if he were my son! Even if he were. A man has to sow his wild oats like a trooper, especially if you've never been to war. That's the problem with men today. They were too late for the last war and with so much peace and the poor rations they ate as a child, they've no idea what a woman is and think they're like diamonds you must pick up with pincers and speak to in French to find out what they're really feeling. If they'd been on route marches, won battles, and raped, and learned all about booty and the hallowed right to loot conquered towns and not just read about it in novels, it would be a different kettle of fish. They'd have a different outlook, I fear, and this little fool wouldn't have just paid my little girl's bedroom a visit, but by this time he'd be long gone and we'd all be terrified, we'd have watched him pass through like Beelzebub, who you can tell from the noise his hoof makes and the scorched smell he leaves behind rather than the honeyed words he mouths. Though obviously if he'd been like that fruitcake, my little girl would still be sleeping in my bedroom and our plans would have changed, and the most he'd have done would have been telling silly Dora some risqué jokes, for she's always game for a laugh, and I'd have wrinkled my nose and told him mine was a decent household and sent him packing like he deserved. But he's not like that, he's our very own San Luigi Gonzaga,[21] and all he needs is a rosary and a bunch of lilies and he puts up with our chitchat and spends his free time in the dining room at night and I wouldn't be at all surprised if he didn't come to me one day, dressed in navy blue, and ask for her hand with a bouquet of purple flowers; that's the color that goes with my age, even though I'm so well preserved."

The immediate proximity of sacred shrines, temples for the celebration of nocturnal Orphic rites, can be divined from a few key, unequivocal signs. The municipal authorities simultaneously help keep good order in the area by prudently reducing the potency of public lighting and no less prudently increasing the quantity of door-opening employees, who, stripped years ago of their luminous navels, still proudly display bunches of gleaming keys and fearless faces riding over thick scarves. Young workers in raincoats—who'd previously have been called journeymen—as well as apprentices to various liberal professions and men from later generations, better equipped biologically than financially, constitute the bulk of that collective onward march plagued by hardships, facing unforeseen reefs, calling for heroic efforts, aided only by limited fly-by-night camaraderie they express by averting their gaze rather than in hearty slaps on the backs from mutual strangers who, nevertheless, feel bonded in their incongruous huddles by the same hundred-percent earthiness of human nature.

From the very beginning, serendipity marks out the complex acts to be performed in futile attempts to placate the nocturnal beast's hunting instincts. Why do we go in 17 and not 19? Who can guess in which doorway we'll dally? Who can tell if the object of our desire, whose pleasant, if hazy, memory we cherish today, isn't asleep right now and couldn't care less if we came? Who can guarantee that, if she isn't there, she may not have been transferred to number 21 or 13 on the same street? Who can be sure the bewildered supplicant will recognize her the second he spots the same tangible body in a slightly modified outfit (tight black skirt rather than red bathing suit; loose-fitting yellow housecoat rather than sky-blue two-piece; black hair and gleaming white teeth rather than faded two-tone hair and screwed-up mouth with broken dentures on the bedside table; heavily talcumed, olive-dark skin rather than the hint of fluff above her top lip; busty breasts under a black French bra rather than tits drooping under a green silk blouse)? Who can predict, if he does, that the fluttering butterfly of desire won't fly skyward again or be poleaxed by disgust when he sees her come downstairs with the man she's just serviced in our absence? Be that as it may, and ignoring such irritating questions, serendipity, not love, is the god lording it over such games of fancy.

Doña Luisa operated as the resident female veteran sluicegate when Saturday-night crowds flooded the passageways, defying all possible calculations or plans to fit them in her house's available spaces, and by simply shifting her elderly frame, she rerouted in the most practical way imaginable all traffic across key crossroads, sending the riffraff from the street to the drawing room, or to a designated waiting room always *sans femmes*, or back to the gloomy stairs in the direction of the realm of night watchmen and her totally submissive helper, a wrinkled old dear who opened the door to the street from the inside and who—when not doing that—stayed seated on a bench like a church pew. In such situations, when Doña Luisa completely blocked the traffic and the sluicegate was both dike and breakwater, the veteran old dear attained greatness itself. Dragons of desire furiously beat their red wings against her, licking flames singed her noble gray tresses, but she stalwartly stood her ground and prevented the entry of anyone undeserving. Maybe a humble stance, a tender glance, an old acquaintance backed by sound finance, or manly beauty matched by the attractions of extreme youth would placate her vigilant zeal on nights when they were packed to the ceiling. That was how Matías engineered his and Pedro's entry into that castle of delights while the plebs were being rebuffed, even though their calloused hands flourished mandatory twenty-five-peseta notes, the fruit of their honest toil.

At that late hour the atmosphere in the drawing room was rank. Odors from bodies piling into that reduced space from mid-afternoon onwards, tobacco smoke finding no exit because the opening of windows onto the world outside was strictly punished, dust scattered from the mud slowly drying on visitors' shoes, cheap perfumes, coughs spraying thousands of microscopic, spherical particles, and brilliantine dripping from most male heads formed a dense miasma through which customers admired sculpted bodies barely veiled by the astonishing, flimsy attire of the white women who were lined up along a wall and whose trafficking was on the agenda. In contrast to the hubbub on the heaving staircase, helped by a cornucopia of tactile, aromatic, and visual elements, a discreet, embarrassed silence lent the scene an even more liturgical air. Mute desire expressed itself in sidelong, furtive, almost pretend glances. Sometimes two or three customers, more impressionable than most, chatted intently, hiding from the barefaced stares of the women trying to identify their future victim-executioner as fast as they could. Provocation was reduced to a minimum: a single, brazen glance by a complete stranger, an ingenuously perverse, half-opened mouth, shoulders and hips swaying maybe in an attempt to conjure up mirages of exotic isles, trembling breasts that shock only because of the scant material draping hesitant stirrings. Despite their palpable, perfumed presence, the silence pervading the room reduced them to a threatening vision of phantoms about to vanish. But a magical intervention of will by any of the males ensured that the woman in question halted her primal antics, and as he tilted his head firmly to one side, she grabbed with one hand a skirt that was too tight or hair that was too loose or any other part of her anatomy unprepared for such a move, and began walking quickly towards the dungeons of love pursued by her purchaser, who on that very same staircase could, by placing a hand on the swaying hip before him, verify the physical, not phantom, nature of the item he'd rented, to be followed by a ritual surrender of the aforementioned twenty-five-peseta note, together with occasional cash surpluses for the acolytes bearing towels and buckets of water. "A good catch today," crowed the spiteful acolyte, who paradoxically wielded power and authority over the high priestess herself, as the latter handed over a round aluminum token which the former carefully put away in a cloth bag hanging from her belt, where the token joined its mates in a small but sonorous pile, at once a symbol of the priestess's exploitation and the expectation of an unredeemable future.

But Matías was like one of the family, and the simple selection ceremonies just described couldn't be applied to him so summarily, let alone on a day like today when his prodigious skinful and gift of omniscience allowed him to demand a more sophisticated preliminary to his eventual encounter with a strange body. He broke the religious silence that had descended over the drawing room—as was only right—by spouting oratory out of place in a cheapskate brothel.

"Don't weep for me, virgins of Jerusalem, weep rather for yourselves and your children! Like a Madonna lily among irises I seek you out, o stranger in the night. Where is the one my heart has chosen? Where is the warm bosom on which I can rest my weary head?"

A skinny old louche sitting in one corner, loath to attempt a suggestive wiggle of her bodily parts, placed hope not in these questions, but rather in the excess demand that was forcing her fellow workers to migrate to upper levels, and she just had to smile, lift her white arms, and lasso his neck, contravening the draconian rules over that area of the house, as she said: "Come on, you cheeky thing!"—and, more sotto voce—"Want me to try a few little tricks?" like a weary lioness flinging herself at the only opportunity to touch a young man that—despite her trade—had come her way in recent eons.

But Doña Luisa's adjutants rushed violently towards the sacrilegious couple, who were breaking the sanctity of a spot destined for mere visual titillation, and, prudently dressed in black, they pushed them, together with Pedro, into the visitors' room that was set aside for people too important to be thrown out and too dubious to stay in the selection zone, where they would only upset all those focused on that uplifting hocus-pocus.

Spheroidal, phosphorescent, booming, darkly luminous, gristly, tactile, a mass of folds, caressing, soothing, paralyzing, swaddled in protective folds, odorous, maternal, impregnated by alcohol spilled by a mouth, bluish counterpane, sometimes gilded by an anemic bulb, its glow searing nighttime eyes, lulling, fit only to mumble, to denigrate, the prostitute's cup of disdain for the drunkard, a place where madam becomes reverend mother confessor again, setting clear norms by which the sins of the flesh are avoidable, longitudinal tunnel along which nausea rises, earthen colored when the worm body enters into contact with the masses imprisoning it, with no gravitational pull as if in an experiment that's still ongoing, gyroscopic, turning towards a goal, chosen for a secret crossing, Stygian lake, gifted with a metal bench where the languid, elongated body slumps onto a softness that's no less soft, wagon-lit compartment traversing the Bordeaux landes at a eighty miles an hour, log cabin in the Far West where no scalps remain, cabin rocked by a storm in the Indian Ocean when typhoons halt the flight of the yellow cormorant, wicker skiff montgolfiering into the sky, elevator hurtling to the top of a dilated rubber skyscraper, dank dungeon where man's solitude is plain to see, basket of filth, dregs where, reduced to excrement, the inmate awaits the black water that will take him out to sea, past gray rats and sewers, a cell where he again uses a nail to slowly etch, laboriously removing slivers of lime, the same profile of a siren with a female fish's amazing tail, watched over by the stout figure of a woman who is cradling her, caressed by the figure of a plump woman with a child on the tit, cradle, placenta, meconium, decidua, matrix, oviduct, pure, empty ovary, inverse annihilation by which the egg in an antiprotonic universe splits into two previous entities and Matías has unbegun his nonexistence, thus the private room, the visitors' room, the trash room, the room for drunkards from good families who drop by on a packed night and are marooned with the only whore who's unemployed and who, with baffled gaze, observes them as they make peace and are saved among orange rind and potato peelings.

"Sweet servant of the night, solace of my sorrow, tell me: How did you find the secret of eternal youth? Who enabled you to preserve those full red lips after years of kissing? How is it, after visiting so many bedsheets, your flesh isn't a sponge soaked by an idiot child's pee? Tell me all! Reveal your secret to your admirers."

"You'd be amazed. Touch me here!" she said, baring a thigh. "Feel how firm it is. If only you'd seen me in my prime. But you're so silly! Why do you drink so much? You do get into such a state."

"It's incredible. Who invented flesh like yours? What substance is it that can cross the fires of hell and emerge so fresh and flowery?"

"Golden willy, golden willy, you imbecile," she roared, with a horrible laugh, exposing the vast expanse of wrinkles hitherto hidden by a fifteen-watt bulb conspiring with the rouge caking her cheeks.

"Beauty, eternity, luxuriant beauty! Time-conquering goddess! Lasciviousness incarnate! Tell me, tell me, do. Open your heart and explain. Did you sign a pact with the devil?"

"Jesus wept!" she cried fearfully. "What are you saying?" and she suppressed (almost involuntarily) an (almost unconscious) wish to make an exorcizing sign of the cross.

"When you laugh, I have to avert my gaze," Pedro informed her.

"Laughter is healthy," the old woman retorted.

"Can *you* look her straight in the face?"

"I love her. I love her. I want to possess her," Matías assured him, stumbling in a frenzy towards that beat-up body, collapsing to the ground in a drunken stupor, slipping on peels from oranges mysterious visitors had consumed in a not so distant geological period. He made no attempt to get up but flailed with his only available hand, the other being strangely twisted and entirely deadened under his own body.

"Why do you drink so much?" she repeated gloomily, as if imagining the oceans of delight she was being denied by the sad state of those limp youngsters. "Why do you drink so much? It means you're fit for nothing."

Hearing which, Matías split his sides in serial guffaws.

"What would *you* do, learned sage, if you hadn't been drinking?" he asked mid-hiccups.

"Me?"

"Yes, you."

"Let her be! Don't laugh at her!"

"I desire her. I'll do anything."

"Come on, ducky," said the old woman. "Why on earth did you drink so much?"

"Call the woman on duty. Tell her to reserve us the best bedroom in the house. I'll go with you, and let death sunder me if I'm not the happiest man around tonight when everyone else is on their last legs... Wimps!" and he waved his long arm threateningly. "Wimps! Don't you know that life is short, that it only occupies the time of a rose between two equidistant stars? How do you use your time? *Postume, Postume, labuntur anni!*[22] Don't you know the body dies and the soul enters eternity?"

The woman stooped over the form prostrate on the sodden mat of orange peel and placed his head on her immortal thigh, the malleable firmness of which time had yet to undo. She wrapped her—extremely withered—arm around his head and stroked his disheveled hair, which fell over the drunkard's greenish temples like a crow's wing. For a second she forgot Pedro, who was looking on, half shell-shocked, half in the clouds, and said: "Are we really bound for bed?" with a soothing, inevitably sultry voice.

"Yes, enchantress," confirmed the loving gallant.

At which point Doña Luisa came over to shoot the breeze; the female sluicegate had finished her watch once the front door had been barred and bolted and the municipal employees had dispersed frustrated bands of hopefuls with gestures of contempt and vulgar jibes. Entering the magic sphere where the three had been journeying, she reestablished an equilibrium between the realm of reason and the realm of unbridled passion, and now, from the way she sat down on the metal bench, it was evident—despite all her savoir faire and savoir vivre—that she was going to break the mystic atmosphere they'd shared till then.

"Good evening. How's it going?" which their enervated state prevented them from answering. "What a crazy night! You shouldn't visit on nights like this. You really shouldn't! The girls are all spoken for. And everything goes so quickly. Saturday's fine only for bricklayers, I reckon. But not for you. Naturally you're always welcome in this house. I don't know how I stand it, people get more discourteous by the day. Naturally! If only they were all like you... But you can't imagine the people who've passed through tonight. So coarse, so foulmouthed, my God, so foulmouthed. And all drunk... and that shows too. You must be able to handle your drink. You know what I mean. But I'm not up to this kind of lather. Christ, I'm sweating like a pig. Hey, Charo, my love, fetch me some fizzy pop from the kitchen!"

"Right away, Doña Luisa!" said the swooning lover, getting up and letting the august head she'd shed thud on the floor. "I'll bring you some right away," her anxious look revealing the fear Doña Luisa inspired in those of her flock who were ripe for retirement.

"Did the consolation of my dotage abandon me? Did the staff for my stumbling steps depart? Woe is me, will I ever see the light of the sun again, sad Oedipus? Electra, my daughter, do not abandon your aged father," declaimed Matías, striving to impress the hard-faced Doña Luisa with the depths of his hallucinations.

"They'll all be in bed by now," said Don Pedro, wanting to keep the conversation going.

"They'll all be fast asleep by now, except for those canoodling, and that poor thing," explained Doña Luisa benignly. "That poor thing's past it but she's still game," she went on. "Indeed, she's mad about men."

"Yes, that much is obvious . . ."

"Not like others. Like the young girl you must have seen previously, tall, slim, and blond, with protruding bones. Doesn't she ring a bell? She's here but might as well not be. My girls must be ready for anything."

"She doesn't have the vocation."

"Too true, not even to be a nun. But Charo's been worth a mint."

"Your fizzy pop," said Charo obsequiously. "I took the one next to the ice."

"Would you like some?" asked Doña Luisa. She started imbibing that spiritual beverage in step with the rise and fall of Matías's Adam's apple.

"Don't worry on our behalf," responded sad Oedipus. "I can neither feel nor reason."

"Why do you two drink so much?" Madam asked.

"It's our youth," said Pedro.

"Yes, of course, that makes sense . . ."

"Why the hell do you think I'd be necking this celestial creature, if I wasn't plastered?"

"Shush, you silly," said the old woman, resuming possession of her gallant in repose.

"Well, I think you two should go," Doña Luisa went on, turning towards the no less plastered but less literary Pedro. "I mean, if you're not staying, you should leave, because it's four o'clock. You sure you don't want a sip?"—holding out her bottle of pop, its rim smeared by her shiny saliva—"It's so hot at this time of night."

"Let's be off, Matías!" said Pedro, standing up.

"*Dieu et mon droit*," answered the latter, by way of a no.

"We should be going."

"You know, no need to force yourselves. You can go when you feel like it. You're the well-mannered sort and can stay and chat awhile."

"I am what I am."

"If it were down to me, but you know very well, we have our regs."

At that precise moment (it being the time for electricity cuts) the small assembly point was plunged into darkness.

"There we go again. The cuts," said Doña Luisa. "I'm going in search of light," and they heard the muffled shuffle of her babouches and her knuckles scraping the walls as she groped her way.

When the light went out and the ogress disappeared, that humble space smelling of vomit and oranges regained its ideal dreamlike state.

"I knew it! The gods were preparing my punishment!" shouted Matías energetically. "The time is nigh for me to be struck cruelly blind."

"What's that, my love?" said the ardent Charo, seeking out his mouth with her own.

"Sad Oedipus, never again will I see the light of the sun! I've gouged out my eyes, the right one with the nails of my right hand and the left with the nails of my left, and they still feel warm in my hands though they no longer give me sight. Electra, Electra, come to me!"

"Shout as much as you want but it won't come back till six. But Doña Luisa will bring a candle," the daughter-lover said soothingly. "So what? There's time enough for what *we* want to do."

Pedro took advantage of their climaxing ecstasy to slip out. A small crack of light indicated the path to the door. Groping his way along the passage he managed to find the stairs. On the various floors flickering flames lit up scenes of life being lived. Each postcoital woman guided her hour-long gallant towards the street, her left hand round his male waist, her right raised slightly so the light cast its light farther and they didn't stumble. Wrapped in their negligees, flushed and meek, they said polite goodbyes, while sullen and sour, ears bright red, in threadbare raincoats, the men slunk off silently, didn't look round, as if pursued by a curse, sensing that only the cool darkness of night could cleanse in the way the ocean cleanses.

Pedro walked gingerly back. Frightened by what he might have left behind. Rattled by retching he was holding in check. Trying to forget the absurdities of life. Repeating: it's intriguing. Repeating: everything has a meaning. Repeating: I'm not drunk. Thinking: I'm on my own. Thinking: I'm a coward. Thinking: I'll be worse for wear tomorrow. Feeling: it's cold. Feeling: I'm tired. Feeling: my tongue is parched. Wanting: if only I'd lived a while, found a woman, been capable of giving myself like others do. Wishing: not to be on my own, to feel another human's warmth, to be caressed by velvety flesh, desired by a kindred spirit. Afraid: tomorrow will be another wasted day and I wonder, why did I drink so much? Fearful: I'll never find the key to life, I'll always be on the margins. Affirming: despite everything, one didn't, despite everything, maybe I; despite everything, who'd ever desire someone like that? Affirming: I'm not to blame. Affirming: something is wrong, not just me. Affirming: evil exists. Asking: who can explain evil? Reflecting-remembering: that woman who was there and who shouldn't have been, because it was as if she wasn't, because she was no use. Insightful-forgiving: he was no angel because apart from not having wings, apparently all he longs for is to be annihilated. An angel can revolt against his god, but this half angel only revolts against his mother. Accusing-dissolute: she was a loathsome old louche, just a loathsome old louche. Conclusion: I'm the pits.

He crossed empty streets where dimmed lights barely picked out facades. Fleet-footed, frowning, lonesome men, hats pulled down, avoided him. There were no cars. Only the odd, silent, rectangular shadow passing by in the distance. Night watchmen had gone off to sleep in unknown dens from which the incessant clapping of those they'd marooned failed to fetch them. Maybe a cigarette-selling beggar might still be hiding behind the jutting corner of a house on Calle de la Reina that shielded her from the wind. Maybe a beggar with a stick and stinking of wine might still be trying to scrape up some shekels using a reverse technique to the one he'd use in a church atrium. A woman in an astrakhan coat, olive skinned, neat, dark brilliantined hair with a carnation, offered him anisette as if she were supplying a drug. This woman smiles as if also at the ready to sell—out of hours—another kind of goods. But everything is out of hours now, and he can only pull up his coat collar, pretend he wasn't tired or drunk and hurry up the street to the distant boardinghouse, towards the Plaza del Progreso, across the too-broad, too-bright Calle de Sevilla, then more pleasantly along narrower side streets whiffing of food frying, churros, and hot *porras* soon to be sold by heroic street sellers who went to bed at five p.m., before he finally reaches the familiar doorway on that empty street. Thanks to maternal forethought he has a front door key and one to the apartment. All he has to do is open the heavy door with the big key, an aluminum copy, so it doesn't weigh heavy, of the ancient iron key in the keeping of the concierge, who never lets it out of her sight. And then shut it, hearing the bang echo, more startling than by day. He must climb the stairs, gripping the rickety banister. Feel along the wall for a button he must press to produce light. Think for a sec to ensure it's not a doorbell. He must hold off because of such doubts and go blindly up, counting the steps in the pitch black, while his hand is impregnated with acrid wall plaster that's always rough, covered in pencil squiggles, enigmatic inscriptions, and caricatures. Some miraculous skill allows him to open the door at the first attempt. His nose encounters a familiar stench. Damp smells from the kitchen laundry room, the breathing of the commercial rep and childless couple, the cheap perfume of the maid and the more expensive one—though it's hard to tell the difference—of the daughter of the house, and the old lady's, which smells of violets. He's back, suddenly immersed in the tepid domesticity that serves him as home. He leans on the doorjamb and stops when he feels the visceral heat. The whole house is alive, all those bodies in their beds. He hears a grunt, a gentle whistle; the ensemble can't manage a snore. But everything is in sync, serenely, blindly, mutely expecting his arrival. There, close by, is his place, his white sheets, his thick blanket, his pillow where he will finally find rest, a glass of water now tasting of warm broth, his old books. And all those awkward, unaesthetic items, the arms of the coat stand pointing upwards, the sideboard with its dreadful porcelain figurines, a green plant, an embroidered mat on a coffee table, a chair upholstered in oilskin on which nobody ever sits, an artificial cactus that nobody has to water because it's plastic, a gilt umbrella stand with Greek figures in relief, a glass bowl on a shelf above a radiator that's never switched on—except on New Year's Eve—await him, all visible to his inner eye (no need to switch on a light that might disturb someone). "The third eye," he reflects, shutting the other two, which are so pointless, even tighter. As he makes this seemingly external, inoperative contraction, an image lights up on his mental screen. Dorita is sleeping in her bedroom, her curvaceous body resting on the best mattress in the house, which the dowager made available for her body and no other. The body (which his everyday eyes can't see because it's covered by blankets, sheets, a shift, and maybe even a threadbare overcoat) appears well defined and complete to the third eye struck by wonderfully accurate vibrations. He sees her whole, in repose, offering herself on her eternally rocking chair, where she always awaits him. The house endures in a silence as solid as a casket. Invisible or purple-velvet shadows shroud it so completely that when he hits a corner, or a table, he barely feels a thing, barely an echo in the muggy early morning and she awaits him from a parallel deep space and the reminiscences in his feverish brain. The image of the young woman appears duplicated by stereoscopic vision: along one tunnel spreads an almost indefinite succession of conversations, silences, knowing maternal words, brightly colored housecoats exhibited one after another, enveloping that young, ever-blossoming body; along the other tunnel comes only the frozen image of what he has never seen, a naked body in the shape of a bud, an archetype of exactitude. Like a silent siren, the summons from this body echoes across the world's perennially erotic literature, a waiter's sly grin, the unknown model for the pink ladies, the convulsing neo-expressionist mantis, the plump compactness of a sweaty madam, the last glance of a hopeful old whore. Is *this* love? Could love be a hasty assembly of meanings? Could love be the world unifying around a symbolic being? Could love be the annihilation of the most individual part of the self, annihilation that strips bare another reality, one completely incomprehensible in itself, but one we insist on ensnaring in the spider's web of our vacillating existence?

No. That isn't love. He knows it isn't love. Alongside that accumulation of grotesque nocturnal phenomena, alongside those magical, familiar objects and that heated atmosphere, alongside all that vinous inebriation and unsatisfied eroticism, lies a small part of his self, the basest, the most passionately poetic, shameless like those plants that exhibit their sexual parts and are enhanced by an obscene aesthetic that creates beauty from what we animals know only too well to be ugly. The construction of a more essential life, the project of going further, the deluded sense of not being part of the dingy reality of that city, that country, and those times lie elsewhere. He is different and has nothing in common with this tasty but empty tendril of the lame, consenting classes. He exists in another world, which a young girl doesn't enter simply because she's languid and tasty. He's chosen a more arduous path, at the end of which is another kind of woman, whose value derives not from elemental, cyclical energies but from clarity of mind that is free and decisive. He mustn't fall on this half-opened flower like a fly and dirty his little feet.

Be that as it may, at the moment his right hand—which holds the world within its grasp—wants to open the door of the ascetic sage's cell, his left hand gently levers open the coveted chalice.

Dorita is hardly surprised when she feels his hesitant hands on her body. She shudders, then whispers: "Is that you . . . my love!"

Pedro plunges in, barely able to tell flesh from welcoming warmth. But the woman's awareness (she is ever alert, even when being raped late in the night by an irresolute drunkard) jars him when she demands he answer the essential prior question: "Do you love me?"

"I love you, I love you, I love you, I love you, I love you," Pedro feels his mouth affirm, promise, let slip, while far from himself, far from her, in a lucid corner of his mind, he observes two abandoned, solitary, robotic bodies not possessed by him but by a demon, two bodies swaying—incubus and succubus—so distant, alien, and lost, yet, for all that, the most violent pleasure granted to man isn't unleashed and doesn't burn him, across that distance, in the tiny space where he seeks refuge, where the freest part of his mind still holds on momentarily, before inevitably he yields his freedom—like a communion wafer to a black dog—and collapses exhausted.

He is immersed in an immense void, he floats, then sinks, pursuing the depths of a dream that never comes, until a "You must leave" awakes him inexorably, transports him back to the nauseating salty dribble of cognac coating his mouth. But still she has questions for him. She places two hot arms on the back of his neck, kisses him, and insists: "Will you love me forever?"

"Forever, forever, forever, forever," he says, as he reels towards the pitch-black passage full of familiar objects and smells pouring out of half-opened doors of bedrooms where aging, inglorious bodies persist in expelling air at regular intervals.

The crannies in an old woman's heart and brain. The trap. Femininity turned guile when flesh is no longer flesh and only nondescript matter. The procuress who procures so as not to starve to death or have to remove the lace curtains from her windows. So as not to scrub floors, being a widow now. The hunt. The advantages of the hunt over selling or renting. To have him in your clutches, because finally he's fallen and, being who he is, he won't be able to escape. And he will do his duty. How right she was not to sleep. Old women must be tough. They don't need sleep. Why would your weary body want to sleep if you cannot tell tiredness from rest? Why would your keen ears shut out those whose bones have yet to feel the cold? Why close your eyelids with their blue bags and drooping folds if you can still see in the dark and frighten him who you stare in the face, knowing you know what he knows too: what you have *seen*. She's so innocent! Her flesh is no longer what's on her bones, but what sticks to the best mattress in the house. Her flesh has leapt generations and landed there, still the same, ready to feel exactly what she felt, what she remembers and still imagines, but no longer feels. At last! Revenge on that repulsive effeminate dancer and chancer. Quits with the fat, bespectacled banker, wily prospector of soiled goods! At last! The laugh's on you in your grave, braggart soldier, flirting with Tagalog women, collecting photos of naked natives, poisoning the blood of your wife, dishonoring your daughter and your widow sodden on Rhum Negrita! The laugh's on you because everything's been reset, and the dubious legality of your name will soon be tactfully reclaimed, witnessed, and signed off on, from this generation to the next!

"Good evening!" said the old woman's cracked voice. "What time of night is this?"

"Yes . . . I . . . I know; it's very late. Good evening!" And he slammed his bedroom door more loudly than he'd intended, a his face bright red, annoyed with himself, feeling pointlessly embarrassed and sheepish in the presence of that old woman, the entire world, himself, and a hazy future of undiscovered cancers and virgins deflowered en passant in a manner that wasn't his style but that now pertained to him.

He bolted his door. He was alone. Rampant male glee flooded him for a second and he felt like a rooster perched on top of a wall, stridently cock-a-doodling at the land-bound animals roaming down below and smirking up at him: cat, fox, and vixen. What's that cock-a-doodle mean? I'm drunk, you know. What about her? She's asleep; she never woke up. Sweet dreams. She's still asleep, and I'm here. Why? What cock-a-doodling or baying at the moon? Why should I accept what I've done? Why rail against my flushed face? Against the snifter of cognac still coming back at me. Against the whole idiotic night. Why? Why did I do it? If I believe love must be conscious, lucid, light, compassionate . . . And here I am drunk and cock-a-doodling. Like a murderer, his knife dripping blood. Like a torero with the tip of the sword he's thrust in once and must thrust back in, time and again, nightmarishly, for a lifetime, though he's being jeered, though the presiding officer bids white handkerchiefs be draped over sombreros, though the band strikes up and the picador's posse pirouettes, and the town hall's watering cart arrives, the torero stands there, still thrusting his blade into the bull that refuses to die, that grows and grows and grows and bursts, spattering him in black stuff like an amorous octopus, without horns now, oh my love, my love, while the crowd laughs and asks for its money back.

He filled the washbowl with water. Cold water from the pitcher. He splashed his face. He poured water all over his head. He looked at himself in the small cracked mirror. He swiveled round. The water streamed down his soaked face from his shiny black hair. The water spilled down his neck and slipped between his skin and his shirt. He took off his tie that was still comically neat and tidy. Its diagonal blue and red stripes hit the ground. The image of Dorita's beauty still floated in his bemused mind. Not like someone loved or lost, but like someone who's been beheaded. She'd stayed there, separated only by a partition and linked to him by a stupid episode that should be buried out of sight, but would inevitably come back to haunt him. Her head—as if axed—rested on the turn of the bedsheet. She was so beautiful! She was asleep. Everything about her was natural: she was waiting in her silent rocking chair and nothing could take her by surprise.

He splashed more water on his face. Water is so refreshing at first light. It clears the head. Everything swollen deflates. Inebriation disappears. The forehead becomes a forehead again and not a battering ram thudding away. Cold water. Primitive remedies: cobwebs on wounds, sheets between legs, saliva on bites, pigeon chicks opened on rheumy chests, leeches for strokes, purgatives for severe colic. Ablutions, baptism, resurrection of the dead man on a cart who falls in when fording the river, the pool in Siloam, the immersion of the hunchbacked girl with Pott's disease in the gurgling water of the Lourdes grotto, the sacrificed bull, the bloodbath beneath the big idol's sacrificial altar, the river Jordan with a shell from a sea that isn't dead, the voice from on high explaining that this is His dearly beloved Son, rain, and more rain. And this land where it doesn't rain. This land that is waterless. Into what river will a suicide fall if he jumps from the viaduct onto the Roman tiles below, next to where a cathedral should be and the only light is the glow from the palace?[23] A viaduct for trapped drunkards. I too am in heat, warm as toast, like Snarler's mice, caressed by whores, pampered by old women, robbed of animals for my experiments, brooding on experimental cancers but a buddy of the literary crowd, living in a modest boardinghouse but out drinking on a Saturday night, dependent on little bags warming up on the city's edge, until the president orders me to do my unavoidable duty and, as an honorable man brought up to defend family and status quo, make sure everything is done according to the finest standards and regulations on the statute books, for the good of humanity and nations, from that remote night in the Middle Ages when swords were raised against Moors tilling the fields of Toledo and more southern territories where they had begun cultivating orchards, to form a new nation, a chosen people, an aseptic city, without orchards, where man has been fed on spirit and pure air forever and ever. Amen. More water, more water to wipe the taste from my mouth. Water brought from distant sierras down long canals paid for by men who sweat in distant climes, so it arrives so pure it doesn't stand out from the local pneuma and doesn't stop them wanting to give orders, doesn't turn heads into sponges, nay, those upstanding men breathe pure air and remain clear-sighted, swords held aloft and steady, leading the way, giving shape to the inert, veined corpulence of distant viceroyalties. Water not for bathing, only for drinking, water that doesn't fall like mist or from a nearby cloud, but enters the body's delicate pores, cleansing but not soddening, neither swelling nor fattening skin, nor basting the hard, almost leathery carapace of an arid empire.

And he drank it, as if he too were an eagle that must fly far.

That night was to be especially eventful. It was a Saturday that elastically extended into the early hours of Sunday, infecting it with sabbatical substance. Pedro hadn't managed to fall asleep and was still looking at himself in the cracked mirror, refreshed by Castilian water, or maybe he was still lying fully dressed on the bed turned back by the maid, or he was naked by now, trying to stifle his retching, or thinking about Dorita and Dorita's body, one he'd seen rather than touched, when there was loud knocking on the apartment door, after the door to the street had been breached by a resourceful nighttime errand boy. And after that din, the dowager herself, accompanied by the maid, ushered into Pedro's presence the messenger sent by Night to gather him once more into its sinful bosom, because he'd yet to complete the odyssey destiny had mapped out for him. The messenger who'd taken on this mission and been able to assume the tone of urgency necessary to overcome various barriers—the distance, the unseemly hour, the locked doors, feminine caution and reserve—and violently invade the intimate space where Don Pedro had retreated to rest was none other than Snarler, who spoke emphatically and exercised his facial muscles in a surprising panoply of grimaces, communicating his distress with a final plea of "Don Pedro, I beg you, Don Pedro," a moment that restored the *Don* which friendship, a whorehouse, a drunken binge, and love had snatched away.

And the panic visible on Snarler-man's face was the panic of the proud Snarler-father of two nubile daughters, one of whose life was in danger, and on whose behalf he'd rushed there at full tilt, employing various modes of mechanical traction starting with a neighbor's rusty bike and finishing in a retired, worn-out taxi that he'd summoned as a matter of life or death.

The motive (not remote, but very specific) of this new encounter was related to the way in which wise, charitable, protective Don Pedro had helped out Snarler and his family—wretchedness personified—in their hour of need, prompted in no small part by the girls from Toledo. And also the interest munificent Don Pedro had shown in the mice-breeding those same girls had generated thanks to their natural bodily heat, a reliable guarantee that the physical health of those incubators would ensure his genuine, most generous support.

But what had led Snarler to take responsibility for dragging a man of such stature from his bed, from the depths of the five-star establishment where he lodged and the company of the proprietors he'd also disturbed—fully understanding their scorn at his audacity, which was only natural and in keeping with custom and practice among upper echelons of society he rarely rubbed shoulders with—was nothing less than the alarming amounts of blood being lost by the elder of the two modest consolations for his old age, who, pallid and trembling as a result of the absence of that vital fluid, was being sustained only by ham-fisted, spur-of-the-moment care provided by other females in the family, who were applying cold towels, binding her with laces blessed by San Antonio, laying freshly cut slices of potato on her temples, force-feeding her extract of celery achieved through the most primitive pounding process, praying profusely, and welcoming superstitious acts of magic such as the laying on of hands by a man reputed for his blood-stemming powers.

And although one might have assumed that nurses, midwives, and other members of the profession undoubtedly existed in the immediate geographical area, not to mention barbers and other trained personnel and even—in the neighborhood inhabited by the petitioner—a man of science blessed with autodidactic or natural knowledge who successfully intervened to cure nonlethal afflictions, the serious pallor he'd noted on the sick girl's face and the affection and close ties binding him to her made it quite out of the question for him to resort to professionals not blessed with the enlightenment illuminating the gray cells of an erudite researcher, like the one seated there, pulling on his nylon socks and impulsively preparing to resume his nocturnal odyssey to the yet-to-be-explored Nausicaa.

He grasped that the time factor wasn't negligible, that with each moment her blood soaked the only two sheets the family owned, the unfortunate girl was increasingly in danger of breathing her last, and though maybe it would have made more sense to move her to a casualty ward, an intensive care unit, the emergency department of a general hospital or other such institution that the generous collectivity places at the disposition of its most needy offspring, Snarler knew that many youngsters from dodgy backgrounds served their apprenticeships in these places and later graduated as renowned handlers of scalpel and needle but who, for now—and particularly on a Saturday night—were necessarily wet behind the ears, so he'd not hesitated to opt for Don Pedro's hands, whose experience would easily compensate for the more extended period of blood loss and a location less perfectly disinfected than others that had been treated by copious quantities of bleach.

If it ever crossed Don Pedro's mind that it had been a mistake or malice on Snarler's part to choose a man who, as the creator of a future science yet to be consolidated, wasn't obliged to stoop to such humble tasks as directly serving members of a marginal community, and that was undoubtedly the case, the dehumanized father or offending aide-de-camp might feel his righteous wrath, but, being mindful of the baptismal innocence of that unworthy girl in agony whose fate the stunned father had dared take into his own hands, inept as they were filthy, out of gratuitous love or Christian charity, or simply on a whim inspired by his benign nature, he was inclined to err on the side of benevolence and set off towards that pool of blood on which her still-not-quite-a-corpse was floating at that late hour.

To which end, even at risk of ruination, Snarler the lowly pauper had managed to secure a retired Automedon at vast cost who, while his purring engine consumed priceless liquid from the other side of the ocean, waited outside the entrance to the regal mansion with the night watchman—whose palm the same hapless father had also greased—and two or three bystanders always ready to stick their necks where they didn't belong, even at that late hour, one of whom, a baker on his way home, added an untimely white stain in poor taste, according to the man gossiping, but what can one do if people will behave like that.

And what Don Pedro feared might be a dearth of essential surgical tools, swabs, sutures, or dressings didn't materialize because a handy telephone call had mobilized the distant relative—who honored his family by his institutional proximity to science—the much-loved Amador, who at that very moment was loyally plowing his way through the midnight Madrid selva to seek out at the Institute to which he was privileged to have a key the required materials, which, though appropriate for dogs and other superior animals useful to science, could equally serve without complaint or false scruples the lowly stock of the back-bending Snarler who continued to apologize for his rudeness.

Since the preparations Don Pedro was making were clear proof that he was fully committed and would follow Snarler to the couch of suffering geared up to end all evil that exists in this world, it became Snarler, grateful father and enthusiastic acolyte, to throw his dusty cap into the air and bellow a thousand Jesuses and a single "Praise be to our Lord and Maker!"

Dynamite had been on the prowl all night, as if the shindigs hadn't been only on the Calles de San Marcos, Reina, Villarrosa, Tudescos, or Echegaray but had spilled over into remote areas on the city outskirts, to places so poor it would be impossible to collect from their motley inhabitants the price of a single brothel token, where hunger rather than the death drive shapes the round-the-clock helter-skelter. He'd stationed himself on twists and turns aspiring to be paths, along which he'd watched shadows pass that—oh woe—he thought were heading towards—oh woe—the place he already knew, where—oh woe—he suspected what was afoot: the dealing of goods over which he wanted exclusive control. Though he wasn't at all sure what the hell he really opined and walked into a watering hole and relaxed over a nip of anisette or moonshine and, when he'd almost spent all his scant cash on firewater, "What's happenin' at Snarler's?" he asked the guy acting as waiter, not in a tuxedo but in a corduroy jacket with a high black fur collar. "They're plotting something or other," explained Furry-man. "That guy just walked in." He didn't ask who "that guy" was, but perked up when the roly-poly consort emerged muttering to herself or to whatever deity heeds women, and returned with another unfamiliar matron in black and then another chubby dame appeared until nobody else could have piled into the hovel or people would have outnumbered the mice. "They're tryin' to pull a fast one," Dynamite remarked to the pseudo-waiter. "I'm gonna have a word." "Let them be and let them sort it out," replied the dispenser of firewater. "What difference does it make to you?" "No, I don' want that guy or anybody else spittin' in my patch." "If I was you, I'd keep well out of it." "I've had it up to here" "Florita doesn't belong to you." "The man's yet to be born..."

It was almost closing time and, obeying regs that weren't municipal, but to do with exhaustion plain and simple, the man was putting his concern's ten bottles, six glasses, and one wineglass in the wooden box that served as a counter and announced he was going to switch off the consumptive lamp: "Because my earnings goes on fuel." Dynamite said calmly: "Let it be," an order rather than a suggestion, peering through the window-door on which TAVERN was emblazoned in blood-red paint.

Much later Dynamite returned to the twists and turns, walked along, one hand fondling his skinning knife and the other around his freezing member. "They're tryin' to pull a fast one," and "The man's yet to be born," and "If they're damagin' her, they're damagin' me, and every virgin that's damaged goods," and "When I see who it is, I'll knife him," and "Snarler may be tough but he's nothin' on me," and "He better not think he can outsmart me or I'll have his guts for garters," and "Fuck his mother's twat," and "I shit on his father's grave." And he swore, cursed, and belched, and conjured up Florita's soft skin that he'd felt up and was gorgeous and he knew what it was like because his hands were a little rich boy's as if they'd just slipped out of his mother's belly, he'd never got them dirty, which was why he could feel the softness, not like a guy with calluses from mixing cement. He'd had his fill of her one way or another and kept an eye on her, although he'd not done her yet, out of consideration, heaven knows how, him being so up for it, but what if with him being so ready to lay her, she'd been having it off with someone else? And he kept winding himself up and touching the sore spot. "My blade'll slice through whoever put that bun in her oven, because someone *has* put her in the family way an' they're tryin' to deal with it, an' it weren't Dynamite, and if it turns out they can't fix it an' it sticks inside her, it won't have this sinner's gizzard."

It was still pitch black, but a hint of early morning pink on a patch of light to the left competed with the glow the city spewed up to the right like phosphorescent stale breath from a drunkard's mouth and laid bare all the sinfulness. The air was so clean it went in deep, brought a chill tickle to the back of his nose, the bottom of his throat, and even penetrated his chest. But that air was a friendly thing his dry mouth needed to breathe, as he tightened his lips and lowered his brows, as he waited for the fog to clear and the coming bombshell to explode.

Against the opinion of Swedish hospital architects, who in recent times have preferred to construct hexagonal or even circular operating theaters (to facilitate the movement of auxiliary staff and rapid conveyance of required material), the one where Florita lay was rectangular or oblong, slightly flattened by one support pole, with a ceiling fixed in rough-and-ready fashion to slope all down one side. The patient about to go into labor didn't enjoy a nickel-plated or stainless steel table with thigh supports securing the gynecological position most surgeons prefer, but lay on a surface made from Galician pinewood boxes previously used to transport citrus fruit from the region of Valencia and later adapted into a bed supporting a spring mattress and sheets stained by her own abundantly flowing blood. The shadowless scialytic light had been substituted to her advantage by two acetylene lamps that spread a smell of dust and animal-ridden forests much pleasanter than the scent of ether and nitrogen dioxide, and that gave sufficient illumination, despite the flickering caused by the entry of intruders (unequipped, alas, with mandatory face masks). As she was a healthy female of Toledan stock, she needed no anesthetic—which is always quick to glaze the patient's mind and make her forget who she is—and it was only at this point that best precepts were followed: the wonders of reflexology, previous upbringing, gymnastic contortions to relax the perineal muscles, and jaw contractions at the most difficult stage leading, on occasion, to the most exquisite examples of painless screams. Less cultured, our young woman bellowed uncouth words (not delicate sighs without a curse in sight) that skewered the serenity of the many attendees. These folk could be categorized, according to a range of criteria, as "family and non-family," "experts in provoking abortions and those unskilled in the art," "neighbors from the plain of Toledo and immigrants from other regions of arid Spain," "people equipped to give moral advice and cynics who understood that such is life," "women offering vague solidarity and men furtively hoping to see the patient's breasts," and, to conclude this string of dichotomies, "those who knew Florita's father was on the cusp of becoming a father-grandfather, and those who simply suspected that almost self-evident truth."

Rather than being in the position earlier indicated as best to ease out the uterus's contents, the young girl was lying on her side on the mattress, curled up like a cat. Her vitriolic screams had gradually weakened as she lost vital fluids in the hours after the operation performed by the Wizard armed with a needle had got off to such an unsatisfactory start. This Wizard must surely have miscued his sharp instrument, or maybe its point, blunted by overuse, was less efficient than usual. Her excessive youthfulness may also have given her tissues and their products abnormal consistency or elasticity. Or maybe the contraction of the matrix, often sufficient for pain-stricken females to give birth, had on this occasion acted only to dilate her blood-letting veins and make her hypersensitive to the rhythmic pains suggested by her spasmodic screaming. The truth is that the crestfallen, even shamefaced Wizard had ceased all therapeutic activity and was simply stating that nature should be allowed to follow its course, like any doctor of repute from the seventeenth century. The live wires at which he'd aimed this pearl of wisdom had been duly unimpressed and resorted to violent procedures that incited a flood. Before seeking refuge in oral platitudes and exorcism, the Wizard had tried to round off his needle's destructive actions with what were currently regarded as the most highly recommended practices. He had the roly-poly consort sit on her daughter's belly, in the belief that this met the requirements of gravity and all due modesty; he used a cord to squeeze the young girl's slender waist from the navel down, tightening it as he eased it round and down her ample hips; once he'd withdrawn the cord, which bubbled the skin on the end of her coaxial bones, he massaged the affected area with both hands, rapidly and forcefully sliding his hands down until he'd expelled all remaining fecal matter and urine; he administered scalding drinks made from a secret recipe that burned (only slightly, to be sure) the roof of her non-motherly non-maidenly mouth; he poured cold water on her belly and boiling water with a drizzle of mustard onto the lower part of her thighs; and sweating, though not throwing in the towel, he declared he would extract *it* with his hand, which turned out to be completely impossible, thus provoking Snarler's departure to his distant savior and the anger of his consort—invisible to that point—which reduced the Wizard to innocuous inaction and the summoning of life's vital spirits.

The consort, conversely, thought it a good idea to place a sprig of green fennel between the girl's legs to lure out the baby with its fragrance. But the green sprig soon lost its color or was plucked away, or maybe aromas aren't perceived at such a tender age. She also gave the nod to the rosary and a prayer to Santa Apolonia, which was known in its entirety by one old woman who—so she said, though nobody could verify this—had been a sacristan in her youth and who, being so long in the tooth, had forgotten the prayer was, as far as anyone knew, helpful in bringing relief to toothache. Apart from these remnants of primitive medicine characteristic of animist minds, the rest of the therapeutic activity pointed to an empirical-activist Weltanschauung typical of hunting and animal-breeding peoples and was, as such, completely of a piece with the hovel's pedigree fixations. Failure can be ascribed only to a highly uncommon fatality, but aren't there also very painful, unexpected deaths in the state-of-the-art hospitals that are the pride and joy of American industrial cities? Yes, there too, beneath duralumin and cobalt, young girls continue to perish who'd previously been assured (as had their loving mothers) that it would take only a moment.

After arriving, once he'd emptied the premises, Don Pedro proceeded, following the book, to establish a diagnosis for the hemorrhaging that was clearly afflicting the young incubator of his experimental mice. On his journey there he'd toyed with the idea that maybe a viral infection had been brought on by such close cohabitation, and he'd gently chided the gentleman farmer for the way in which he managed the perpetuation of his stock at the expense of his daughters and their life-giving warmth. But he was soon confronted with the shocking reality of the facts and a light flashed furiously in his ingenuous brain. Maidenly blood—once again—made him queasy. He felt a rush of insight and fear. He turned angrily on Snarler to say: "Scumbag!" or shout: "Get an ambulance!" or yell, like a torero: "Transfusion!" but Amador was already in the doorway, flourishing the instruments with which, in that dire emergency, despite his inexperience, he ought urgently to do his duty. He bent over the motionless girl. She'd stopped screaming. She was asleep or dead. He uncovered her chest. He applied the stethoscope. He saw the mice's bitemarks. Her heart was beating, dimly. He lifted up the elastic. He stood still. Amador whispered in his ear: "She needs a scrape." Yeah.

One must first place her in the correct gynecological position, then dilate the neck of the womb provident nature had tightened, and finally clean the inside of that recondite nest with a spoonlike implement. As the latter grazes against tissue it makes a scraping, grating, tearing sound that seems to suggest the matter being removed isn't alive but is stringy, woody, or stony. This sense of non-living matter, much to Don Pedro's disquiet, could become non-life at any second. The end of the hemorrhaging could be as much down to the success of the therapy as to the exhaustion of her emptied veins. He'd have liked to be able to look at the girl's almost-dead face as he worked, and he asked Amador: "Is there a pulse?" Amador held the girl's hand and applied his four fat fingers, such tamers of dogs and mice, to the fragile dead girl's wrist; he felt no beat, but nodded his big head benevolently and his thick lips cautiously puckered in an affirmative to which Don Pedro's eyes clung in order to continue his labors. "The tubal corners," he repeated, knowing these corners—which he'd once studied—might conceal a fragment of living matter (though not of a living mother), might reinitiate hemorrhaging, infections, and dangerous internal putrefaction. A surer instinct than Amador's nodding told him that niceties like carefully poking the spoon into corners where life streams into its most elemental source were of no use whatsoever. The dead girl's thighs had fallen like big petals and the small spurt of blood had halted completely. "Is there a pulse?" "Carry on, carry on," Amador replied, not daring to keep lying. "Carry on, you're almost there," because Amador thought Don Pedro would feel more tranquil if from thereon, in the days, months, and years left to him to reflect on that night, he could be sure he'd acted according to standard practice. Don Pedro made every effort, in consummate skilled movements, to probe as with a finger in case any fragment of velvety, bleeding mucous remained through which the life of the dead girl might escape—if there was any. Time dragged endlessly. He kept testing dark inner surfaces, imagining the form of the now-clean cavity, listening as his hand felt the ripping of tissue vibrate along the implement. The dead girl was no longer in pain and meekly let him maneuver in ways that no longer related to her. After yielding her last breath to the air and her last blood to the world, she was now resigned to being of modest use in the training of a knowledgeable man who (though he'd studied it in detail) was performing that operation for the first time. Grasping the meaning of Amador's solemn nods and with an angry awareness of which he was in denial, he thought: "I'll do better next time," and "A transfusion at the right time might have revived her"; he continued scouring mechanically and once he'd finished, he plugged the space with clean gauze destined for mice, applied a dressing, washed his hands, laid the body in a more decent position, turned to the roly-poly mother who'd watched everything, then looked at Amador, and everyone was waiting for his face to react, for him to make a dramatic gesture, throw the instrument on the floor or curse and unleash a mournful chorus of wailing women.

"She was already dead when I got here" was the first thing he said, denying all the evidence, and blushing shamefully because that was a mere excuse to appease a mother who in any case hadn't been born to hate, and who tried to console him: "You did all you could," before she started to scream, threw herself on her dead daughter, kissed lips she'd probably not kissed since they were a baby's and tasted of her own milk, and slapped the man at her side and scratched his face, which he allowed her to do despite the airs of master of the house he would inevitably adopt in the morning when he'd continue to pinion her to the ground like an iron wheel.

When the mother began to howl, the wailers howled with her. As if they were always primed for premature deaths, the wailers were already wearing black when a maximum (smallish) number of them burst into the morgue.

"Scoundrel!" shouted one, standing in front of the surgeon as if she were about to spit at him, raising two tensed hands that, before they hit him, struck hard against her own face. "What have you done to my little flower?"

"Look at her! A real angel!" a bare-armed woman, her sleeves rolled up, cried blissfully, who, because she'd collaborated in the Wizard's handiwork, maybe thought she'd been party to a work of art.

Indeed, the poor girl did look more beautiful now she'd shed the puppy fat that comes with puberty and home-cooked fare.

"She looks as if she was sleeping, she—"

Such remarks were punctuated by the nonstop refrain of "Daughter, Daughter, Daughter, Daughter" that hiccupped from the open mouth of the mother who'd scratched Snarler and told the doctor what had to be said, before finally descending into inevitable despair.

Ever the calm, sensible type, Snarler filtered the entry and exit of bystanders, and to help matters he took one of the lamps from the medical theater and placed it in the anteroom to the hovel. He then decided the remaining lamp was inappropriate and lit two tallow candles so no oversight on his part might blemish funeral honors that were duly deserved. A little later he started moving the cage-palaces of the mice that had been so tenderly conceived into the outside air, although the occasional difficult pregnancy might now be interrupted by the dampness of dawn.

Having now revived, the matrons began to take up strategic positions, huddle on the floor, and whisper inaudible prayers, while the woman with the rolled-up sleeves and another, thin as a rake, began to wrap the dead girl in a winding sheet.

Pedro and Amador watched on in astonishment, contemplating the confirmation that there's life after death and that—in its wake—you only have to follow time-honored routines for life to resume its orderly round. But for Pedro and Amador, death was more than pure grief or the mere making of arrangements: it was a technical problem. Don Pedro was there, his hand still squeezed into a metal item of dubious import; Amador was there with his half-opened canister of swabs; the mother's "Daughter, Daughter, Daughter, Daughter" had turned into a continuous purr like an engine's or a waterfall's that soon fades, and was sorely missed after the wretched woman was led out into the temporary spaces that acted as squares or streets between rows of flattened sheets of tin and uralite and planks stolen from construction sites. Snarler didn't look Don Pedro in the eye and couldn't bring himself to say (though he *knew* it was the right thing to say at the right moment, which his consort did not): "You did all you could." The younger sister, on the other hand, stared at her father and pressed both hands against her belly as if to protect it against ill-doing. She wasn't crying. She watched her father conscientiously doing what he had to do, finally bidding her: "Fetch the doctor something to drink."

She brought another glass of bitter lemonade with sugar and cold water, which he drank nervily.

"Bring me some too," requested Amador.

She obeyed.

Don Pedro didn't leave because he sensed there was something else he had to do. He suddenly remembered.

"Who performed the abortion?" he asked Snarler.

"But, doctor, sir, you saw what happened. You yourself did what . . ."

"Who did it?"

The matrons looked witheringly at Don Pedro. They broke off their prayers. The dead girl in her shroud was witness to the debate. Two or three men who'd been standing around until that point, neither helping nor wailing, filed out and disappeared.

"The hemorrhaging began," Snarler said, "because it was God's will. Nobody touched her. It was her doing, it started slowly, sped up, and turned into a river. That's why I fetched the doctor, sir, because I'm a miserable fellow who knows nothing. And the poor thing was saying she didn't feel well, that it wasn't going well. The poor dear's life was bleeding away."

The little sister glowered at Snarler: her mouth opened and she began to hyperventilate between trembling lips. She was pallid. She suddenly leapt on him, screwing her face up.

"It was you! It was you! You, Father! You were the one who..."

Snarler knocked her to floor, where she wept, howled, and wailed inarticulately, and suffered insane panic attacks, scratching, biting, tearing her clothes, wetting herself, while Snarler blindly kicked her living, twitching mass of flesh, but didn't manage to stop her fit.

Don Pedro finally dropped that bloodstained nickel-plated implement and rushed out, at the end of his tether, wanting to leave that night far behind him and all the lunatic adventures in which it had involved him, wanting to sleep, to be alone, to be in a warm bed unaccompanied, where, when he woke up, everything would confirm it had been one long, far too vivid nightmare, like those alcohol inflicts on individuals not in the habit of drinking.

Dawn was breaking. In the corner of another hovel, helped by two of her peers, the banished mother sobbed tearlessly, emitting the same staccato lament: "Daughter, Daughter, Daughter," and didn't notice the doctor's madcap departure. Cold air and daylight seared his eyes. The hovels were pinkish in the early morning light, as if bathing in a mother-of-pearl reflection for a few minutes, until the hidden sun's true rays revealed them in all their ugliness. The taxi was still waiting for him at the end of the road. He got in, and spat out his address. He was driving off when Amador peered out of the hovel and shouted in vain: "Don Pedro! Don Pedro! The certificate...!"

He slept through the morning undisturbed. The dowagers wove the necessary silence around his room. Dorita also stayed in bed until very late, and while her fool of a mother went to Mass—maybe followed by a walk along the Paseo del Prado or even an aperitif in a café in the Retiro with a friend from the old days to whom she spoke at length about past glories—grandmother entered the same bedroom Pedro had entered, whispered in her granddaughter's ear and made her respond, gave her some advice and smiled wanly, then wept a little, but always with the restraint of a worldly-wise woman who understands the simple things that motivate men, and never gives up on seeing her longings crowned by a happy outcome, provided on the way there are no unscrupulous, immoral dancers or stupid women addicted to Rhum Negrita who refuse to deploy their charms rationally.

When it was time for lunch and her chatterbox of a mother had come home and all the lodgers were back too, and had eaten their chips or even grilled prawns, money permitting, the dowager duly instructed family, servants, and illustrious clientele to be reasonably quiet in their movements and conversations so as not to disturb the repose of the man who'd been summoned in the early hours to carry out an urgent operation and was now recharging his precious energies that would be required in an immediate future to galvanize a splendid career garlanded by one professional success after another. To which end, she reflected, he must finally say goodbye to an already overlong period of life devoted to research, laboratory experiments, and fine-tuning theoretical studies and, leaving such paths to those ill equipped to succeed in life, welcome with open arms the glittering clientele that was waiting for such a move so they could descend upon him and overwhelm him with their glittering gifts. These remarks were received by the non-working classes with understanding grunts, nods, or shrugs of the shoulders with which they communicated their unanimous agreement that this, and no other, was the proper path for a young man whom they all thought of as a stepson and protégé and who'd exemplified honesty, gravitas, and good habits from the very day—now distant—on which he'd landed at the boardinghouse entrance, dressed in drab provincial fashion and dragging behind him a trunk full of books and clothes that, thanks to advice from his well-intentioned landlady, he'd gradually shed in favor of others more in keeping with the brilliant career that awaited him.

But once cloths were cleared and the table talk slowly petered out, it became evident that the young man's slumbers were unfortunately at odds with the equally unavoidable need to feed a young body braced by a lively metabolism and a relatively hectic existence, posing the question of whether to send in the maid with a tray laden with supplies so he could satisfy in bed one need without completely abandoning the delights of the other, and this decision was precipitated by the arrival of another young man, already familiar if not exactly adored, by the name of Matías, elegantly attired and demanding to be let into his friend's chamber of rest. Although it was perhaps this young man—as immediately suspected by the luminary surveying all these events—who was responsible for getting the late researcher and newly born surgical practitioner into bad habits, the agreeable social cachet wafting from his well-ironed suit, silk tie, and immaculate haircut, as well as the cultured inflections of his voice and rich lexicon, were ample reason not to prevent the encounter with any specious excuses, with a particular regard to the potential good company he'd provide the newlyweds the moment they were over their honeymoon raptures and their opportune collocation in a suitable social universe easing the path to a plush consultancy with clientele that—as previously mentioned—were already lining up, determined to surrender themselves to the expert care of the man who was still asleep, but was about to be brought back to the problematic world of wakefulness.

Once the expedition had been agreed upon, the party members positioned themselves in this order by the bedroom door: first, the lucid old lady, an imperceptible smile curling the corners of her upper lip; second, the said Matías, with a very clear idea of how he wanted to occupy his friend's afternoon and early evening; third, the scowling servant, somewhat annoyed that unusual event had been given the go-ahead as it would delay the time she could leave on a Sunday, when management should have treated her leisure time as sacrosanct. Immediately they entered, an unpleasant, acidic smell mingled with alcoholic vapors led them to anticipate what they were about to see, sheets stained by vinous vomit and a snoring, supine archangel sullied by his own excrement, a woeful image of the human, scarcely divine, condition our first forebears bequeathed us.

"Poor man! He'll catch his death!" was the landlady's rapid reaction. "Run a bath for him right away."

"That will use up all the hot water. I've not done the washing up yet."

"Don't answer back."

"Baths are taken in the morning."

"I told you to shut up."

"So when can I leave, if you don't mind?"

"Clear off and leave us in peace! The young lady will run it."

The pointless tray of food sat on a chair. Pedro slowly stretched his arms. Matías had a laugh on the quiet. The old woman went to see to arrangements. Life resumed its usual round and while Dorita filled the bath, mixing cold water with hot, her hand testing the ideal temperature for a renascent body, the old lady extracted from behind piles of bed linen in a wardrobe a flask of blue bath salts she still used occasionally that brought a voluptuous nostalgic joy when the bubbles tingled her skin, which might have hardened but could still feel cold or shudder.

Dynamite belonged to the most doleful territory among the different districts of the shantytown. While Snarler's mortuary had been established in a legal, dignified fashion as corresponded to an honest immigrant, Dynamite's (or rather Dynamite's aging mother's) was a precarious, crabbed quasi-cave. These filthy, marginal hovels didn't even aspire to look like small houses, but were resigned to their nature as stinking holes with no pretense to dignity or self-esteem, in strict correlation with their inhabitants' lives. A luxury that never fell to these sub-hovels was a division into compartments like the gentleman farmer's, which, as we saw, comprised kitchen-dining-living room and bedroom-tabernacle-incubation chamber. The one occupied by Dynamite was formed by a single space, and stolen items couldn't be moved to a special unit, but had to be buried beneath a round stone (also used as a seat) or entrusted to a fence or thrown into the lake in the Retiro. The wretched inhabitants of these neighborhoods didn't display the stigmata of unskilled workers on their calloused hands, but rather showed off their bodies in pretty poses, ever sexually ambiguous and ripe for commercial exploitation. They wore tight pants with zips on their calves and rocked to folkloric rhythms. But when they were past their sell-by date, and hadn't secured a stable mooring in the city's vice-ridden backstreets, and age had erased any residual charms, only panhandling (now severely repressed by an eminently progressive society) or scavenging could prevent their total extinction or bodily wasting by early morning cold—inside or out. These wastelands weren't home to highly skilled individuals—pickpockets, shoplifters, thieves, burglars, bag snatchers, or hitmen—but to petty delinquents ill-suited for any kind of criminal success because they lacked the requisite mental level or grit. They were, then, people who'd never gelled, who swore, or were exhausted by occasional remunerated labor (loading or unloading lorries, transporting coal to hotels), and never achieved a stable status, banished both from circles that only accepted their own kind and from underworlds framed by unintelligible codes of honor, lingos, gestures, and provisional constituent assemblies. Gypsies passed through on their way to the big wen. When they'd made their mark, they stopped here, then progressed almost respectfully, and disappeared down its streets. Later on you'd see old Gypsy women back from the big city that had shaken them from its skirts like crumbs from a snack. They arrived with faces sculpted a thousand times more powerfully than those of women who'd never given themselves rumbustiously to life or illuminated (by the art and perfection of their own readily offered bodies) the passing of the years that gradually stripped them of their boobs, fangs, bras, and dark velvet lamé dresses.

One such was Dynamite's mother, now in her dotage, squatting on the round stone, beneath which her son had hidden the knife he'd used to kill Pretty-face and others nobody knew about. Her son brought her hunks of bread buttered with loads of swearing, and as she couldn't get up, she'd wait there for him to bring her a variety of tiny spoils: a ring, a watch, an odd payout earned by the sweat of his brow, a small-scale fraud, a frustrated sale and purchase, a toy sewing machine, the purse of a maid who'd saved up to buy it, then taken it to a dance with a curly dark-haired lad fond of dancing. A bastard child of a single mother, clinging to the tree of life where he'd sprouted, like a clown through a paper hoop, into a circus where he can't even crack jokes, he loitered between the stones in the morning, watching out for someone to leave the morgue where he'd heard shouting, which had led him to conclude that someone was interfering with what was rightly his, and that sparked his fury.

Amador sauntered out with his burden of canisters, swabs, and sorrow to the metallic clink of instruments he'd washed thoroughly with water a woman had drawn from a nearby well. The death wasn't on his mind as much as the certificate that should allow everything to proceed in orderly fashion, even in that forsaken spot with fool people who start things they don't know how to finish. He'd spoken to Snarler and they'd come up with a procedure that would deal with the matter properly, even without a certificate. But a lot of people were in the know and Snarler had also involved the Wizard in the conversation. Snarler and Amador talked quietly, and gradually reached an agreement about what to say if a situation arose where they had no choice but to say something. The mother was still intoning a dirge that even Snarler found distressing, though he'd lived with her so long and by now ought to have got used to her whining. But, generally speaking, she'd been the quiet sort, and Snarler couldn't recall a piercing screech like that since their early days together in the wheat fields of the Tagus Valley. He arranged for her to be taken to a region relatively far from the shantytown where he had cousins who owed him one and a distant cousin who'd indulge her howling. The young daughter, after her fit, was so deeply asleep that, despite all the scratches and bruises, she seemed harmless enough. And a father always feels warmly towards his remaining daughter when the first has just departed. So the three men discussed the uncertain future and made their plans, being the sensible men they were.

Dynamite followed Amador and his illegal burden of state property, which, with the generous donations received by the Institute, seemed to assume that the natives in its territory, educated at their own expense, though in buildings it had made available, can contribute to the growth of that carefully catalogued mountain of knowledge that was an almost unknown quantity in his neck of the woods. And as he walked away from the scene of last night's events, he slowly drew closer—with no cash at hand to spend on a taxi, in the unlikely event he could find a taxi in that backwater at first light—to a subdistrict of sub-hovels where Dynamite reigned as undisputed master and his most outrageous deeds had buried the odd body and brought him, albeit on a temporary basis, to a shady den where he could rest and recoup his energy.

He hurled himself at Amador when he was least expecting it and pressed the tip of his knife into his left flank. He said: "Walk!" and forced him to walk. He said: "Go in!" and Amador went inside as far as the spot where the old single mother was squatting on the round stone, toothlessly slurping cold garlic soup.

"Who did it?"

"It wasn't me! I swear by my mother it wasn't me!"

"Put that down there."

Amador dropped the packets on the ground and the mother began to unwrap shiny items, swabs, bandages, and a bottle of iodine.

"It was you! Don't you lie to me."

"I swear it wasn't!"

"So what was the point of all this?"

"Snarler decided it had to be done because she—"

"Whose was it?"

"I've not a clue, I swear —"

"Tell me whose—"

Unflappable, the mother returned to her soup. She was swathed in vast petticoats that hung on her frail body like a snake's unshed skins, and in whose folds she could sleep divinely.

"Don't let him go, son," she interjected. "Make him shell out."

"Let me go or I'll inform on you!"

"Try it! Rat on me if you dare!"

"Let me go!"

"Reckon you can scare the living daylights out of me? You're the one who's gonna be sorry—"

"It wasn't me."

Dynamite behaved as if he could effortlessly ease the point of his knife into Amador's skinny belly that was far too soft to resist. He hadn't a clue where that man in black had come from, rained down from heaven or spewed up by a mine, and now pushing him against that disgusting old woman; he felt the sweat of fear streaming down his neck. What was his connection to any of that? This guy was in love with the dead girl. Shacked up with Florita. He might be the father. But Snarler didn't know. This guy and her were an item and Snarler had no idea the trouble they'd brought into his house. He looked like a wild animal and anything was on the cards, God knows what savage...

"It was the doctor," said Amador.

"Don't lie to me."

"The doctor..."

It was covered by a prickly carpet, the thick pile of which gave when stepped on. Red-faced and clean-shaven, the blue-uniformed porter bounced gently over like a rubber ball and, with a deep bow, opened the elevator door. The lobby smelled of refined pine-ozone quite unlike the ersatz stuff used in local fleapits. The elevator went up silently and slowly; it had mirrors on three sides, a thick red carpet too. A small, velvet-lined bench at one end offered exhausted aeronauts a point of repose. Alerted by a mysterious mute mechanism, a flunky in a gray, tight-fitting, metal-buttoned jacket opened the elevator door. This skinny, willowy fellow had curly hair and green eyes. He bowed, but not like the porter; he puckered his mouth into a combination of smile and ironic rictus. He drawled a few confused words in which "the young sir" popped up, then vanished among vaguer ones. He seemed to be able to bow yet stay straight-backed. His tight-fitting gray jacket squeezed his neck like the uniforms worn by bellboys and officers in long-defunct armies. With amazing ease he closed the cabin's inside doors and the metal grille to the stairs and placed himself by the apartment's front door (which he opened wide), while they sped along the landing, whose main carpet had been overlaid by a second layer of lighter-colored material for some unfathomable reason, perhaps for protection, perhaps for a sophisticated touch beyond the ken of feet not used to wearing made-to-measure shoes. As he walked along, the flunky balanced nimbly on his ankles, hands by his sides, their long fingers ready to offer any unexpected service, such as resiting a piece of porcelain that had drifted out of place, offering an ashtray that was suddenly required, taking charge of an overcoat, surreptitiously pressing a switch hidden under a gilt molding, or pointing out the direction the young sirs should take to reach their desired destination.

Even for Matías—whose home it was—the passageway must have seemed too wide and the servant too ubiquitous. Pedro moved awkwardly in the midst of so much splendor. Huge curtains seemed to preserve a special quality of air by preventing the entry of ordinary, fume-ridden air from the street. The indirect lighting met its own reflections, which rebounded off old oil paintings and intensified their patinas which seemed to crack more quickly than from the normal passage of time. The end of the long corridor opened on to drawing rooms similar in size to a convent refectory, but rather than housing a series of thin, white marble tabletops, they were furnished with leather armchairs ready to comfortably seat the bodies of giants that had survived from the Iron Age, next to which objects difficult to describe and English illustrated magazines were piled high on absurdly small, short-legged tables.

Matías gestured to him to occupy one of those armchairs, which he did, feeling his body sink slowly into layers of duck feather, welcoming cushions, and silent springs made in Britain. In the meantime, the somnambular flunky managed with divine simultaneity to put on a record to Matías's taste and offer two tall glasses of carefully measured, opalescent cocktails, whose clinking attested to the excellent quality of the cut glass. That beverage found favor even in a stomach as sick as Pedro's, and as soon as Matías placed a sweet-scented cigarette between his fingers, the flunky disappeared, leaving personal tasks like lighting the cigarette and knocking gray ash into the arty ashtrays to hands less deft than his own.

Pedro had hardly said a word on their journey to Matías's house from the dismal depths of the bedroom where he had puked. When he reflected on recent happenings, he discerned no coherent pattern, only an assortment of jottings and impressions an imaginative journalist spreads over his desk while he waits for creative inspiration to tease out the as yet not entirely transparent meaning behind his story. Although more buoyant, Matías was still feeling the aftereffects of his nighttime shenanigans, and being in no mood to broadcast bright clarion calls of lofty-sounding Greco-Latin or Latin periods, he mouthed utterances in the vulgar vernacular: "What a malarkey!" "What an old perv!" "Literature pure and simple . . . !" and "Nothing funnier than a boring German."

With the healing passage of time, the pain in Pedro's temples moved to the nape of his neck, and when he closed his eyes he felt (though it was an illusion) his body was sinking into even comfier layers of a bottomless armchair, and when he intuited rather than heard nervous footsteps approaching hesitantly, then forcefully, Matías sprang up almost to attention, obliging Pedro to snap out of his reverie and try to follow suit. A lady in a tight-fitting black dress, buttoned down the back, with the whitest triangle of flesh above a swooping neckline, from which rose a delicate neck, a well-appointed head, and an artful hairdo, was walking towards them, her delightful smile flitting from one to the other.

"Mama," said Matías. "You do know Pedro? I believe I've mentioned him to you."

"Yes, of course," said the lady, raising the slenderest hand to a height that meant Pedro barely had to incline his head, while deciding whether to kiss that slim hand or simply pretend to with his mouth, so as not to make the slightest vaporous smack.

"You must be the researcher," the lady said. "How interesting! You must tell me about your experiments. It's a subject I feel most passionate about. My son tells me you are a genuine sage."

"Not at all; I'm merely trying to demonstrate whether the hereditary factor is dominant in transmission in a particular strain of cancer-bearing mice or if environmental factors are more pertinent. It really isn't that original. Americans have studied this before me, but..."

"How absolutely enthralling... Yes, you have the face of a sage. Does my son see to your every need? Why don't you let him help you? This son of mine is quite a wastrel even though he's so intelligent."

"Of course, if that's what he would like. I..."

"Will you stick around? If your sister comes with her little girlfriends, please make a fuss of them."

The lady kept spinning round, seemingly of the opinion that those armchairs, despite her slim figure, weren't going to be comfortable enough. A luminous halo of blond hair carefully arranged around her round face, straight nose, large bright eyes, and arched eyebrows gave volume to a face that perhaps bordered on the over-ethereal, where her nervousness expressed itself in the contracting and almost constant quivering of the corners of her mouth, in the transparent, blue-veined skin on her forehead, in a slight rash under a double chin she kept upright, ensuring (a victim of habit or Sisyphean punishment) that the fluff there was never more than a trace, rapidly erased by an unceasing desire for perfection.

"Do sit down," she said. "I prefer to stand."

"Sit down," Matías said, reassuring him, used to this woman's ways.

"I'm expecting a call; then I'll be off."

Turning her back on them, she went over to the mirror on the marble mantelpiece (near the unknown place from which the music was blasting away that still flooded a drawing room too large to stay empty) and kept a sharp eye out for anything that might blight her looks. At this point, the smile that seemed more like a mask pinned to her white face, a necessary appendage rather than an intrinsic element, suddenly vanished and the corners of her mouth sagged and stopped quivering. Her concentrated gaze was tempered by a proportionate descent of her arched eyebrows. For a moment she seemed to stare at herself, at a point equidistant between her eyes, but a moment later, she reviewed each detail, and began reshaping the complex harmonies within the idea of herself that she'd created, resuming an infinite game. She appeared to have identified something crucial in the fraction of a second, something that guaranteed she'd endure beneath the mask as the same woman with her hidden pain or a steel point sunk into a sensitive place.

Pedro hadn't sat down but looked on in fascination at the mother of Matías—forgetting her son was there. She noticed he was gazing at her.

"Are you studying me? You scare me. Clever men always scare me. They seem to know things about us that we don't."

An embarrassed Pedro stepped back and slumped into an armchair—something he shouldn't have done—his lit cigarette fell on his knee, he clumsily tried to retrieve it, knocked ash on the floor, then stamped out the cigarette on the carpet. He gazed at her again.

"Will you be going to the lecture tomorrow?"

"Yes, of course I will," Pedro said, not knowing which lecture she was referring to.

"Excellent. Come here afterwards. We'll be having a get-together. It's an intellectual get-together, so you'll feel at home. Don't be afraid you'll be bored. Bring him on here, Matías."

"Yes, we'll come together," Matías said, "but your get-togethers do bore me."

"Then don't come. But he'll like it if he's as intelligent as he looks."

She abruptly put them out of her mind, and returned to the mirror to stare in all seriousness at that secret, intermediate zone, destroying at a stroke the entire facade she had erected. This time she stood looking at herself for much longer.

"Goodbye! Goodbye! Don't stand up, I'm going to be late," and she moved off as nervily as ever, straight-backed, svelte, her legs close together, self-engrossed and very conscious of the secret work of art she constantly secreted, like the wonderful mother-of-pearl slime a snail leaves in its wake.

"I'm sorry! I didn't think she'd be home," Matías apologized, before she'd completely disappeared. "She's a real drag."

"She's so young!"

"No, she's not that young. Let's go to my room!" And he walked in the direction opposite from the one into which his mother had disappeared.

"But didn't she say we should wait for your sister?"

"So what? Let's go and look at my Goya."

Matías's Goya was a large, full-color reproduction tacked on to his bedroom wall, showing complete contempt for the Empire furniture and pink wallpaper. Surrounded by entranced women, a big ram at a witches' Sabbath was welcoming them, gesturing haughtily, his raised head peering down not only at each woman prostrated on the ground but also at any unwary spectator who dared to gaze at the painting.

"What do you reckon?" Matías asked.

"Let me take a look . . . ! I hardly dare."

Scène de sorcellerie: Le Grand Bouc—1798—(H. 43 cm; L. 30 cm). Madrid. Musée Lázaro.

Big ram, big male, big he-goat, scapegoat, well-endowed Hispanic billy goat. Sacrificial goat. Not he! Big ram in all his glory, at the height of his powers, enjoying being the cynosure of female adorers. His horn is no ominous horn but a sign of glorious phallic power. And two horns means double potency. His vigilant eye watches the bunch of auparishtaka females[24] lying on his chest, ripe for it, whose aborted fetuses seem genuinely to beg for repeat performances via contact with the One who (maybe the reincarnation of the malign one or the mighty prince of the night) likes to rest a benign left hoof on the still-warm, skinny, underfed bodies of rickety kids from countless *mauvaises couches*, the mummified leftovers of which hang at regular intervals from a willowy sapling. Why are they strung up like that? What keeps them strung up? Maybe life-bearing cords that bubble and flow with deoxygenated blood from veins and oxygenated blood from arteries. Can a little waif be strung up by his navel if he is yet to use his throat to scream, to breathe, to cough, and to cry, but only to ingest slowly and imperceptibly the liquid that keeps life afloat? Bats hover in threesomes, fly down and perch on the same horns that are such a source of fascination. And while his left hoof saves, his penetrating stare indicates that the pure air from distant mountains, the very same air he breathes, shows how we are all bonded to this earth, are all its children and fated to become earth again. But why are the sated auparishtaka so besotted? What truth does his open, motionless eye emit? The women are in a hurry; in a hurry to hear the truth. Precisely those who are left completely unmoved by his truth. He'll raise his other hoof, his right one, and place an apple on it. And while showing the apple to that most select gathering, he'll speak for an hour about the essential and existential qualities of apples. The quiddity of his apple will be revealed to those women who couldn't care less about quiddity. Let's accompany those angst-ridden, refined, select women to listen to his inspired peroration! Let's bow our heads before the grand macho metaphysician and let his honeyed words gush purifyingly over our foreheads. He has something to give he alone can give. Faces will be illuminated by an impossible sun at that hour of the night. But it's there, it shines, it glows, the truth is he wears a mask. Only his eye belongs to the reality beneath the mask. And from there he observes us as through a periscope, all the better to enthrall us. So why does his eye burn so bright? All the better to see us! So why does he lift his horn so high? All the better to horn us! While his eager eye looks on, aborted bodies wither and writhe, dream of resurrecting renaissance. While the defenseless masses are said to be revolting, choice bodies in repose enjoy laidback penetration. While the nocturnal sun renders vitamins and powdered milk redundant, the peel of sucked-dry oranges drives the continual growth of elephantiasic geniuses. Because in Elephanta there were Brahmin temples though in Bhubaneswar children starved mercilessly to death, but in those temples they celebrated great rituals for provident mother nature ever flowing with milk—as described by Vatsyayana—yet starvation and death by other means never kneaded the suffering people into fermenting, rebellious dough that was cannily segmented (into sects) like the rings of a repulsive reptile, an inferior beast that slithers and coils, so it never ripens and bursts and suddenly demolishes or puts to the fire what art has hallowed as noble. Prophetic proclamation delivered precisely so that the prophesy is never fulfilled! Silver-tongued dissector of the future! I denounce you as a traitor! I summon you to treachery and the conclave in the flameless Barceló.[25] You're not a scapegoat, you're a rutting goat. You raise your left hoof benignly but goatishly threaten with your right, and time and again you refer personally to the secretary of the learned corporation. With the eyes of an assegai you see moldy Visigoth blood circulating through our umbilical veins, as in an amusing X-ray, and you're too smart for a people with such shrunken brains. And since you're made of a nobler substance, o goat, you feel contempt for us all. Yes, really, you do, you saw the light: we're all fools. And there's no cure for fools. And it will never be enough for foolish folk to eat, dress, be piously educated in luminous new seminaries, or be nourished on select vitamin-rich juices and protein extracts the blender squeezes from a range of raw material, nourished on juices, fruit, fricassees, sausages, roast beef, fresh fish, fresh beans, squid, oranges, oranges, and more oranges (and not only the peel), since as the victims of their poor Gothic blood and inferior Mediterranean stock, they will remained entrapped in their Asiatic mindsets and vegetate miserably, a prey to one-line gags and deprived of the repulsive technology from the northwest. *Cante hondo, media verónicas,* pharaonic females with hordes of children, a torero's loyal old rapier bearers, hospitality galore, equites, centaurs from Lower Andalusia, all phantoms from Elephanta, caste after caste after caste, and not just the torero caste, but the panhandling caste, the vagabond caste, the clod-splitting caste, the caste of the seventh child of the seventh child, the caste of Chinatowns from every Marseille in the world and the caste of dark-eyed females soliciting on Parisian pavements who can't roll—still can't, the dimwits!—a properly rolled *r,* the grand Gilbert and skinny Mary caste,[26] the only touch of Europe in the most European of our cities put to the sword and whose knives were secured (by a better caste of noble Nordic monarch) by rings of iron on tables so they could be used only to cut dry, worm-eaten bread. You know all this, goat, with your subtle insights, and you prescribe one huge therapeutic antidote, our phenomenological incorporation into the great, nutritious Germania, covens, goats, and all. And your spiritual Carolina Isles can be our temporary jails.[27] But you are a good man, and that's why you raise your left hoof a little higher than your right. That's why you don a disguise that isn't yours but entertains those who observe you so admiringly. That why you play the "amateur" and inveigle people so effusively into philosophy, like a straight-from-the-heart youth in short sleeves,[28] so graceful, such a sublime style, such flourishes of the pen, such mind-blowing metaphors that dead children will forgive you for not explaining what was the cause of their deaths (not looking at your mask, but at your eye), and we will ignore your two horns and carry you to your grave singing a dirge that's almost bound to sound sad.

Like any well-arranged cosmos, the one where the event took place was also organized in a hierarchy of spheres. There was a lower sphere, a middle sphere, and a higher sphere, peak and dynamic arc-boutant of the entire edifice. Very classical too, as inevitably happens in every theocracy; the lower sphere was devoted to the hells in which—setting aside every excessive Ormuzdahrimanian tendency[29]—the kingdom of sin, of evil, of the perverse, of all those condemned to lengthy, richly deserved sentences, can simultaneously coexist with the terrestrially vital, the genetically engendered, with what can be voluptuously relished before punishment hits it too. In this way, the lower sphere of the cosmos to which we refer, where no (apparent) alignment or relationship with the two higher spheres existed, was occupied by a servant girls' dance. Oblivious to the Maestro's imminent exordium (simultaneity of time and elevated space), the sweating throng beneath swayed, sashayed, and shimmied to the sound of a pseudo-Afro-Cuban cha-cha-cha. In this lower sphere, sounds and smells were created that would have struggled to impregnate the higher middle sphere, had it been empty. That was far from being the case, because the middle sphere was packed with a crowd almost equal in number to the lower sphere's, even if it was a most diverse lot. Before this event began, the crowd jostling in Brownian[30] disarray in the hall's far-from-sumptuous spaces and bustling passageways produced a considerable buzz, blotting out all but the occasional thunderous bugle blast or drum solo that slipped surreptitiously through a window opened over the inner courtyard. In terms of smell, the middle sphere's was a potpourri of various expensive perfumes (some imported from Paris despite the balance of payments deficit), medicinal lotions and male hair restorers, a welter of non-black tobacco smoke, and almost imperceptible, though de rigueur, whiffs from the sweaty armpits and necks of students keen on philosophy but not on water, long before the vogue for the existential was at its height. Finally, and to conclude this summary survey of our theocracy, the third, highest, and climactic sphere—in a variety of senses—of the ensemble was constituted by a movie-house scenario where, next to a desk that was home to a lamp, a jug of water, a glass, and an apple, a blank blackboard made its menacing presence felt. This third sphere existed only virtually or allegorically until the exact moment the Maestro occupied his pedagogic hotspot and kick-started the event.

Those condemned to the basement had no inkling of what was going on three yards above their heads and consequently no clue that the sharpest mind in the Celtiberian world was about to make a conscious attempt to raise the intellectual level of the society to which they also belonged (unworthily, it has to be said). But the phenomenon was mutual and perfectly symmetrical, because neither the crowds in the middle sphere nor, God knows, even the powerful Maestro had the slightest idea of the fascinating reality being simultaneously forged beneath the soles of their feet. Because it must really be crucial for an adolescent who has scraped together three pesetas to have a chance to inspect for himself the makeup of the female members of his race who've entered those Elysian Fields gratis. Because it is from these encounters and no other—neither spontaneous generation nor the flight of storks—that the elemental biological continuity springs, the germinal thallus on which the remaining spheres sail and are satisfied in their diverse bodily needs and provision of creative artists, painters, toreros, and chorus girls. But things being what they are, the people, engrossed in themselves, were unaware of the philosopher and the profusion of luxury automobiles outside the fleapit's door, and simply experienced new obstacles when crossing the road and drew no useful insights from that historic moment.

The two friends—included in the intermediate sphere—sat between an ex-seminarist in a dandruff-speckled black jacket typical of the defrocked fraternity on their right and a sophisticated lady from the très haute on their left. In front, behind, on every side they were surrounded by ladies of a similar stripe and poets of varying genders. Dressed à la Balenciaga with a hat specially chosen for the occasion—featuring a small Pallas Athena helmet, its single frivolous note a tiny red hummingbird feather worn in trophy mode—a lady incessantly waved her exquisite hands in front of her face. While she informed her adjacent colleague of her ideas (assuming she had any) and philosophical inclinations, her hands, like live animals, described broad, unpredictable whirls. Never settling, the toys in flight chased each other and revealed a svelteness of line unblemished by nicotine, oversized cuticles, or the spurious, swollen bumps engendered by even the most delicate of work implements. Pedro admired for a moment the fingernails adorning her hands. Longer than usual, more convex-concave than usual, more scarlet-red than usual, they gave him angst as if they reminded him of something.

However, now that the great Maestro had stepped onto the stage, that micro-universe finished perfecting its spheres. Harassed by hisses from highly indignant, punctually respectful folk, the last coxcombs took their seats as the welcoming salvos faded. The circles of purgatory (as we might designate the cheap seats, higher than the stage only in appearance) received their burden of tardy souls and the Maestro—grave, hieratic, self-preening, ready to lower himself to the level of his audience, haloed by an aura of consummate grace, with eighty years of European idealism behind him, endowed with an original metaphysics, endowed with a following in the wider world, endowed with a big head, a lover of life, a rhetorician, an inventor of a new style of metaphor, a sampler of history, revered in provincial German universities, oracle, journalist, essayist, conversationalist, the one-who-had-said-it-before-Heidegger—began his peroration, which went more or less as follows:

"Ladies (pause), gentlemen (pause), what (pause) I'm holding in my hand (pause) is an apple (long pause). You (pause) see it (long pause). But you see it (pause) from there, where you are sitting (long pause). I (long pause) see the same apple (pause), but from here, where I am standing (very long pause). The apple you see (pause) is different (pause), very different (pause) from the apple I see (pause). However (pause), it is the same apple (gasps)."

The audience had hardly recovered from the impact of this revelation when he condescendingly resumed, with more pauses, before delivering the key to the enigma: "What is happening (pause) is that you and I (long pause) see it from a different perspective." (thumping of desks).

Given the lack of a medical legal certificate signed by the doctor who had attended her in her last moments, the removal of Florita's corpse (simultaneously the cadaver of a crime) could be secured only by one of three procedures: falsification of the official document, bribery of a professional colleague not implicated in the intrauterine homicide, or clandestine burial in unsanctified terrain. Snarler's hyperactive brain ceaselessly searched for a solution, helped by Amador, who—loyally—returned after his assault/interrogation at the hands of that evil-looking character. Each contradictory solution brought its own complications. The best would have been to ensure that Don Pedro signed the document, but that was impossible because he was a full-time animal experimenter and lacked collegial recognition and consequently couldn't give the demise a due legality. "If there hadn't been so much blood, we'd have called the guy from down there," opined

Snarler. "It could have been something sudden." "We've no choice but to bury her ourselves, but we'll all go to jail." "There's room in the yard." "Somebody will rat—I didn't like that fellow one bit." "He won't rat, but I bet he's plotting something." "The old woman and that know-it-all will keep quiet or they'll be landed in it."

But the roly-poly consort had already departed and, bareheaded, had trekked many a dusty mile until she reached the area inhabited by beings not demonized as immigrants and who could hear (like in her village) a church bell toll and proper prayers and responses to accompany the body of her ill-fated daughter when professional gravediggers, with the rapidity and skill brought by years of practice, would throw the first shovelfuls of reddish earth over a casket she was all ready to buy to accommodate the bloodless body, despite the avalanche of legal complications this irresponsible, though heartfelt, desire of hers might bring upon the heads of those who'd decided her daughter's fate in her presence but without her consent.

In the meantime, Florita's body was perfectly at rest, and the secret movements that follow death had yet to start. Grimacing, her sister arranged a few small flowers around the body and stared at it hard.

Gleeful, jubilant, victims of verbal diarrhea, vaguely conscious of their high IQs, the invitees rushed into the domain of that nimble flunky and struck a variety of poses on the seats of the giant armchairs, or on their arms and backs, chairs that comfortably accommodated the cultural fowl perched there holding glasses of bird feed, chirruping in every direction, their different voices distinguished by the sonorous lilt of their trills rather than any specific content. "How easy it was to understand him!" warbled the young, pink-beaked fowl, eager not to ruffle any feathers, humble even, in disbelief at how easily they'd flown to the lowest boughs of the tree of knowledge; "I followed him perfectly," suggested a higher level on the scale of smug self-belief and grateful approval of the way the philosopher had explained his truths; "He's better than ever," croaked a connoisseur who sampled fruit on the tree and could tell if they were avocados, mangoes, pineapples, or other kinds of tropical fruitery, as well as whether they'd reached optimal ripeness, whether the slicing and peeling of what was on offer respected the rules of good taste; the man who declared, "The apple thing was brilliant, nobody has ever explained so clearly and precisely how the Weltanschauung of each and every one of us depends on our location in the cosmos," was a hallowed bird of the night, the wisest and biggest of owls ensconced in the darkest depths of the treetop. Not pigeonholed by any category, lovely little bird and deft bird fancier, the lady of the house flew from branch to branch humming more complex tunes that, while fulfilling the purpose—like the other birds'—of self-glorification and enhancement, also served more useful goals in terms of pairing and matchmaking groups, sometimes imperfectly constituted, continually shifting, forming, breaking up, constantly changing the dynamic equilibrium. Taking care that neither one silly bird's excessive isolation nor an irresponsible ostrich's unpremeditated kick disturbed the harmony of the whole, she distributed her flocks around her large stoves that ensured temperatures where birds ascribed from birth to elevated social climes felt as at ease, as did those whose risqué fluttering, overanxious pecking in dining rooms or outrageously intelligent trills revealed a provenance from less exalted climes, silted ponds and mean and murky streams. These pretty birds could only scale such heights, for which they'd never been destined, thanks to the special allure of their plumage or cheeping, whose "fascinating" aesthetic value compensated for the fundamental mediocrity of their species. So just as infrequent mutations within a family of earthen-hued partridges give rise for no apparent reason to a mother-of-pearl-feathered specimen, or common sparrows may produce an unexpected great-great-great-grandson with a lovely fire-colored chest, so torero birds, painter birds, and even, on rare occasions, poet birds or writer birds (if their poetic gift comes with a numismatically noble profile), could—despite being children of the fourth estate—rub shoulders with birds of paradise and the most aristo of pink flamingos, who always succeeded, come what may, in distinguishing themselves from social climbers by the refinement of their wings, the length of their necks, and a plumage cut by the finest couturier.

"So I see you finally made it," the main bird fancier said agreeably, her gaze lingering on a Pedro in penguin mode with creased, tight-fitting, sea-blue suit. "Did you enjoy the lecture?" she asked, desperately scouring the horizon for someone to introduce to an unknown researcher, a close friend of Matías, with no other saving graces—unless she dropped *cancer*, that cruelest of words, into a conversation, which might very well stir the entrails of an ancient marquess on track to her final wrinkling, still cosseting a carcass she'd cherished with kid gloves from time immemorial. No sooner thought than done, taking the arm of the alarmed young man whose unintelligible muttering fell on her deaf ear, she simply smiled as they cut a path through the cocktail party's leafy boughs, some tangled branches already set afire by the sparky, flame-throwing laughter of squawking parakeets in awe of their colleagues' incredible wit.

When Pedro saw himself plonked in front of those two noble, self-engrossed ladies and failed to achieve the mandatory half bow, half kiss of hands and heard the word *cancer* trip off the lips of his kind introducer, after she'd disappeared, he recognized to his horror that (though the hostess with the mostest) she'd made a miscalculation, and the two leathery old cranes were engaged in swapping personal impressions about an ongoing situation that necessitated hawk-eyed concentration, and were reluctant to grant him a scrap of attention. After an excruciating (for him) period of time, the old ladies interrupted their confused chatter and stared at him, fixated by the quality of his tie and his shoes.

"Are you Dolores's nephew?" asked one.

"No, madam—"

"What did Matilde say? That what Dolores has is cancer?" the other asked her companion, at the same time as she said to him, indirectly and blankly: "Poor thing!"

"No, she said I'm working on cancer."

"Aha. So you're . . . a doctor?"

"I'm more of a researcher. I'm preparing studies of cancer in mice that—"

"But you *were* at the lecture," declared the first, seeking clarification.

"Yes."

"So what is the connection between cancer and philosophy?" she asked, leading Pedro to feel a vague need for a witty riposte that hovered on the tip of his tongue but never came to fruition.

"You can make as many experiments as you want, but there's no curing it."

"Not yet."

"So you say Dolores has got cancer. What treatment has she been given? In any case, the poor dear's obviously on her last legs."

"I didn't say..."

"Why bother to deny it? Everybody knows. Breast cancer. It kills all the women in that family. But they insist on saying it isn't, it isn't, that it's pneumonia. Everyone knows her mother had cancer and her sister, the nun, too... Hey, Matilde!" And with an agility belying her appearance, she jumped to her feet and pursued mine host, who, pretending not to hear, was flapping her wings in the direction of a renowned lawyer pontificating to a bevy of ladies, closer to that unforgiving age than they cared admit, about the marriage rights of women historically when a contract of separation of assets hadn't been signed at the right time.

Pedro turned that flight to his advantage and detached himself discreetly from the other, apparently deaf old dear with a polite nod, an empty glass his saving excuse. Like a Bedouin hastening to an oasis he made his way to Matías, accompanied by a slim young blond whose eyes were devouring him, whose svelte hand was even touching his strongman lapel as she asked him the odd question, which he, either preening or presumptuous, took his time to answer. Smiling ingenuously, Pedro sidled over, wanting to stop drifting around that room full of strangers like a buoy on the loose, but when he raised his hand and half opened his mouth in greeting, his friend's stony glare halted him in his tracks, indicating complete nonrecognition, acknowledging him neither as an individual being nor as a physical body, freezing him to the spot. For a moment, Pedro wondered if he'd made a mistake, one of those hallucinations that only lead us to project onto a stranger's face the features and familiar gestures of the individual who's on our mind. But he hadn't; it *was* Matías, without a doubt, but a version he'd never seen before. It wasn't simply his eyes that sent out different messages, he'd also changed the shape of his mouth and was clearly not voicing Latinate but more commonplace words, in a secret language whose value can only be discerned by the initiated, and that includes among its many virtues the ability to make a delightful creature tremble with desire and magnetically steer her graceful neck with its luminous halo towards the individual holding forth. Matías's body had also realigned its limbs in another way Pedro had intuited fleetingly the other day when his mother walked into that same drawing room that underwent such an abrupt metamorphosis. As if obeying a universal categorical imperative, Matías held his glass differently, raised it differently, drank from it differently, with minute attention to detail: carefully rehearsed gestures performed slowly like a rite any modification of which would seem sacrilegious. That same Matías with whom he'd shared his astonishment at the emptiness at the heart of the Maestro's lecture now seemed transformed, revealing a surface as unknown as the other side of the moon, which, nevertheless, surely exists. And as if to confirm the presence of his old friend under that facade, which was maybe more real than the one he was familiar with, Matías suddenly winked, in a way that suggested: "This pain in the neck won't let me come and chat with you about the usual, but if you knew what a turn-on she is, you'd soon forgive me."

Pedro slumped into one of those infinitely giving armchairs where the posterior descends to the remotest depths. He had to admit the unease he felt was pure Envy: the yellow beast medieval artists placed in allegories in which Lust is a naked woman holding an apple and Pride a clothed woman with a crown on her head. That whole universe, where words hold a meaning he can't grasp (though he might one day) and where gestures achieve a beauty that he can't see (though he will one day, once cured of a color blindness he can't accept), constitutes a fortress of beings from another species who act benevolently towards him and are prepared to help him up the steps of a very long, but not insuperable, ladder. True! It only needs an act, an act of will. Just like the angel of temptation saying: "Eat of this fruit and you will be as gods." And he simply has to take that step, make that gesture, or take that bite and put himself in the line to reach that destination. He merely has to decide to be like them, go to the fruit, join in, assimilate, espouse a new nature. But he doesn't want to. It pains him that he doesn't want to. It pains him that he forces himself to scorn what at the moment he—pathetically—envies. But does he scorn this other way of life because it's truly contemptible or because he's incapable of getting sufficiently close to be part of it? Is it only the envy of the dispossessed, or does his moral stand have an absolute value? If he is so certain that what he wants to be is what he should be, why the pain? Why the envy? He feels so much pain because of this small world where he could walk but can't, because of these gilded bird women who are stupid and vain. To be heard and admired, to know how to kiss a hand, to be admitted into their insidious conversations, to be in the room at the top, one of them, the select minority, those who are beyond good and evil because they dared bite the fruit of vanitas or have been brought up with it, breathing it in like the air we breathe.

"What are you doing here all on your own?" asks the bird fancier in chief.

"Matías was very busy," Pedro explains vengefully.

His rancor allows him to be aggressive, because on reflection he's not prepared to admire anyone or be afraid of anyone, only to put on a show of insolence.

"Don't tell me you're angry?"

"I don't see the point of these society gatherings. Didn't you say it was to discuss the lecture?"

"But people have been speaking of nothing else . . . you've been in dreamland. Didn't you speak to the professor?" And she points to a large huddle around a bald man who is still holding forth. "Would you like me to introduce you?"

"No, thanks all the same. I must be off."

"You *are* angry. You think we have ignored you."

"No, not at all."

And all of a sudden, finally falling into the trap, the act of making himself seem interesting, in a preening display of his own, albeit splattered, feathers, he adds: "I carried out an operation last night."

"Did you really?" says the lady luminary. "Do tell me!" But before he can start telling his tale, she gets up. "Sorry!" The professor is walking away; he is going to leave the gathering. Surrounded by his wisdom, like a great vessel swaying slowly before setting out to sea. "How disappointing! Why's he leaving so soon?"

"Madam..."

"Don't go yet. I've not had an opportunity to talk to you. There is so much I need you to explain—"

"Just a moment; just a moment..." And he leads her into a corner near the door, where, steely-eyed and gesturing limply, he informs her of knowledge she finds totally uninteresting. Pedro watches her possessively; he now thinks he has rights over this woman, that the attention she's paying the other man has been stolen from him. He'd like her to listen to him. He was on the verge of telling her... but Florita's corpse surfaces in the middle of the drawing room. She's resting on that deep, thick, springy, luxuriant carpet more comfortably than in her own bed. Obstinately naked, she lets her blood run capriciously between the furniture and the legs of the over-the-top members of this social set. Naturally, it's an item the latter have learned to ignore, for although they walk past it or absentmindedly tread in it, it's something that passes them by. Not one of the laws governing this world of gods and birds references corpses.

Matías looms before Pedro, alarmed, distraught, he's forgotten the blond fairy and the hand she's resting on his chest, he seems to act more normally, and looks anxiously at him. He says something, alludes to a serious, most urgent matter. Somebody has come who has something to tell him. It's very important. He is upstairs in the same room where the big he-goat is still lording it over the becalmed witches' coven. Matías is very agitated. Why is he so pallid? There's someone who wants to see him urgently. He is struggling to exit that deep armchair. The layers of silence are so dense that Matías's words barely reach him. He guesses what he's saying from his mannerisms. Matías grabs his arm and leads him away from the festive throng, away from the presence of those deities, towards a reality that awaits him close by, in Matías's bedroom, in front of the great all-conquering billy goat.

The difference that exists between factories that mass-produce and those that produce more limited quantities of manufactured goods isn't only—as one might imagine—of a quantitative nature, because there are qualitative differences thanks to which the application of the rules arising from Bedaux-Taylorism achieves infinitely higher efficiency levels that are of quite another order.[31] Manufacturing reaches a volume that is properly *mass production* when the production line allots one or more workers to each of the minimal operations into which analysis of the process breaks down its wholly integrated system. It is only then that the principle of time and motion fulfils its virtual promise and prevents the entire factory from "having to function at the rate of the worst of its workers." Proper planning of the ensemble; schematic indexing of the relative complexity of each operation; paring back of displacements, movements, pauses, decision making; and banning of any appeal to craftsmanship ensure the results we all want. Such a rationalization has perhaps never been established in our city with complete exactitude because of the failure to reach a critical mass of production. Consequently, to gauge its basic principles, we will review an organization that may not properly speaking be manufacturing, but that deals with a sufficient number of items for rationalizing norms to consolidate due levels of proven efficiency. We are referring to the vertical burials that are common for people who, having belonged in life to the least elevated social classes, were unable or did not wish to acquire a grave that is their own property and are thus destined to be randomly consigned to nondescript, ill-defined terrain for the number of years necessary for the processes of putrefaction to finish their work and later to be moved to the ditch that is known by the elegant, resonant name of ossuary. Since the terrain available (despite the vast extension of desert around the city) is necessarily restricted, while the number of dead can be considered to be practically infinite since, thanks to the relentless passage of time, every day generously or parsimoniously brings its contribution, it has been deemed vital to fine-tune a technique of exploitation that, while limiting the spread of the putrefying zone, diminishes the cost to the public purse of this most innovative service afforded to every citizen. The cornerstone of Bedaux-Taylorism—as is well known—depends on every worker not having a single nonproductive moment (whether it's waiting for tools to arrive, or not having immediate access to the next part he should be slotting on, or the negligent lighting of a ciggy), and while he works, each movement constituting this uninterrupted activity must have a precise outcome in modifying the material that forms part of the manufactured item. In line with these norms, the Este Cemetery gravediggers, rather than playing around with skulls or femurs and cracking macabre jokes almost always in dubious taste, act in step with a nonstop, rational, scientifically determined rate of output. While one of the squads, which we will designate as A, creates in the reddish earth rectangular graves in three rows of two to a depth of approximately four yards and a width and length that long experience has shown to be the most suitable, another squad we will denominate as C transports the displaced earth in barrows to terrain where the excess soil—which amounts to seven-eighths of the total—is used as backfill, at the same time as squad B is devoting itself to what is, properly speaking, the burial, which, being the phase in the process that requires the most skill, deserves a more detailed description. Following their predetermined schedule, each of these workers applies himself exclusively to his specific task and other subsidiary services supply the material to be worked on, at a rate that must be strictly monitored if optimal output is to be achieved. This rate can be achieved because all those items are stored in a spacious depository from which transfers depart at regular intervals, shifting at a uniform speed along previously designated paths. The time invested in each oblong item is rigorously controlled, constituting the length of its time slot, to which a minimal corrective coefficient is added based on respect for the human grieving of relatives, to ensure that the funeral corteges don't bump into one another or coincide beside the same trench. This sense of respect is perfectly preserved through the use of divergent, rather than criss-crossing, routes for each couple of successive transfers. When the item has reached the foot of the parallel grave squad A has just left in order to excavate another similar one a reasonable distance away, squad B workers start on their contribution. With rapid, efficient movements they manipulate two thick ropes they pass under the casket: one at the putative level of the neck or lower, at the point where the top of the vertebra juts out and marks the beginning of the back; the other in the putative position of the back of the knee or popliteal cavity. Both ropes thus in situ ensure that the load is perfectly balanced. Each of the four in the squad grabs one rope end and the casket descends quickly (it's made of thin pinewood that facilitates the swiftest penetration of all the elements that must be present to secure a rich and rapid process of putrefaction: moisture, earth, plant roots, seed buds, insect larvae, white maggots) without knocking or brushing against the sides of the pit. Once the casket reaches the bottom and they've checked its horizontal state, the ropes are easily removed via the procedure of pulling one end while letting go of the other. Meanwhile, a resonant religious accompaniment to the burial is chorused, and after briefly giving a few closer relatives the opportunity to cast down a handful of earth to test the precarious intangibility of the lid, the four synchronized workers, never getting in each other's way, cover the item with a layer of soil sufficient to hide it from the peering eyes of inquisitive, occasionally impertinent relatives intent on leaning over the hole and glimpsing a piece of black wood, but not dense enough to significantly reduce the space available and cause a decrease in the output from their labor. After depositing this layer of earth that tightly embraces the deceased (leaving the necessary space for air to enter to secure future necrophagous life), squad B workers mouth an "OK," a "finito," a "done and dusted" so expressively that all bystanders still scrutinizing the ocher color of the earthen substance that's just been spaded down become aware of the inanity of their behavior, look up, and, after a moment of hesitancy, follow in the—surer—footsteps of the chaplain of that place of rest and his acolyte, who are striding away towards the depository, in search of the next load. And it is high time they did so, because surreptitiously, barely visible to eyes still misted by sorrow, the next convoy is approaching, which the expertly chronometered schedule requires without delay. In this way, the vertical burials pile into the smallest space, with the least physical effort, the largest possible number of dead bodies without affronting religious ritual or ethical concerns. And these humdrum operatives achieve the—almost unattainable—ideal of a job well done without fuss or hoo-ha.

Subject to this common fate, Florita's bloodless, pseudo-virginal corpse reached the aforementioned depository at an unremarked moment and was placed on the serried ranks of sarcophagus tables. In the sunlight, the Este Cemetery had spread out all its oneiric magnificence of an enchanted garden by Hieronymus. Pointed roofs of pagodas raised their colored tiles towards an Oriental sky. A motley crowd of mourners ambled leisurely along the paths in small groups admiring manifold marvels: those chessboard niches displaying every little home of the dead, with their individual doors on which one could knock, accessible thanks to stairs spiraling down to the earth, allowing whoever can pay the price to rest eternally on a third-floor left apartment; those sharp-pointed trees surrounded by beds of preferably yellow flowers; those barren zones where no permanent gravestone is allowed, only temporary wooden or iron crosses or small iron railings around body-sized private plots; those buildings conceived by an insane architect at the time of the apotheosis of fin de siècle bad taste; all those diverse elements succeed in creating the appearance of a landscape from a Japanese fan from which they've banished artificial lakes, rippling brooks, hunchbacked bridges, and weeping willows.

The roly-poly consort and three other old women, the corduroy-clad barman from the big tavern, a female cousin from their village, and Amador's wife were the only witnesses to the deft operation by which dust was returned to dust like an illusory phantom of tempting flesh. But just as the earth that was to accompany her on her long journey was thrown on her casket with alarmingly hollow thuds and three companions of diverse sexes had been laid above Florita's young body, the exhumation order arrived signed by a judge on dull but duly legal paper in a distant, dusty courtroom, the result of strange skullduggery, now delivered to the necropolis by a policeman on his bike. In this ridiculous manner the—ever-inhuman—law of the land interrupted the rhythm of work and prevented the day's toil from reaching its accustomed degree of efficiency. Once again the loose earth had to be half removed by B and C squads since A alleged it wasn't its responsibility, while new caskets, a beautiful, smoky black, were shamelessly lined up in unaccustomed tawdry promiscuity, displaying in the light of day what should never be eyed again.

"It's this one," declared the overseer of the three squads fearlessly and decisively, underlining the error-free nature of his orderly mind, once the grave had been reopened; Florita's corpse began to retrace its steps along the path of no return, not towards the same depository, but towards an adjacent, equally Asian and effervescent construction where forensic doctors ruled the roost during their shift, in the uninterrupted presence of the fat autopsy porter, a ruddy, jovial fellow, inured to all sense of repugnance and a skilled connoisseur of the human body and several species of maggot.

The great accusing eye (which by day occupies the zenith of the astronomic vault and projects its insidious light on flat surfaces exposed to its gaze—whitewashed housefronts, the flimsy roofs of shantytowns, the sandy arenas of bullrings, as well as shady spots where sensitive souls seek shelter—and with that same luminosity pursues its deceptive acts to their limit, stubbornly asserting to every astonished spectator the self-evident truth that the only reality is the opaque surface of things, their form, their size, the spatial disposition of their parts, and that, conversely, the deep symbolic meaning, the essence such entities embody in the night, is devoid of truth) extended in an everyday way its transformational energy into the navel of the world of shadows, into the palace of the daughters of the night, where, becalmed and providential, singular and sweet Doña Luisa rested like a large, off-white-bellied queen. Like her counterpart in the other realm of shadows, she was capable of transmuting blossoming young girls from white-veiled, white-costumed, honest dancers in nuptial flight into indefatigable wingless workers, and also like her counterpart, to perform this sad but profitable transformation, she had no need to resort to mutilating surgical operations, the removal of organs, or metal chastity belts, but through simple changes to eating habits and daily routine (including a thoroughly researched alteration in the timetable that orders the asleep-awake dynamic) she easily achieved the desired effect. Just as the placing of a glass partition in a beehive or an ants' nest triggers an immediate response from the community, which quickly smears the translucent wall with an opaque substance, restoring the dark atmosphere such places need, the only one suited to their specific activities; so too the entry of the great deceiver and his distorting rays into Doña Luisa's anthill was carefully blocked by the presence of lattices, green raffia venetian blinds, wooden shutters, and heavy drapes. Its denizens' aesthetically pleasing blue-lined eyes, black-toned eyelids, and dilating pupils didn't have to suffer the inexorable affront with which daylight punishes their solitary, would-be freewheeling sisters, who for want of any organization appropriate to their nature, the second they depart a room in a cheap boardinghouse or a helpful widow's house, accompanied by their deflated punter, risk their client seeing in lethal daylight the lascivious houri dissolve and vanish, as in a fairy tale. Now he's arm in arm with a housewife from his block who's going to the market, or a cook horrified by the price greens now fetch there. Only one room had been preserved from the sun's deceitful activity, where its malevolent might wouldn't happen upon beings susceptible to such metamorphoses. In the kitchen where the maid toiled, the sun penetrated via the inside yard and consoled a cat that lent its heat, during the unpleasant, even horrific hours of daytime, to Doña Luisa's plump thighs. In her queenly hierarchy it wouldn't have been right for her to spend her time mending and sewing or knitting scarves like the ladies in the Lectures[32] who toil to gain heaven through an existence that's never idle; it rather became her to caress the furry backs of noble animals that have always found a welcome in palaces: greyhounds, gazelles, and elegant, untamable felines. Sitting in a corner of the kitchen, the one nocturnal creature able to confront the light, she was relaxing, her batrachian eyes barely half-open, stroking the back of the black cat, who replied with a secret music, at once tactile and sonorous.

Matías and Pedro stood before her like two pages bound for the Holy Land seeking a bed in her castle and promising to distract the ladies of the court with their graces. Ushered into the kitchen, less resistant to the sun than the matriarch, weaker, paler, and pensive after a night of fear and reflection, wary of the dangers ahead, giddily attempting to avoid the inevitable, they'd finally embraced a foolish subterfuge, a senseless flight towards the other world known to them, where time possessed a different rhythm and concepts didn't coincide with the boundaries of a quotidian reality marked out by death and punishment. Unawares, Pedro was following the path usually pursued by a felon who, after committing a crime in another sphere, returns to the world he is primed for; like animals whose eyes have atrophied through lack of use, blind buds beneath the skin on the neck, his invisible organs of moral discernment hide beneath his forehead and never open for want of proper exercise. Habitually, such reptiles or ophidians feed on small prey in the cracks of slate rocks, but when, rather than devouring the profits of their fellow creatures of the night, they nibble at the lesser, distinct currency of a bank clerk or tram conductor, they are mercilessly crushed, not because of the nature of the crime, but for daring to do so in the light of day.

Matías and Pedro, accomplice and criminal, after walking down half-dark passageways and stairs that stank of stale tobacco, after striding over women scrubbing floors on their knees, after slipping on wet floor tiles, after sniffing on the wooden parquet the smell given off by dry earth after a downpour, after witnessing through open doors the daily change of sheets that characterizes cheap, well-managed brothels, after bumping into the only male inhabitant, a wizen-handed retard, an errand boy from a convent out of the *Decameron*, who was also heading towards the distant kitchen with his basket of victuals, dragging his game leg along the floor thanks to the vigorous efforts of its healthy partner; after all this, Matías and Pedro finally stumbled headlong upon the Buddha bathed in light. The rays of the sun entering the kitchen created that visible trail of minute particles that betrays its presence in dusty haunts. From beneath drooping eyelids, Doña Luisa watched them walk in and didn't budge, drawing on other qualities besides her business-driven nocturnal affability and quasi-tender spot for youngish men. Matías rushed at the idol and his noble arms hugged her tight, while his queasy stomach heaved.

"Here we are. Where are the girls?"

"It's not the right time," the matriarch sternly informed them.

"No matter. We've come to eat with you. It's on us. It's on Pedro..."

In walked the errand boy, and Doña Luisa gestured to him to come over so she could inspect the contents of his basket. To get a better view she pushed Matías away with her other hand. Pedro stayed by the window, flummoxed and shocked by the existence of a kitchen, an oven, a black cat, and a basket of provisions. Doña Luisa sat there, lifted the lid, and gave a grunt of approval. She picked up a tomato and lifted it in the air so the sun beat down hard on the small red sphere. She looked at one side of the tomato. Pedro looked at the other. Both saw it from a different perspective.

"These tomatoes are overripe. I prefer them greener."

"So what? It's on us. We'll order in a meal. We'll eat with you and a few of the girls. We'll stay the whole day."

"It's not the right time," insisted Doña Luisa.

But Matías was already ordering the errand boy to go buy cold sausage, tins of sardines in olive oil, tins of peaches in syrup, cheese, and red wine, slipping one or two notes into his palm. Doña Luisa's motionless eyelids slowly fluttered in the direction of the door. Then she fingered another tomato.

"All right. In any case we can always make a salad."

Turning to the sub-women around the stove, she told them: "You can take your pot and eat downstairs."

And added: "Wake up Andresa and Alicia and tell them to get a move on."

Doña Luisa struggled to her feet, forcing the black cat to jump on the floor. Underlining how hard it was for her to circulate, how difficult it was for her feet to establish contact with the ground, she shuffled over to the window, where gently, but ever so self-consciously, she shut out the sunlight, and restored her role as the mistress of the night.

When the pleasant, pervasive darkness of twilight reestablished the predominance of truth and precision in the house's kitchen, and things could proclaim once again their symbolic nature as *objects*, jettisoning the spatial imprecision of their forms, corners, and dimensions; when Doña Luisa reassumed the providential, reassuring presence of the great phallic mother who invites to drink from the chalice of life all those who—overcoming their natural sense of deference—cling to the hem of her dress and, respectfully supine, kiss her purple ribbons, apricot-colored lace frills, pruriently pink garters (at her age!), never a lascivious black; when her batrachian eyes finally opened wide, unfurling the curly fans of her eyelids and displaying the ever-present shine of the wisest of pupils; and when—at last—the now *de trop* cat returned to its usual hunting forays in adjacent rooms, Matías knew the time had come to reveal all. And with heartfelt sorrow, despite the absence of all future intent except his eternal espousing of the enjoyment of love (elevated by honest artisan labor to a work of art), he told the chatelaine of the reasons for their arrival at that untimely hour and the nature of the crimes (not entirely unfamiliar to that establishment) and the bizarre but lethal machinations behind an autopsy protocol certified by an unknown forensic pathologist, that had put the police on the tracks of the friend by his side, pale faced, trembling, huge bags under his eyes, short of sleep after a panic-stricken night spent in the company of nocturnal *porra* sellers, barely improved by a number of anisette shots courtesy of a monkey, now in need of a more substantial meal, of shelter, of protection, of warm skirts that would unfold in a welcoming gesture, then wrap him in a warm maternal embrace. Matías detailed the circumstances; the age of the young victim; the innocence of the accused; the unlikely fact that he'd never had sex with the one scoured so roughly; the sly sleight of hand of the incestuous father; the commercial connections that existed between both men, mediated by the loyal Amador; finally, how it had been impossible, given the advanced degree of hemorrhaging, to prevent the inevitable. Apprised of these criminal deeds, Doña Luisa observed the doleful swain as if a halo of fire or gentler gold encircled his disheveled locks and thought she glimpsed a devilish beauty in that new denizen in semi-perpetuity of her half-open inferno. Slowly extending her black-clad arm's jewel-laden hand—which glistened purple and amethyst only at night—she took Pedro's cold hand, caressed it, contemplated it as if admiring the power lodged in its fingers. Pedro's delicate hand, though not to the degree it might have done, had he been the skilled surgeon preparing to pursue the victory road that was the dream of the other (boarding-house) old woman, communicated outright repugnance to Pedro's shrunken soul through sensitive nerve endings. But he shot down an immediate instinct to flee and let his hand be stroked, contemplated, relished, and cherished by a calculating, senile mind already foreseeing how useful he might be for curing the ravages that carelessness or fate, on occasion, brought upon her worker bees, leading them to abandon momentarily their headlong rush to inevitable sterility. But she didn't yet dare wield any power she might have accumulated over his cursed hands, and was content to enjoy their pure, unexpressed potential for the moment, with that sensuous tingle a hired killer feels when he caresses a shiny revolver he has yet to fire.

"My dear boy!" said Doña Luisa.

And Pedro bowed his head as if about to rest it on that well-upholstered knee, as if about to kneel before a real mother, as if a soothsayer's lips were about to issue an oracle revealing the only route from sorrow to salvation.

"You can stay here for a few days," said Doña Luisa. "Until it's all sorted."

Pedro felt he was weeping gratefully, though no whimpers came from his lips, no tears welled in his eyes, nor did his heart miss a beat, except that mysteriously he seemed to have stopped breathing, marooned in a submerged space where everything (food, air, love, breath) was being fed to him through a rubber tube while he remained inert. Doña Luisa made the gesture he'd so longed for, the grand gesture towards which he'd walked all night, and over so many years; she put her stout arm around his young neck and drew his head to her bosom, to the soft pillows of her breasts, pressed his nose against her neck's wrinkled skin, gave him a whiff of the residual mix of perfumes she'd wiped on her flesh since the age of fifteen, when—a simpering songstress—she was already selling it professionally in the emancipated huts[33] of the Republic when—mistress of a city counselor—she'd hid her dewlap under sumptuous silver fox and peered down from a box in the Eslava, when—now sitting pretty—she changed her fingerboard of scents and scaled the heights of crushed flower petals and ditched the aftertaste of a musk deer's scrotum.

But Matías laughed and threw himself upon her: "You make me so envious!" landing a sardonic smacker on her flabby cheek and laughing as if the path were clear, and as if all he need do was pirouette, make a lethal jump from the top of a chair, bid farewell to his respectful audience and be immersed in the day-to-day world that mysteriously insists on existing beyond the canvas tents of circuses and their music.

Knocking tentatively on the door—a warning or humble alert—then half opening the door linking the rooms and making a cautious entry, two sleepy women revealed themselves in the glow from the light bulb, the ones Doña Luisa had requested join the party (and quasi-banquet), after which Pedro would be consecrated as the jewel in her crown and a valuable hostage. The plain-faced houris came with long tresses hanging loose (blond at the tip; black at the root); their genteel, polychrome housecoats (peony and poppy patterned) unbuttoned; their large red mouths yawning, gaping, saucily sticking out sharp tongues; they languidly stretched their long arms, barely swayed their fat hips as they sat down—slightly sprawling their legs—on the pinewood chairs set around the kitchen table, and gleefully greeted Matías, whom they knew so intimately, and with equal alacrity a Pedro whom they'd yet to get to know. However—realizing their moment hadn't come, that they were mere decorative pawns moved by their mistress's bountiful will, that long hours must pass before the irresistible power night conferred on them could restore their true standing—they acted with schoolgirl modesty and naiveté, and rather than employ the metaphysical language and *de haut en bas* mannerisms of complex organisms, they spoke unsurely and shifted awkwardly like chrysalides awaiting their moment to leap out of their uncomfortable carapaces beneath which, notwithstanding, their future appearance is already delicately shaped.

The errand boy, eunuch of the netherworld, brought in a cargo of victuals and placed them on the table without anyone seeming to notice his arrival.

Doña Luis broke bread and gave thanks. The girls saw no need to be grateful for the gifts received. They held their hands out to the loaves where the chatelaine had left her mark in chorizo fat. They ate in a prudent silence, barely opening their mouths as they chewed, their jaws emitting small sounds, leaning back to drink red wine, although it wasn't from a wine decanter but a blue plastic glass that might well be used for dentures, which Doña Luisa had brought from her pantry, thinking to share the wine round fairly.

"How tasty!"

Pedro ate with the hunger that follows a night on the tiles, and as the chunks of bread disappeared, his body felt a comforting warmth after being so cold. Besides, it was hot in that kitchen. The lit stove ensured, from then on, hot water for bedroom bidets. The kitchen maid walked in as silently as the errand boy had done and threw in some more coal.

"Enjoy your meal!"

"Go downstairs!" rasped Doña Luisa.

And after they'd had a drink, they began to say a thousand sweet nothings or perhaps to hear the sweet nothings the women had been saying that they hadn't been able to hear before, how tasty, it's lovely, hey you, help yourself. Until Matías tried to feel Alicia's plump leg under her housecoat. "Hey, keep that hand to yourself!"

After that vitamin-rich offering had been consumed and the dregs of wine returned to the pantry, Doña Luisa gave a blessing and wished them peace.

Pedro began to walk reluctantly upstairs to his hideout, an inhospitable room whose number the old woman had solemnly spat out, hoping he would enjoy a siesta that would imitate in every way the real sleepiness that's born from the night.

Amador's manfully thick lips kept his wife happy. She admired the paternal Asturian's affectionate ways, she admired his social status, superior to a security guard's, she judged her tall, strong, powerful man absolutely capable of guiding her through the imperfections of this life to an honorable special third-class burial with her own grave thanks to his regular payments to the Ocaso insurance company. Amador was a generous fellow. Without quibbling he'd as readily give his time to a hyperactive researcher as buy on a whim a coffee-colored plastic purse for his darling wife. He could equally pinch the bottoms of scrubbers polishing the floors of a hectic Institute or slope off to a box at the Monumental with a servant girl from the far northwest, and after such dishonest philandering, effortlessly make his wife forget the late hour of his return. A wary Celt, a brave Astur, though born in the very heart of this nation, his atavisms allowed him to pilot his way more cannily than the mass of natives of the steppe. His late, extremely tall father passed on to him—along with his northern blood—a love of life, a readiness to laugh, a huge capacity to hold his drink which the parched womb of his Toledan mother had never noticeably diminished. His unexpected gloom was then all the more remarkable as he now meandered through the relatively comfortable rooms of the distant apartment he'd inhabited for so many years in the district of Tetuán de las Victorias.

"What's up?" asked his wife, a childless womb that still lusted.

"Poor Don Pedro, poor Don Pedro," he repeated into his coat, making sure his thoughts were inaudible to his wife, and responding to her with an impatient shrug of the shoulders that, though disdainful, he was able to soften with his tender touch.

Then out loud: "Let's go to the Glorieta for a beer."

"No, you go by yourself!" his beloved said with a smile.

The sun shone down on the usual mishmash of trams, taxis, and shabbily attired people in the square. Amador drew near, walking hesitantly, almost wearily, breathless from overweight, grinning all the time at the tiny wooden folding chairs and rickety tables without plastic covers or Cinzano ashtrays. Hordes of workers were alighting from a 43 tram that had just pulled up, wearing blue or dark brown overalls, carrying empty lunchboxes wrapped in green or yellow checked handkerchiefs, and disappearing down nearby side streets. They were longtime construction workers, electricians, or plumbers, and had inherited apartments, small homes of their own. Only the odd Korean mingled with them, prepared to pay a sublet or rent a room above a bar.

"Poor Don Pedro." Amador's brain kept mulling over those words, irking his remorseful conscience. Not realizing his wife was no longer watching, he gave another warm yet scornful shrug.

"That's him," said a young boy, a neighbor, pointing to him.

"There we go. The police."

The young man accompanying the boy was smartly dressed, and far too smarmy (when he came over) to allay Amador's suspicions.

"I'm a friend of Pedro's," he said, as if such a simple lie could dispel any fears and prize open lips Amador pressed oyster-tight. "We must help him. He's got into a mess. He told me to fetch you."

"And which Pedro might that be?" protested Amador.

But by now Matías had started to tell all: the pseudoresponsibility for the pseudoabortion and the reason for Snarler's betrayal or whoever the bastard might have been, because Pedro would never believe Amador had . . .

"I know nothing," said Amador, convinced only a policeman could be so well informed.

"He's hiding. I found him a hideout. Amador, he's expecting you to go and clear up the mess. He told me Amador will explain what actually happened and why the girl died. You must come to the police station with me and clear all this up—"

"*Must?*" said Amador, feeling the hair bristle down his back. "What can I say? I'm a poor sod who knows nothing, and you want to implicate me?"

"I beg you!"

"What do you expect me to do?"

"Come with me!"

"Why me?"

The pine processionary caterpillar has long white hairs and looks harmless, but when touched it stings like a nettle and blisters the skin, and can even inflame eyelids if a wayward naturalist rubs his fingers over his inquisitive eyes. As it advances, each little beast, which is apparently blind, secretes a thread of shiny, transparent matter. The individual behind passes the thread between its tiny feet and thickens it with its own slaver. As does the next one and the one after that of a blind flock that follows the leader whom happenstance has transformed into their captain. Despite their blindness, the caterpillars reach their harbor and on cold nights, huddling in the nest, keep each other warm. Any entomologist would have been enthused by the similar procession (through the city, guided by a thread that behind each of them changed its character, but not its direction) made up of Matías, Amador, Dynamite, and Similiano.

"People who hide the most should be punished the most. Judges don't know or don't want to know how hard we frontline cops work and the dangers we run or the ones they expose us to. But you can only keep mum, say, 'So be it,' completely disregarding your health, in the middle of the night, as if you were made of steel, which you're not, because I don't know how I stand it and don't put in for early retirement, and just keep repressing the feeling. Because it's not so bad when I'm on duty. It's as if I shrank and became harder and can walk and walk and never get tired. And even lose all fear, when I was always such a scaredy-cat."

"He thinks he'll get away. But he won't."

"Poor Don Pedro must be holed up somewhere, I can tell you. But I don't believe what this guy says about him wanting to see me. This fellow's probably hidden him in his place, that's more than likely. Let's see if I can find him and we'll get to the bottom of this. It's all because there's no death certificate."

"I don't think this will lead anywhere, but he did say: 'Follow this guy and he'll take us there without realizing.' The fact is he's never been in the vice squad and doesn't know how it works. So what if he's a neighbor if he's always been into crime, stealing or sticking his knife in. But I can't imagine he's got involved if there's no money to be made. The bar owner said he spent the whole night there keeping an eye out, but he reckoned it was because he was jealous. He had a soft spot for the girl and now he'll be prowling around with his knife, I bet you, with his switchblade in his pocket, trying to find the guy who did the dirty on him. It's got to be the doctor. Otherwise why would the doctor go there if those people had no money to pay him? It makes no sense. But my job isn't to think but to follow that guy and he's got a peculiar way of walking. He hops and jumps. I expect he's seen I'm trailing him."

"They can't hoodwink me. He'll pay for it. That guy doesn't know who he's messing with."

"And he's such a nice guy, the only thing he likes doing is peering at mice through a microscope. That's his only vice. And poking the lumps they get in their intestines. I can't think why he got mixed up in this. Apart from not knowing how to do it, it was obvious it was his first time. I'd have fixed it, but he kept saying let me have a go, I'll scour her with the spoon, he didn't check her pulse, ask for help, or get her a transfusion."

"*Audentes fortuna juvat,* but *perseverare diabolicum.*"

"Now it's starting and that fellow keeps going. I'll take a pill. They say opium's not good for you, that it's a drug and poisons you. But what would I do without my shot of laudanum? It relaxes me and keeps my nether parts in check. They should transfer me to warmer climes, Málaga or Alicante . . . The worst thing is the apartment. I can't leave my wife there and start boarding. I could sell the apartment and my wife could buy one in Alicante. I'd even make money... He's going to jump on the tram. He just has! Now I've got to run, my belly's rumbling, and I've got to run flat out. Course, he gets to rest. The best cover is running after a tram. Nobody thinks you are what you are."

"He thought he was gonna give me the slip by gettin' on the trolley. I mean me. A goat like that guy. I mean me. I don't know why I've not stuck my blade in..."

"It's what you call existence! This enriches existence. A situation limit, on the edge of the abyss, the decision of a lifetime, the first real moment of life. The moment! The crisis point that changes the life project... Choice. Freedom incarnate. Death, death, where is your sting? Muse, sing of the ire of Achilles."

"He was the one who fucked her. Right in my face. And I was afraid it was Snarler. And I just couldn't get enough of her tits. What a mess."

"So you wanted blood, man. You liked playing bloodstains. The original blood. Virginity restored. What a hoot and laugh at them that get off with old whores!"

"It was all because of the mice. His being so interested in the hovels gave me bad vibes. Each to his own fancy, and like with like. He had no reason to go. And he was so excited: 'Hey, are those the hovels?' Young kids, wet behind the ears, and they think they're men."

"If I go to Alicante, I'll lose my housing and Madrid allowance and never get any bonuses, for what could ever happen in Alicante for them to give me a bonus. I can see I'll have to give up going on holiday and get a little afternoon job. But Laura won't stand that, you bet she won't. If it makes her ashamed here where nobody knows, how will she stand it in Alicante where everybody is bound to find out. Though the climate would do me good, feeling the sun on my belly as that doctor recommended who was the only one who understood me. Sunning my belly all day long, seeing off my stomach cramps and excruciating bouts of wind. Because I know it's only wind and, as my mother liked to say: 'Cover your fat with your cat.' But she could do that in the village, in her low chair in front of the fire, cat on lap and killing time. But how on earth do I put a cat on my lap chasing after this guy in a tram. I'd feel better inside. Being on the platform is killing me. But if I go inside, he'll see me. A technical error. He doesn't know me, but he'll smell something is up. I mean, I'm the invisible man, as the 'spector said: 'Similiano, you're a pro at camouflage. You look like a broker. But no promotion for merit or anything. Your rank's your rank and you keep saluting. You've got a posting in Madrid, what more do you want.' I think the guy's going to get off."

"Twinkling stars guide him through the night. I bet he's still in bed. As if he were ill. He might or might not have touched her. He probably never did. But I think he did. You bet he threw himself into her arms. Returning to the maternal bosom. Wanting to regain the original matrix. Searching for prenatal annihilation. That man is always after the same thing. (Laughs to himself.) It is his fate."

"I told him. I say: 'How pleased he'll be.' But I didn't think he'd be that pleased. Snarler is an animal. He's got us into this pickle. And it's all down to sleeping in the same bed, that's not healthy, no, sir. I did well to get him out. No subletting. 'You don't have any children.' And I tell him: 'That's why, so as not to.' It's incredible, but it's not the first time. I've seen it all before. Poor Don Pedro wasn't implicated but nobody dares help him now. They hang someone out to dry for the least little thing."

"I expect he said: 'Sorry, miss, I know it's not time, but Doña Luisa was adamant.'"

"I get that a doctor aborts a duchess or a black marketeer's daughter, but a doctor aborting in a hovel is unheard-of. How low can you sink."

"And this guy walks so fast. He's like his friend, if he is his friend. It was better in the tram. Now he's stopping in the bookshops on San Bernardo. As if I were interested in books. What if he's not going to get him and it was all baloney. Know what, I'll tail him a bit longer, but I don't know why I'm meddling in something that's none of my business."

"Now fatty's on the heels of the other guy. It stinks of the fuzz."

"And what about that little humdinger in the boardinghouse? She's in love. The way she came to warn him, hair all over the place, hysterical, a woman on a mission. There's nothing like a woman for the crossroads in life. Pedro! Pedro! What have you done, Pedro? Why are they after you, Pedro? Tell me it's not true, Pedro! Tell me it's not! Not one word of criticism; not one word of disgust. Feminine understanding, compassion, nestling the sad male to her Delphic bosom. Daring is the man who penetrates female flesh, how can he be in one piece postcopulation? Vagina dentata, tender loving castration, possessive emasculation, you're mine, mine, mine, who's trying to take him away from me? Ahh... But she was so pretty, a humdinger."

"I won't get away. I'll end up in the slammer. But neither that guy or anyone else... The guy's not bin born who..."

"Laura sees it straightaway. 'You've been on duty.' I can't stand it, my eyes go under and it takes me three days to get over it. I'll take another pill. Thank God I can take pills without water and I'm not one of those that choke. Their throats are probably screwed. My head's beginning to whirl. I've got to persuade her to go to Alicante, let my belly get some of that sun."

"The woman's so attractive. I like her almost as much as the one in the boardinghouse. I get it that we let them do whatever, even be intellectuals and go to lectures. Was my mother like that when she was young? Yes, she was, but she'd never walk like that gal does. My mother was as attractive, but in a refined way, slender nose, slender ankles, slender wrists... I'm thinking about my mother! You're an Oedipus too, my friend, you too, when will you shed your infantile complexes? When will you stop looking for what you're looking for and go after barely nubile young things and not those whose vast experience makes you think they are superior, for that's only a retreat-to-the-womb obsession your friend's purging right now, and which you will only satisfy on the day when the abandoned ghost of Clytemnestra goes off, wrapped in her veil, and you'll finally see in Eva the pure woman, free of all birthing, possessed and no longer possessive?"

"Just as well he's now decided to walk straight on and not be distracted, it looks as if he knows where he's going. What a woman, my God! The kind they recommended me to cure my cold."

"Not even this gal stops me in my tracks. Pretty woman! We could have a bang-up meal with what you cake on your face!"

"Perhaps he saw me when he turned round. A technical error! Must keep my distance. Luckily I don't stand out. My head's in no fit state to work. It's thudding, and that doesn't bode well."

"How did he get her to fall in love with him? He's hardly fetching. She must have set it up to hook him. But he's got the hots. Sarah Bernhardt's got nothing on her. What a show. I love you, I eat you, I devour you, I sink my teeth into your tenderest parts. And me with a five-star seat on the special proscenium, private performance for yours truly. And she, totally oblivious to the Asiatic luxury in the seigneurial mansion, not at all overawed by the top-dollar drapes, acting at the top of her game, as if all that were theater wings and abstract scenarios. The fool doesn't understand it, let alone deserve it. Thanks heavens I was there. If not, that spectacle would have been lost in the ether. She entered like tragedy incarnate. Deus ex machina. A gesture from her and his fate was decided. Love, anger, terror, dizzy distress, pathetic. And me: 'I'll hide him, don't you worry.' Fascinated by literature. Swept along by the whirlwind. Because what he should have done was give himself up: go and make a statement. What was behind the idiot idea of hiding? We had to put ourselves in her shoes. She'd never have understood if we'd called a taxi and sent her darling to the station. What can that girl read? They're born that way."

"And I need to know if I can do anything for him, provided I'm not compromised. I did nothing. He was the one who did it. I don't know what he hopes I might say. What happened to the girl was just bad luck. Snarler is the one who should own up, but if he doesn't want to, how can I implicate a relative? He'd be better off going to America, he can study properly there and find out what he's after, because that's where the goddamn mice came from. He should clear out, ask for a grant, and leave us to rot in our own shit. That would be the best all round."

The arrest was straightforward, even for such a half-hearted policeman as Don Similiano. Amador hadn't made it into the house, warned off by his instinct for self-defense. Dynamite had: he'd walked in as if he owned the place. Although it wasn't the busiest of times, the odd beggar after an erotic windfall wandered the passageways and stairs like a rogue meteorite, muttering to himself and avoiding all eye contact. Matías was talking to Doña Luisa in the private sitting room, telling her what had happened, how he'd been unable to convince the witness to make a statement and how the best option would be to wait until his clever lawyer friend arrived, a legal eagle and generous soul, who would never deny him a favor. On this occasion Matías completely ignored the high heels tip-tapping down the corridor. It wasn't deep into the night, he wasn't so drunk, and he felt only a vague desire to find out quickly how this was all going to end when the drawing room door was opened by a pale-faced, olive-skinned serving wench and in walked the tall and gangly Don Similiano, flourishing his police badge in his left hand as if it were a magic key or safe pass.

"He's upstairs," said Doña Luisa immediately. "But I wasn't in on it. What a fix!"

"We ought to have guessed," remarked the friendly policeman. "Knowing what we're after him for, it was the best place he could go."

"I don't do that kind of business," the old lady blushed. "Mine is a respectable, legally registered establishment."

But Don Similiano didn't like to argue. Stooping over Doña Luisa, he quietly asked her for the whereabouts of the little room from which his pills could no longer save him. He knew too well how dangerous these tiny spaces are where the most diverse pathogenic germs pullulate in untoward quantities. But his lofty sense of duty prevented him from seeking a more distant spot to drop his load. He couldn't give his prey any more opportunities; though he now lay hypnotically transported in the arms of a lady of the night, he might at any moment cast off his lethargy and pursue his destructive path through an outside world full of untimely, pregnant eventualities.

"Take care!" he said, lifting his forefinger with a knowing shake of the head, before he disappeared into the perilous little room, to which the proprietress replied: "Don't you worry!" in the same tone that at another juncture she'd have used to guarantee a client the undivided attentions of a plump, green-eyed blond.

"I'm going to warn him . . ." said the unwary Matías, turning round.

But the old woman grabbed his arm, smiled, and pinched his cheek: "You, my love, can get going right now. Leave this to me! Get hold of your lawyer! Don't pointlessly put yourself at risk!"

Having managed to avoid any suspicious encounters, and happy with his prophylactic squat, the smiling policeman followed Doña Luisa up to the higher reaches.

"I wasn't trying to hide him," she explained. "You know how we put the longer stays at the top."

"Yes, of course," allowed Similiano.

"My God, what a pickle! One never knows what one's letting into one's house . . . they're all a load of undesirables . . . that's what they are. The things one sees!"

"Of course, madam."

Pedro was technically accompanied by a lady, because it had been a quid pro quo for the help he'd received. The lady was bored stiff and observed the young man with a degree of awe or fear. He was lying there, now fully clothed, on a blue, flowery eiderdown made from some synthetic shiny silklike material. The bottom of the eiderdown was falling apart, worn down by the various shod feet it had had to tolerate over the last months. On the other hand, the pillow cover, changed that day, was surprisingly white. There was a little pink light on the night table. If you pressed the button, it turned white. But everybody—clients and pros alike—preferred the pink light out of a residual romantic longing that made them rebel in the deepest cockles of their hearts against a paucity of poetry. The pink light doesn't simply make blackheads disappear from the nose or crow's-feet from the corners of eyes. It also lends the naked contours of bodies a blurry definition, transmuting them into tactile rather than visual items which more easily match the inner archetype the tireless spirit has in its sights. In that pinkish glow even the shiny white porcelain objects in a corner of the room, redolent of their hygienic functions, looked like small pets curled up and purring to the sleepy lullaby from the running tap. That cool water made you forget the dusty floor, where the linoleum glinted, furrowed by decorative borders and nailed to the floorboards, as well as the mediocre wall and ceiling paintings that were an abysmal attempt to conjure up models from Pompeii, which, way back when, an unknown painter and decorator had decided, after seeing some color photos of them, would be just the thing for a newly inaugurated brothel. Set horizontally on the wall at bed height, an elongated mirror, though rusty and a mass of gray-brown stains, constituted the ultimate touch of refinement in the first-class bedroom and, in the pink light, barely returned a black reflection of the imagined body's silhouette, which was so murky it became anonymous and bountiful, hidden in a quicksilver fantasia, as if spying on the eternal, disenchanted couple, and offering them futile benediction. Indeed, pulling on the finest rubber leotards, their fingers funneled into thick surgical gloves, nose and mouth orifices plugged by layers of absorbent cotton wool, and eyes and mouth entirely covered by a mask that had survived 1918, the bodies never touched, their gazes never met, remaining deeply unaware of an intimate bedmate, whose only function was to brutally ring the bell as a result of which the experience would be repeated. Astonishingly aloof, the man dressed for the street, the woman naked though cloaked in unerring indifference, they made bored gestures and chatted of the same subjects one is constrained to talk about day in, day out: the weather, how pretty you are, how beautiful your eyes are, how prices are rocketing, how much I like Humphrey Bogart, how this leg I broke when I was a kid really hurts when there's a change in the weather.

"Hey there, come on out. Police," Similiano declared decorously, averting his gaze.

The frightened girl wrapped herself in her peony housecoat and looked aghast at the man lying on the bed, as if he'd metamorphosed into a menacing scorpion. Her exit took her to the other end of the room, where the low bidet still lamented endlessly, now ringing out more clearly. At first Pedro stayed still, then he appeared to wake from the deepest sleep as he gathered strength to react. Suddenly he sat up in bed, leaned his elbows on his knees, and stared at the door.

"Come on now, just a few questions," the humane policeman repeated in that soothing voice of his. "Nothing to be afraid of."

And although nothing led him to suspect violent intent, he insisted professionally, gently: "Don't make any trouble. It's the best for you, I can tell you."

Like the dentist who says "Keep still" as he drills into the center of your molar.

Don Similiano was so likable, so self-effacing in his role, that when they left arm in arm, those entering could see on Don Pedro's face only the redness that becomes the flushed cheeks of a contented customer. "We should bring that guy in too," thought the policeman, who'd just noticed the hirsute Dynamite, in a corner of the drawing room, rivet his eyes on the arrestee and etch his image hatefully on his memory.

Each one of the barred doors, bolts, and grilles Pedro met on his descent was the preserve of a gray gnome who, as he passed by, manipulated them as if they weren't rusty steel but a fluid, malleable material.

In the meantime, the fact that Similiano had asked him for some free prescriptions to help him cope with his well-defined infirmities, while other timely, friendly folk had occupied him in exchanges as to his name, surnames, civil status, profession, and abode—and that a routine naturalness imbued the mannerisms and attitudes of all those working in those offices—wasn't sufficiently soothing for the anxiety in his chest to cede to fatigue, sleep, or plain tedium. He remained awake, seated on one of those swivel chairs, while functionaries came over and looked at him as if to say: "He's our man," then walked away after picking up obviously useless pieces of paper or tapping lackadaisically on one of the typewriters distributed in huge numbers across that expanse of zones linked by the corridor where roamed police, prisoners, office workers, and white-jacketed waiters who'd lost their way. The dirt falling imperceptibly settled on all items accessible to their fingers and made them rough to touch and lent a yellow patina. Maybe this sensation, frankly, wasn't about dust, whose reality is always debatable (like that of other invisible organisms), but about the fear that appeared to dominate such areas, populated, what's more, by councilmen and agents of anguish, and eye-catching, subtle, green-hued, bearded beings, born of a race yet to be anthropologically classified, on whose faces, when scrutinized closely, glowed that realm of the absolute, before which Pedro stooped as if before a mirror revealing the nature of his very own metamorphosis, of which he still wasn't completely apprised. So what he noted as a hint of fatigue in the backs of his knees; a tension in the lower eyelids; a protracted prickliness along both palpebral slits; a total absence of hunger on the dry surface of his tongue, now an alien item in his suddenly diminished buccal cavity; an inability to understand simple questions; a desperate desire to be nice to everybody; a sticky sensation of filth in his armpits and on his feet, not from lack of soap but from a strange sweat he exuded as he nervously and queasily observed all (but all) the faces of the functionaries, trying to discern signs of a distant sympathy that, in any case, they did casually communicate; an excessive closeness of his shoes to his feet, which had apparently lost all mobile traction since no movement driven by will levered his leg muscles, only a magnetic force emanating from the deft directors of traffic along such pathways; the excessive proximity of shirt collar to flesh on a neck that had also lost all natural propensity to transport air, food, etc., retaining only the ability to perform as pivot to a circular movement and capture as often as possible signs of goodwill on surrounding faces; and a trembling or else stiffness of lumbar vertebrae were only inner indicators of that same terror that contorted the faces of those he could see, offspring of that despicable race to which every man can be recruited as a result of guilt that's been publicly exposed and dispatched for punishment.

"We'll get this done in no time. You're an intelligent fellow," said one of the omnipotent inhabitants of those offices, signaling an overwhelming sense of sympathy, an especially welcoming smile, a more sophisticated, benign magnanimity.

Pedro turned towards him, interrupting his search for other sources of compassion since this one seemed more significant and was drenching him so copiously.

"So you . . ." (surprising, insidious supposition).

"No, I didn't . . ." (indignant, shocked rebuttal).

"But you wouldn't want to lead me to believe that . . ." (unlikely, even absurd hypothesis).

"No, but I . . ." (concerned recognition).

"You know perfectly well . . ." (logic, logic, logic).

"I didn't . . ." (a simple, palpably insufficient denial).

"You must recognize . . ." (logic).

"But . . ." (barely viable negation).

"I want you to understand . . ." (warmly human).

"No."

"In any case, it is futile for you . . ." (declaration of superiority based on personal experience of many cases).

"But . . ." (far from convincing denial).

"Of course, if you insist . . ." (possibility of having recourse to other means, jettisoning the use of intellect and friendly interpenetration).

"No, no way . . ." (alarmed denial).

"So we can agree that . . ." (overcoming the almost nonexistent obstacle).

"Well . . ." (first dangerous step to acceptance).

"Absolutely. So you do . . ." (triumphant).

"Me . . . ?" (horror at unforeseen deductions).

"I'm beginning to tire of all this!"

Suddenly and quite unexpectedly, the well of sympathy dried up, and Pedro observed before him a facial expression he'd feared from the first moment that death agony began, which he'd been unable to perceive behind Similiano's bland facade, or behind the diligent, honest toil of all those who had inquired previously and on more than one occasion after his age, profession, abode, civil state, place of birth, and—even—his parents' Christian names.

And after the blinding vision of Jupiter-the-thunderous, Moses-destroyer-of-golden-calves, Father-giver-of-generous-succor-that-was-vilely-rejected, Virtue-shocked-and-astonished-by-the-almost-infinite-enormity-of-human-evil, quite rightly and naturally Pedro was swept out of the august presence and taken to the tempestuous hell where his descent, though swift and uninterrupted, followed the meandering complexities rehearsed by the fable.

The first of which was but a long, labyrinthine corridor along which treacherous zigzags plagued all forward movement, as well as the depths of another spatial dimension, via concealed, slippery steps that went up, then down, with no clear rationale or pattern. Out of that corridor, for a moment, he crossed a yard full of cars and static, leather-jacketed drivers who looked but didn't see. Then, a fresh mouth, closing in on the final maw, swallowed up the shuddering souls of those descending in one ginormous act of suction. After which another set of stairs led to a space set up like a clip joint, on whose bar counter they leaned for a moment, with other, sterner functionaries than those upstairs, using better-oiled typewriters, engaged in the ritual dialogue over Christian name, surnames, age, etc., keen to avoid all avoidable human error and oversight and the subsequent submission of anyone to a mistaken fate. Followed by a fresh snaking, subterranean passageway, with neon lights simulating daylight, granite walls barefaced daughters of this earth, which led to the first of the doors that were only transitable thanks to the by-your-leave of the silent gnome, at whom his savvy guide had to flash a sheet of yellow paper. The next mouth gave way to a tortuous, tiered gizzard through which, without any need to clear the throat, ingestion was galvanized by the peristaltic movements of the granite, leading—after a fresh series of iron bars—onto a broad gastric square where digestion of the thoroughly masticated leftovers commenced. Here they proceeded to strip off all recent purchases, relieving him of a burden of precious metals, fountain pens, ties, braces, belts, spectacles, and any other object conducive to a suicide attempt, by which the denuded individuals of the intellectual caste felt particularly belittled, clutching at their pants, feeling cold round the neck, glancing around, spectacleless, and penguin-like, fearful of offending the well-intentioned law enforcers by virtue of their well-spoken, excessively well-modulated voices. The man overseeing these maneuvers then said a number and the prisoner slithered beneath concave crypts, down vaulted corridors, until he reached his final resting place in this inferno where, unlike those where more guileful demons torture shrieking prisoners, all was silent, a profound silence broken only at intervals of several light-years by the request to go pee or be given a match—that is, when the supreme courts have, with unaccustomed generosity, allowed tobacco to be excluded from the list of lethal objects relentlessly to be requisitioned.

The cell is on the small side. Its ceiling means it doesn't have a perfectly square prismatic shape. The latter has a skewed surface, the highest end coalescing with one corner of the square room above. As a result, each of the two cells seems to comprise one of the semidomes supporting the thrust of the huge mass of the large building above. Domes and walls are made of granite. All have been recently whitewashed. Only graffiti hurriedly scrawled in the last few weeks points to the residue of artistic creation by previous occupants. The cell's dimensions are more or less as follows. Eight feet to the highest point of the semidome; three feet from the door to the opposite wall; five feet in a perpendicular direction to the previous vector measured. Given these dimensions, a man of normal stature can stretch his arms—without encountering solid matter—only in a diagonal direction. On the other hand, the tallest man could never touch the ceiling. The bed isn't placed in that diagonal line, but parallel to the door's normal position and resting against the opposite wall, as a result of which a reasonably tall man must slightly gather his legs into the fetal position if he wishes to sleep. The door is high enough to walk through without having to stoop and is made of quality hardwood. Halfway down is a peephole six inches wide by eight inches high. This peephole, though crossed by three iron bars, gives perfect sight of everything in the cell's habitable space. The height of this peephole forces guards of statutory height to stoop their heads to see inside. If the prisoner is standing on his bed, the guard can see his body only from the navel down and must stoop even lower to get a full view.

This visual inspection is possible thanks to a bulb placed in a niche above the door frame. As a result, the light illuminates both the cell and the narrow corridor. This corridor is organized in such a way that there is always a blank, whitewashed wall and not a cell opposite. Between this blank wall and the door is a sixteen-inch space the guards must negotiate. In apparent contrast with the massive thickness of the granite walls and the depth at which the strange labyrinth has been installed, each individual door is locked by a modest, low-quality bolt of the kind that might be used, say, for a chicken coop. If the prisoner presses his face against the bars, he can see the bolt but not manipulate it, unless he has something useful to hand—wire, a length of rope or a piece of wood. However, nothing in his cell can supply him with such material. The glassless peephole ensures ventilation and allows the guard to light cigarettes the prisoner may have brought to his temporary accommodation.

The light is eternal. It never goes out, night or day.

Inside the cell, apart from air, the prisoner, the lime on the whitewashed walls, and the drawings sketched thereon, there is only a bed. This bed is solidly constructed to resist the possibly overweight load a hypothetical Greco-Roman wrestling champion or fraudulent treasurer of the "Club of Fatsoes" might bring to bear one day. The basic idea behind the manufacture of this standard bed deserves detailed study. They have succeeded in constructing a bed that cannot be pulled apart and that even cuts out the painful creaks a prisoner's tossing and turning might cause. Similarly it is impossible for bugs to lodge or breed in its cracks. Its solid build makes it very unlikely that it can be raided for materials that could be used as missiles or hooks. This silent, indestructible, unmovable, fireproof, shockproof, waterproof bed, beneath which nobody could ever hide, and which a malevolent jailbird could never treacherously hurl at a guard, is entirely manufactured from masonry stone sealed once and for all by a layer of cement lovingly applied by a master builder, with the same precision as a maid in a five-star hotel daily smooths a counterpane. In this way they achieved a perfect union of the art of lavish living and architecture. Out of a sense of humanity and to give a tolerable rest to the limbs of their guests, the pillow at the far end of the bed has likewise been made of cement, in keeping with the rest of the room and at a height recommended to ensure a perfect physiological sleep: one to two inches. Other advantages: The perfect alignment of bed, walls, and cell floor ensures the nonexistence of a gap through which coded messages, Protestant Bibles, pornographic photographs, or cyanide capsules might be slipped. And not only that: The solidity, the robustness, and the reinforced cement provide (once that grayish mass ceases to be considered a mere bed and is seen from an equally useful perspective as a habitable landscape or a geographical accident) a firm base and field of exercise for anyone wishing to practice the various kinds of gymnastics a solitary confinement cell allows an inmate: breathing exercises, yoga, golf swings with an imaginary club, purposefully simulated epileptic fits, rapid descents into the abyss and fresh ascents of the mountain. If the inmate stands on the bed, he achieves a dramatic change of perspective. The air in those higher regions is undoubtedly purer, and the wall drawings fewer; the guard's feet can be glimpsed through the peephole as he walks by, though not his brawny shoulders; and the cell floor with the odd breadcrumb, grease stain, or venomous cigarette butt becomes more remote. The pillow itself seems a small, arid hill trod by a Gulliver finally traveling in a world of human proportions.

Another possible use of the bed simply consists in giving the inmate an opportunity to stare at the slit and (beyond it) the bare wall and (beyond that) the concentrically ordered world outside. Now by raising his sight, minimally, obliquely, towards the passageway's highest regions, he can see the warden's face (at obscenely frequent intervals) before he stoops down, bringing into view his lips, nose, mouth, even his forehead.

The third possible use of the bed is unsurprisingly the recumbent or sleeping position, a function never entirely impossible, even in the most adverse of circumstances.

Although, during your first hours inside, you might think silence reigns in that labyrinth of galleries, that's a mistaken impression, a result of the dearth of significant acoustic signals and the scant importance of noises and sounds that do nevertheless exist. In this respect, one can rapidly draw up an inventory. The constant sound of running water, a result of leaking bowls and sinks. The echoes and hollow resonances of voices one might call "external": the wails of the blind man selling lottery tickets, the monotonous cry of the stout woman hawking newspapers, and hooters muffled by distance. Other voices, conversely, are "internal" and much more interesting. The most constant are those of off-duty guards playing cards night and day in the labyrinth's small central square. The most unexpected come from the underground kindergarten, the laughter and playing of the children who, because of their young age, accompany their mothers in a shared cell. These children run, shout, and laugh in the most restricted of spaces, but their voices reach the remotest cell. Finally, one always thinks one can hear the name of an inmate being summoned, to make their statement, be transferred or released. Hope configures the raw material of such vibrations so each inmate believes, when listening hard, that he hears his own name on the lips of one of the immediate servants of the powers that be, a few yards above his head.

Once night falls, the inmate is given a gray-brown blanket. When day breaks, it's removed after he's been instructed to fold it properly. These happenings and the more banal ones of grub up or peeing provide the semblance of a timetable to what is, otherwise, uniformly framed by angst and theological virtue.

Fateful destiny. Resignation. Be still as long as it takes. Learn to look at a fixed spot on the wall until, gradually, your thought is absorbed into a void. Autogenic relaxation. Yoga. Lie flat and still. Touch the wall slowly with a hand. Relax. Overcome angst. Think slowly. Know nothing serious is afoot, you can only remain silent and wait, nothing serious can happen, until the knot is undone as it was tied. Be calm. Feel calm. Find refuge in solitude, comfort in the walls. In a state of stasis. It's not so bad. It's not so bad. Why think? Only be still. Why think? Try to act as if you long to be still. As if to be still, hidden here, were a wish or a game. Hidden as long as it takes. Still as long as needs be. While I'm still, I'm fine. I can do nothing by myself. Keep calm. I can do nothing; therefore I can do no wrong. I can make no wrong decision. I can do no wrong. I can commit no error. I cannot prejudice myself. Be calm deep within yourself. Nothing can happen now. I can't influence what may happen. I'm here until they throw me out and can do nothing to get out.

Why did I go?

Don't think. There's no point in thinking about what's done. It's pointless to go over the mistakes you've made yet again. Everyone makes mistakes. Everyone gets it wrong. Everyone seeks their own perdition along complicated or simple paths. Draw the siren on the stain on the wall. It looks like a siren. Her hair is falling over her back. With a sliver of metal from a lace dropped by somebody whose shoes weren't removed, you can scratch the wall and give form to the shape suggested by the stain. I've always been bad at drawing. Hers is the short tail of a small fish. She's not your usual siren. When I'm lying here, the siren can look at me. You're fine, you're fine. Nothing can happen to you because you've done nothing. Nothing can happen to you. They must realize you've done nothing. It's obvious you've done nothing.

Why did you have to drink so much that night? Why did you have to do it drunk... so totally drunk? It's illegal to drive when you're drunk and you... you... Don't think. You're fine here. It makes no odds; you're relaxed here, more relaxed by the second. It's an adventure. You're broadening your experience. You now know more than you did. You will know much more about everything than you ever did, you will know what others have felt, what it's like being down here where you knew other people have been, something you could never have imagined. You're enriching your experience. You're coming to know yourself better, plus what you're capable of. Whether you're really a scaredy-cat, whether you feel terrorized. If they can have that effect. What fear is. What a man is behind his fear, beneath his fear, on the other side of the frontier of fear. That you're still capable of living calmly, of being relaxed down here. If you're relaxed here, it's hardly a failure. You're triumphing over fear. The imperturbable man, the man who remains imperturbable, intact, can say he triumphs, even if everyone, but everyone, says he's shit-scared, is a jerk, is a loser. If he can preserve his basic freedom that allows him to decide what happens, to choose what crushes him. To say: Yes, I want this, yes, I want this, yes, I want this, I want this, I want to be here because I want what's happening, I want what there is, I truly, sincerely want that, it's fine as it is. "What is it that all pleasure seeks? It seeks deep, deep eternity."

You didn't kill her. She was dead. She wasn't dead. You killed her. Why do you say "you"? I.

Don't think. Don't think. Don't think. What's done is done. Don't think. Don't think so much. Keep calm. Rest your head. You feel fine. You *are* fine resting here, not thinking, you can shut your eyes, though it makes no odds if they're open. It makes no odds. If they're open, you see the little siren. With the sliver of metal from somebody's shoelace they forgot to remove you draw on the wall, slowly scratch the whitewash. Scratch slowly because you have all the time in the world. Scratch very slowly, the unpleasant, grating sound of the metal, the little strip of tin doubled by some machine over a brown shoe's brown lace, sliding slowly over the wall, making a drawing that assumes a semihuman form and that makes for company, because a moment comes when it has an expression, a moment comes when it takes shape, and a moment comes finally when she—the poorly drawn siren—does indeed look at you and claps her large, moist girlish eyes on you and she looks your way and you're lonesome no more. Her tail comprises two tightly closed thighs. The girl with the tail is not prepared to slice it down the middle with a knife because she's not in love. She stays still like that, her thighs beneath a mass of scales. There's nothing on the wall until that moment when the form crystallizes and a human being is recognizable in the patch of scored lime and she glances and stares. Yes, I do want this, I do. It's as if I did. What difference is there, who can prove it's not true, who can be convinced, however much they scorn me—however much they insist on scorning me—however much they laugh when they discover that I'm here and say *that's him*—that I'm not here because I want to be, because I wanted to be here and still want to be? Although I hid, although I was in the arms of a whore waiting for time to go by, for days to pass, although I wanted them never to remember me, to forget me and give me a grant to go to Illinois and stay there to watch the groins of mice forever and ever, where you say "I want" and a super cyclotron of a hundred million dollars tumbles from the clouds and you say "I need" and a whole family of tropical simians descends with their quasihuman brains for me to study and outside in an enormous purple car a super-duper girl awaits me, the latest model of well-nourished humanity, combining perfect beauty in the same body that harbors a healthy, democratic heart and the generosity of people who invite you to their parties and you're the sage playing golf and the sage eating hot dogs and the laboratory like a large smiley cafeteria where cancer melts in the mouth like ice-cream soda. But I wanted to be *here*, a failure, not touching cancers, or the Iberian microscopes of minor Iberian scientists, which are now beyond my reach, because what I wanted was to be here alone, thinking; no, not thinking; merely deposited here, prostrate, as if I'd died and now knew what it's like to be dead, with my body so tangibly stretched out like the body of the dead girl who knew why she died and not because of a stupid accident when I put my hand in, a hand that wasn't as steady as it ought to have been...

I was drunk. *I was.*

Don't think. Don't think. Look at the wall. Pass the time looking at the wall. Don't think. You have no need to think, you can fix nothing by thinking. No. You're here and feeling calm. You're good, you wanted to do it well. You've done everything wanting to do it well. Everything you've done has been well done. You had no evil intent. You did the best you could. If you had to do it again...

Idiot!

Don't think. Don't think. Don't think. Stay calm. Nothing's going to happen. No need to feel scared of anything. If the worst happens. If the worst possible happens. The worst. If they really think you did it. If they're waiting to bury you with the heaviest sentence in the book. Put yourself in the worst-case scenario. The worst possible. The worst you can imagine, the most catastrophic, the most serious. If what happens to you is beyond words, even so, what *then*? Despite that, nothing would happen. Nothing. *Nothing.* You'd be like this, for a time. Like you are now. And then you'd go to Illinois. That's all. And you're not hurting here. You're good here. Back to the cradle. To the womb. Protected. Nobody can hurt you, nothing can happen here. You're relaxed. I'm relaxed. I'm good. Nothing can happen to me. Don't think so much. Better not to think at all. Just let time slip quietly by. Time does that anyway. Nothing can happen. Even if things get worse. Even if things take a turn for the worst. Imagine the worst. Let's imagine the worst happens. I imagine I'm in the worst-case scenario. Nothing happens. Only time goes by. Time that remains outside my life, in parentheses. Outside my stupid life. A time when, frankly, I'll be more alive. I *am* more alive. Life outside has been suspended in all its imbecility. That was left outside. Life stripped bare. Time, time alone fills this void without stupidity and stupid things. Everything has just got to slide over me, I'm not suffering, no way I'm suffering. People will think I'm suffering. But I'm not. I exist, therefore I live. Times goes by, fills me, I go with time, I've never lived time in my life simply going by as when I can sit still and look at that spot on the wall, the dark eye of a siren who's looking at me. Here alone, how great, I think I'm on top of the world. Nothing can happen to me. I'm the one in transit. I'm alive. Alive. With none of those worries, with none of the money I have to earn, without the woman I ought to marry, without the clients I ought to attract, without the friends who were supposed to like me, without the pleasures I was supposed to pursue, without the alcohol I was supposed to drink. If it could only be like that. Stay here. It's where you belong. I have to be here, at this level, finding out what it's like to be alone, but like this, on a more elevated plane, better than before, calmer, much calmer. Don't weaken. I must not weaken. I'm good like this, calm, nothing can happen to me, because all that can happen is that I continue being like this, being where I want to be, calm, seeing everything, calm, I'm good, I'm good, I'm totally good like this, what more could I want?

You didn't kill her. She was dead. I killed her. Why? Why? You didn't kill her. She was dead. I didn't kill her. She was already dead. It wasn't me.

Don't think. Don't think. Don't think about anything. Relaxed, I am relaxed. Nothing's wrong. I'm relaxed like this. I keep still. I wait. No need to think. I'm totally fine. I'm calm like this, time passes and I'm calm because I'm not thinking. It's all about learning not to think, about staring at the wall, about making another drawing with that sliver of metal, any drawing, it doesn't have to be a girl, you can draw something different, though you've always been bad at drawing. You're free to choose the drawing you want to make because you're still free, even here. You're an individual free to draw whatever you want, or to draw a line every day that passes as others have done before you, and with every seven, a longer line, because you're free to make lines the length you want and nobody can stop you . . .

Idiot!

Although the mother thought it was a bad business—she became hysterical, bawled, drank a big cup of lime infusion and the following day had a bad headache—grandmother and granddaughter sensed, each in her own way, that it was true, that he was now completely theirs. The old lady knew a little contretemps makes a man humbler than might be expected. She knew from past experience that nothing is more appreciated than a few words of flattery at a moment of misfortune. If the old colonel's shameful sterility had placed him most dramatically under his wife's heel, then the researcher's surprising debacle would set him up to become the man in the household, grateful to boot, and make him feel guilty and more respectful of the family that—worthy, though disgraced—had opened the doors wide to its warm and welcoming bosom.

That was why the old lady pretended not to see and hear when Dorita—clearly obeying the more generous impulses of a young heart, even though it was past suppertime—ran down the passage, barely protected by her woolen coat and beauty, and into the street soon after hearing of Pedro's arrest via the malicious grapevine. Lots of people were still milling in the streets around movie houses advertising their nighttime screenings on luminous marquees and bright-colored posters. She walked down from the Plaza del Progreso along the street that heads into the heart of the city, and as she walked, she dodged glances, knocks from elbows and bodies, so rent by worry that she didn't notice people were staring at her.

First they told Dorita it wasn't the time. Then they told her to wait. Then they let her through. She went upstairs and along a filthy corridor. She sat on a chair. Some functionaries working overtime looked at her. They let her go farther in. She sat in a yellow-painted office full of dusty typewriters. A wooden rail separated the typing pool, where a stout gentleman sat, from the space possibly reserved for the general public or nosey-parkers. The gentleman had just finished his supper, to judge by the dirty cutlery on one side of his table. He was reading the evening newspaper and listening to a small radio that blared out music and commercials. First he scowled at her. Then he smiled. He told her to sit down. Then he put on the jacket that he'd taken from a hanger. He smiled as he came over:

"Who are you asking after?"

"No. You can't."

"What's your connection to him?"

"No. I can tell you nothing."

"What's your connection to him?"

"Don't you worry, miss. Everything will be ironed out eventually. I can say that because I've seen all manner of situation."

"No, I can't give him a message."

"No, it's not serious."

"Everyone must be incommunicado for seventy-two hours."

"That's right, seventy-two hours."

"It's been only three hours."

"Who told you?"

"No. I couldn't say."

"I already said I can't help you. I'm very sorry."

"Don't worry."

"Go home and get a good night's sleep."
"You shouldn't be crying, my lovely."
"Don't take it so to heart."
"I'm telling you that's impossible. If it weren't impossible..."
"If only I could!"
"That's the least I could do."
"Totally impossible."
"Of course you can! You can come back tomorrow."
"What did you say your name was?"

If a distinguished visitor insists on being shown toreros and their darlings, if the brilliant painter paints toreros and their darlings, if across the length and breadth of this ancient territory there are effectively more bullrings than Gothic cathedrals, it must mean something. One would have to revisit black legends, bow before castanet Spain's tourist-packed picturesque sights, remove the layer of varnish from the paintings depicting us, and decide to what regrettable extent they were right. Because if there is a constant, something that surreptitiously keeps giving vim and virility to a body that's otherwise skin and bones, this something must be scrutinized, brought into public light, measured and described minutely. It can't simply be being poor, or eating little, or having ostensibly dolichocephalic skulls or delicately dark skin that defines us as exemplary of a category of man to which we inexorably belong and which we find so unpleasant. Let's take a closer look at the phenomenon and try to feel in our own flesh—which is just like his—what this man feels when (from inside his skintight suit of lights) he anticipates his body will be penetrated by a horn, and the great mass of his equally swarthy, dolichocephalous peers are screaming for the bull to gore him and reduce him, before their very eyes, to what they desperately desire him to become: a scarecrow stuffed with red rags. It is not by pure chance that this hatred was so perfectly institutionalized at a historic moment when the country turned its back on the outside world and, despite repeated defeats, persisted in constructing grand palaces, though everyone knew no galleon laden with gold was on the horizon, and, frightened by a furious hatred that showed no signs of going away, we had to find a symbolic conduit where the consecrated sacrifice could be carried out in a lively enough way to exorcize the curse and put the damper on deep longings that are still strangling us all. It is beyond doubt that the key event in the years following the great disaster was the polarization of hatred against a single man, and that ambivalent hatred and deification stirred up the untrammeled vengefulness nestling in the hearts of all and sundry. Must we then consider the butt of the people's hatred this individual waddling across the sand under an unaesthetic two-cornered hat, solemn, frowning, and dead scared, to elaborate his outlandish calligraphy before the baleful beast? Maybe, indeed, maybe that does explain everything, because the forces of law and order, the press, the regimental band, the inmates of the workhouse, and even a representative of the honorable civil governor participate so intensely in the mystery.

But what bull must we carry within us that gives power and strength to the thick-necked, muscular animal cavorting around the periphery of the ring? What bull do we carry within us that drives us to want the near miss, the thrust, the rapid touch, the subtle, persnickety precision by which the cognoscenti measures not the danger but—in their book—the artistic quality of the death? What bull can *that* be, sir?

And broad, fat, and tall, the motherly guards came, their large chests covered in thick gray cloth where they hid matchboxes, cigarettes, little notebooks with mysterious jottings, photos of their daughters, long-distance bargain railway tickets, and they comforted him with manly words. "So you're a doctor, well, I never, a doctor."

And the duty guard came whose turn it was to see to him and he looked through the peephole and said: "Ask for whatever you want," provided it was only a cigarette or to go for a pee.

And if he said: "Thank you," the guard answered: "No worries; it's what we're here for," and if he didn't express any thanks, the guard would also come as rapidly the next time he knocked on the door, after asking with a Galician accent: "Number?" in order to ascertain the cell, thus guiding the compassionate helper through the entangled Cretan twists and turns.

And other wardens came, and then others, a new one every two hours, and they were only too happy to take him to the damp urinals any time of day or night, whether they were awake and bored or pleasantly nodding off sprawled over a chair. "Number?" and tirelessly they would come.

And another two came accompanying the aged man who distributed their grub, a man whose weary legs meant he had to carry out this maneuver sitting on a low chair; he placed the steaming pot between his trembling knees and, in a single movement, stuck the ladle to the bottom, and always extracted with well-worn wisdom the mathematically precise, identical amount he dropped into the bowl humbly presented by the prisoner, and helped by a boy with a rather patsy manner who carried bits of boiled bacon on a platter and dropped one piece in each bowl like a crushed grasshopper, and if a prisoner asked, "Only one?" he told him, "You only get one."

And then came particularly brawny, particularly well-developed wardens, prematurely graying because of their nighttime shifts and continual contact with distress; they spun their yarns, intoning through the peephole in noble Roman style, explaining how they'd been to Australia and fought in Madison Square Garden.

But what every warden most liked to relate was the dire need they all felt to do some other job in their free time, collect payments for gas bills or dues for a mutual insurance company or an upmarket club: "They're jobs requiring honesty, and that's why they prefer us."

And another warden, old enough to be the prisoner's father, told how he'd been operated on by a famous surgeon, and he showed him his scar and told how it had almost emptied his head out and how painful it still was when the weather changed, and when duties were very demanding, and he only had to see the famous surgeon in the middle of the street and he'd stop, recognize him, and say: "Warden," and the warden would ask him about all the residual twinges, cramps, tingling, migraines, and dizzy spells, and the famous surgeon would simply laugh them off as trifles for a man who triumphs daily over death, daily, every day, mocking it in its very own bloody maw.

And the magician of the catacombs would come, the divine shower attendant who forced him to abandon his dingy cubbyhole of a dungeon and the delights of his cement bed, and spirited him away to an aquatic chamber where powerful boilers swathed in steam and vapors cast virginal threads of reheated water over his body, voluptuously burnishing and caressing him, until fatigue obliged him to break off that pleasuring of the skin, and after one barely necessary rub with a clean towel, he was returned and plunged back in his rightful place for the next twenty-three hours and fifty-five minutes.

And there were comforting wardens who soothed the woman in the next cell, who lamented endlessly and audibly and heaved her body: "Come on now, don't be like that, it won't get you anywhere," or the distressed boy who thought more about hurting his father than the weight of the law: "All you need to do is answer any questions you are asked."

Because with an understanding of human nature not derived from being especially intelligent but from their special learning process, the wardens listened bemused to every new arrival as they said they didn't know why they were there and hadn't a clue how the police could have made such an obvious error: "Just think for a mo' and you'll remember; there must be something..." "Possibly it's..." the amnesiac finally confessed and dreamily pretended to think of fresh, hitherto unsuspected possibilities. "Possibly it's... but that can't be it, that was nothing at all."

"When will I get out of here?" asked the now dry-eyed woman three or fifteen hours later.

"Don't you worry," the guard replied. "Ever since I've been working here, which is a very long time, everybody's gotten out."

Matías tried to mobilize the entire complex of social forces that the power of his surname, if not his own personal connections, could rally. Numerous ushers and concierges in ministries led him along portentous passageways to high-ceilinged rooms with gilded chandeliers with fifty-plus lamps, and furniture in the violent, convoluted Spanish style with just as many helmeted warriors' heads and mythological animals sculpted by unknown artisans with a surfeit of skill and a lack of taste. In other, more workaday premises, there were polished marble floors and indirect lighting or lights recessed in flat ceilings over the latest office-style metal desks or elegant French bureaus with green, gold-trimmed leather tops. Behind each of these desks an enigmatic face looked up, with a smile that only broadened when it learned who his father and uncles were, and immediately assumed an attitude of consternation, bewildered by the offbeat social circles this young man moved in, having heard rumors of his flirting with this or that literary trend, his academic failures and consequent rejection from an elite college: "I will do all I can," "Tomorrow I'll dine with the director-general," "I'll find out what I can," came the sibylline sallies from venerable lips intoned from semi-almighty thrones, and in every case one sensed the effort expended to quell a fleeting quiver of genuine repulsion that the word *abortion*, with its barely unimaginable resonances of filth, infection, venereal disease, and taboo relationships, provokes in the pure-of-heart insulated from shantytowns despite their considerable lived experience.

"He did nothing. It was a trap. It was an emergency midnight call. What else could he do? When he operated, she was already practically dead," Matías would explain.

"And you say he reported it to the police immediately."

"No, he was exhausted."

"Of course..."

And after a pause: "So he went to make a statement the day after?"

"No, he was scared or whatever. He was flustered. The following day he was at the lecture with me and then came to the cocktail party my mother gave in honor of..."

"And the police went after him there?"

"No, the police arrested him the following day."

"When he went to make a statement, I imagine."

"No, they arrested him in a . . ."

"Oh!"

After this syncopated exchange (which Matías learned to manipulate more perfectly every time, that is, by better concealing the true circumstances), the individual on the other side of the desk would suddenly turn friendly, overfamiliar, and protective, would lean in and offer personal advice to the effect that he should avoid getting embroiled in this business, because if things were as his friend had said, they'd soon sort themselves out, though everything wasn't quite as Matías believed, because youth tends to be generous in its judgments, and it is well known that friendship muddies the waters when it comes to judging people. It would be better for him to seek friends among people of his own kind, not to imply for one moment that there aren't people outside one's class who are splendid and worthy of anyone's friendship, but simply because such individuals lack a social base and tried-and-tested morals (what we know as tradition or pedigree), and may, whatever their virtues or intellect, be individuals one should steer clear of. No, of course not, we must not prejudge his guilt, but it's very strange that an individual who isn't a member of the profession and who apparently needed the money should have allowed himself to be lured into a trap, as Matías phrased it, into a senseless, ridiculous trap, in circumstances where the only sensible thing to do would have been to back out and report it through the proper channels. If Matías wanted to help, the best he could do would be to advise his friend to tell the truth, and everything would be cleared up without recriminations, but it would be a great pity if Matías, the son of his good friend X, got himself entangled in such a murky matter: "*une affaire ténébreuse*," as one of those gentlemen said, a victim of his French *baccalauréat*.

Matías felt he wasn't winning. At such a moment, he could see that prudent Nestor was only acting out the role of a true gentleman and offering sensible advice, and he guessed the real message behind his words. Later, when he came out from behind his desk, he fawned all over him as he led him to the door, and held his hand, and even gave him a paternal pat on the back with a firm hand only accustomed to grasping a fountain pen to sign documents; that true gentleman (subject to an ingrained habit that threw caution and scruples to the wind) once again adopted his first reflex reaction before a petitioner of good standing, erased his look of distaste, and insisted with a broad smile: "I will do everything I can," and the particularly well-bred even managed an "I kneel at the feet of your noble mother."

After devoting the whole morning and the best part of the afternoon to such gentlemen, Matías set off to find and capture that legal eagle to persuade him to act as lawyer on behalf of his friend, following up on an idea Doña Luisa had suggested the previous afternoon and that he'd put out of his mind, dazzled by his powerful connections, a single word from whom would have made waters flow normally and the tide of history turn without a single catastrophic consequence.

But his eagle had already abandoned the famous law practice where he worked as a junior partner and had gone off to see to some business matter or private consultation and wasn't expected home before supper. Matías tried—and it shouldn't have been so hard in such a relatively compact city—to track down that regular wise guy, and after making several calls and getting a few pointers, he set out again. He walked up from the square along the main avenue. The movies were over and the sidewalks were struggling to cope with the great crowds flocking out of exits beneath neon-lit marquees and huge posters of a four-story-high cowboy from the Wild West brandishing a papier-mâché lasso that never left his hand. American cars with chrome fittings and warm colors braked when the lights turned on, stood still and swayed like gondoliers or Napoleon I cradles for a few seconds, while drivers and the young girls at their side stared, apparently unperturbed, at the jostling throng hurtling in unison across the pedestrian crossing, like an aquarium where it was the fish who contemplated endless stupefied visitors an order had bid walk nonstop. The glances the public cast at the fancy fish in the mobile goldfish bowls were short-lived, sideways, out of the corner of an eye, shy and subdued, while the stares of those sitting comfortably while the red light lasted were one continuous, impertinent stare that encompassed the huge crowd, never singling out an individual unless, that is, it was a sporadic beauty with huge, painted, dark, gleaming eyes and long legs worthy of better use than the occasional perambulation. Surrounded by a herd of shorties, Matías could see relatively far into the distance and was hoping to spot the lawyer perhaps being dragged along by the spectators pouring out of one of the movie houses. The river of people, divided in two by the dark band of cars now on the move again, had for banks two rows of illuminated glass where riches from the remotest climes lined up, separated physically from the herd only by cold plate glass as solid as brick walls or ironclad vaults. Gold, diamonds, silk, the intricate, miniature mechanisms of imported Swiss watches, bottles of whisky, items in exquisite taste, crocodile-skin purses, genuine Parisian perfumes, art books, brochures promoting lion hunts on the savanna, ivory goods and pale-pink York hams were barely a half inch away from the public space but seemed so alien, as if they weren't what they were but their pure essences forever unattainable on the edge of Plato's cave. With the most unlikely expressions of uninterest, a beggar woman laden with newsprint, a taxi-opening boy, a Sunday-night seller of the day's football results walked past. Matías—less metaphysical—looked at these items as one might gaze at an abstract painting which one sees only as the relationship between shapes, lines, spaces, and shades of color. He was forced to stop a moment. It was an order from a red light. And when he felt the endless, roaring throng, the maelstrom that crowns Calle de la Montera, he sensed what it is to be alone. The memory of Pedro and his loneliness came to mind. It had been there all day, but he now grasped it with its true force: *He is alone.* The necessary image of his friend the lawyer focused his efforts to find him, and as if in a metapsychological incarnation, he loomed before him. He laughed behind his learned sage's spectacles. "*Matiotes, kai panta Mataiotetos*" he shouted, splitting his sides. "Vanity of Vanities. All is vanity, saith the preacher," mocking Matías's haughty, serious, tranquil posturing in the midst of the heaving mass: a living image of philosophical man assuming the burden of the short-lived nature of the human treadmill.

"I've been looking for you all day."

"Well, here you have me," the legal eagle declared professionally, without a hint of astonishment.

"We must talk."

"Let's talk then."

And they walked into a bar on a nearby side street, where a young woman was playing a guitar and the atmosphere was more languidly sophisticated than in any cheap and nasty cafeteria.

The young woman wore a skin-hugging black sweater and skirt, and hardly knew how to sing or move, but she did have a distinguished air and circulated from table to table smiling at the gentlemen dotted around, which justified her performance, and the decadent sound of her strumming went well with the tobacco and whiskies Matías and the lawyer were consuming at a reckless rate. The place extended like a tunnel, all twists, bends, and reddish lights. Slippery divans and big cushions were on both sides of the tunnel. Though devilishly uncomfortable, their shiny surfaces encouraged one to lounge and dream of oriental seraglios. But farther in, where the tunnel forked into more surprising byways, the pink lights transmuted into a paler blue, and to get into the mood, it seemed the thing to smoke pot, close your eyes, and whisper to your neighbor. The Moors had introduced this vice, the drug habit of the underdeveloped, and once they'd won their mini opium war, they sold it to ugly, aproned women in the vicinity of their barracks, who then transported it to nearby regions, distributing it to two classes of potential customers: shantytown louts and degenerate rich kids. Grass, unlike other, more schizoid drugs, is gregarious. It's sometimes consumed by bubbling smoke through a wine jar that's then drunk from, rolling one binge into another. When the shindig kicks off, someone, eyes shut, broadcasts his hallucinations, prompting less autodidact addicts to follow the path of his fantasies and enjoy the same collective vision painted bright as in a communal, uncensored, technicolor movie. In the depths of that blueish tunnel you could smoke grass in secret, without making a fuss or toking too much too quickly, so you could boast: "I didn't feel a thing. I don't even feel queasy."

Matías explained to the lawyer the same story he'd told his eminent acquaintances, changing it slightly (because experience had taught him to). If he told it as it was, his eagle friend might refuse to get involved. Jaime listened attentively, gravitas behind huge black-framed glasses that expanded the apparent surface of his cranium and helped impress reluctant clients. Then he declared: "You can't do anything for seventy-two hours."

"Nothing at all?"

"Nothing at all. Find out when he enters the judiciary system. Until the judge questions him and puts him inside, a lawyer can do nothing. Then I'll go and talk to him and we'll see what nonsense he's come out with, what he's confessed to and what he's kept quiet about. We'll have to present a request for his provisional release and pay bail if the judge decides that's a possible course of action. We can do nothing until that's done. For the moment he's not even being tried. If a man isn't being tried, nobody can defend him. Strictly speaking, nobody can until he comes to trial. Up to that point, it's merely a police inquiry. The defense, the defense properly speaking, cannot start now. The wheels of the machine set their own rhythm. We can do nothing. We must wait until the proceedings start. Keep on top of it and keep me informed, and as soon as I can, I'll activate the appeal for temporary release. If possible, which it won't be, I'll appeal against the indictment. But that won't be possible; as you tell it, there seem to be well-founded reasons for suspicion, and nobody is ever going to prevent your friend from appearing in court..."

This welter of procedures, protocols, and depositions sank Matías into a hazy reverie that was interrupted by the appearance of a tall woman with a swooping neckline, a costume pearl (or some such) necklace, and a smile aimed at the legal eagle, who, back on his feet, invited the newcomer to sit down, and after they'd ordered another whisky and offered her an American cigarette, the man in jail disappeared as an object of interest, vaporized in the smoke-filled air, as if he were a phantom generated by dope.

"Jaime . . . !" she mewled after sitting on the divan.

"Introduce me to this pretty thing," purred Matías.

"Who do you think you are," retorted the lawyer selfishly.

And the three sat looking at each other, smiling broadly, so delighted the world is made in such a way that two different sexes exist and that one of them—the opposite one—is so pleasantly supplied with gracious charms. Some slim-hipped, equivocal youths propping up the shadowy bar seemed to look contemptuously at that ravishing sight, as if convinced life might be worth living without such bipartite separations. But ignoring those glances, their sideburns trimmed shorter than those so condescendingly standing in judgment, Jaime and Matías continued to take turns wallowing in the green splendor of that beauty's eyes, happy to share her—for the moment. The guitar-playing entertainer had climbed back up the stairs from the ladies' room that acted as her dressing room. She now wore red turned a gloomy purple by the bluish spotlight, while her feeble voice attempted to fill the place with the Central European lilt of a sentimental old wartime song.

Snarler's roly-poly consort had succeeded by virtue of the visit she'd made on her own initiative to the organizers of such ceremonies in having her unfortunate daughter's body buried in hallowed ground, even at the cost of the vertical promiscuity mandatory for third-class burials in the Este Cemetery, but what her power of foresight couldn't envisage was that the mechanism she'd innocently set in motion was so complex that Florita's body would soon have to be exhumed and, in a backwards march as in a movie played in reverse (always so hilariously), transported again on the shoulders of one of the squads (the organization's perfection didn't reach to the heights of supplying a funeral truck) towards the strange, orientally shaped buildings that comprised the trio of *Chapel, Deposit, Offices*, bypassing these and entering a smaller one dubbed *Judicial Deposit*. By dint of a biological reflex that also affects dogs faithful to their deceased masters, she'd stayed at the foot of the little mound of brown earth in the period between the two contrary operations, never fretting too much about the precise superimposed level at which Florita was resting, and not even wondering at what level of gradual decomposition a dead body no longer merits a vigil. That was why she was there to witness the second exit of her bloodless daughter and see her prostrate next to the policeman who'd come on his bike, guessing from the expression on this individual's mug that he had some inkling as to the *why* and *wherefore* of the ceremony. When the word *autopsy* departed the cyclist's lips and she gathered what such a curious Greek noun means in Christian lingo, she was hit by a fresh wave of despair and insisted on crouching by the Judicial Deposit entrance, almost entirely shrouded by a black scarf and emitting hoarse wails nothing could stop. When the forensic pathologist entered those premises, he took pity on her and recommended she should be moved outside because he didn't want any upsets when he left after performing his duties. But as nobody was available to remove her and facilitate matters, the graveyard porter suggested quietly to the functionary that if he left through the back door "there'd be no issues."

"My daughter, my daughter," she repeated disconsolately, adding in a fury: "They're killing her."

"Madam, in this place we kill no one," retorted the jovial porter.

And he was telling the truth.

But she insisted: "They're killing her. Ay, they're killing her." Later, her lethargic imagination appeared to spell out what she feared: "They're ripping her open from head to toe, my poor dear, they're opening her up." She was suffering more from this profane act than from her daughter's actual death and those profane acts she'd suffered in life. She bellowed in the ears of all those working there and put everyone's nerves on edge. "I expect she was to blame for getting her into such a mess," opined the porter as he gave the team a hand. "This is intolerable," the pathologist finally said, grabbing the telephone and informing the police.

When they took her away, she went silent and kept that same silence on the entire ride to the station. She wasn't trembling, didn't seem afraid, and her heart wasn't racing.

"Will they bury her again?"

"Yes, madam."

After a number of hours, days or nights it was hard to compute, the light in the dusty upstairs rooms—from a sun mottling the housefront on the other side of a narrow street—filtered through the dry air and dirty windows, and was a joy to watch.

"You're an intelligent man," the interrogator began, transfixing him with his shiny, green-gold, piercing eyes. "What would you like to drink?"

The white-jacketed waiter lingered as he might have in any inelegant restaurant, a cloth over his shoulder and a few greasy stains on the lower part of his apron.

"Right away," said the waiter.

And he soon placed the beers on the table.

"No need to drink up, if you don't want to," the affable gentleman emphasized. "Don't think for one moment that I'm offering you beer to loosen your tongue."

"No, not at all . . ." said Pedro, and started drinking eagerly.

"You're an intelligent man," the policeman repeated, "so this shouldn't take very long. We're not going to waste time just to finish up where we should have started. Logic is implacable."

The policeman's neck was flabby and wrinkled, and his face a light red, as if a bloodthirsty temperament lurked beneath his olive-brown complexion. Pedro sensed he was intelligent and strong minded.

"Cheers!" said the policeman, drinking too. "What's your line of work?"

He had another underling at his side, whose deadpan face was bent over a typewriter so dirty that threads of old dust dangled into its scabby innards like so many spiders' webs.

"I'm researching cancer."

"Oh! So there is a cure, is there?"

Pedro explained that there was no cure for cancer. The policeman listened with ominous awe, as if he could feel the crab's jaws biting into his side.

"My mother died of cancer," he said, looking pitiful. "Today, with the progress that's been made, she probably wouldn't have died."

Pedro explained that despite the progress made, mothers were still dying.

"I'm not so sure," said the policeman. "I think they didn't diagnose it in time. Don't think all doctors are the same. We don't have insurance. We aren't treated properly. Do you think they'll soon find an antibiotic?"

Pedro explained there was a long way to go, there were many kinds of cancer, that he was researching a hereditary cancer that appeared spontaneously in a specific strain of mice brought over from America, all the way from their native Illinois. Only a few cancers are hereditary. So even if he did discover something in his research, that wouldn't open the path to curing cancer. These mice contained a specific gene that catalyzed the production of an enzyme that stimulated tumultuous, uncontrollable reproduction that, evading all laws of bodily well-being, via a relatively anaerobic passage into the metabolism, finally destroyed the carrier. Although it could turn out that, instead of a gene, it was a virus, a virus transmitted by the reproductive cells themselves, that lodged in the nucleus of the same cell, in intimate contact with the chromosomes, to such an extent that it was virtually impossible to distinguish it from a gene, since it could only reproduce itself in the heart of the reproductive apparatus of the living cell and because, like genes, it too activated itself from a distance, through catalytic substances that distorted the metabolic norm of deoxyribonucleic acid, until it achieved those monstrous proliferations known as multipolar mitosis, asymmetric mitoses, and explosive mitosis, and—what is quite astonishing—despite the huge damage experienced and the dysfunctionality, without life becoming impossible for the individual cell (the problem thus solving itself), except that the surrounding protoplasm continued, laboriously but luxuriantly, to develop, assimilate, split, grow, consume the blood of the implicated being, even becoming necrotized in vivo when the commensurate growth of blood vessels wasn't enough for it to continue its impetuous trajectory.

"That's all well and good, but what difference does it make if it's a virus or a gene if, as you say, they are one and the same?"

"If it were a virus, a vaccine could be found. But a gene, what is called a gene, forms part of the same organism, the very substance of the living being; it isn't an alien antigen, and consequently an immune reaction can never follow."

"Ah . . . !"

"That's why it's pertinent that it may be a virus. I believed that Snarler's daughters, who were carrying mice in little bags around their necks, might very well have been infected. If they too got lumps in the groin, it would have definitely been . . . a virus."

"But . . ."

"It was a dream, madness. Amador told me: 'They're breeding them. They carry them around their necks so they get in heat.' Because it was cold in the Institute, and they didn't breed. But Snarler stole the mice and he got them to breed."

"But you are saying that they . . . Did you test them?"

"No, I went to buy the litters."

"And that was when you met Florita."

"Yes, she gave me a glass of lemonade."

"And you took a fancy to her."

"I'm sorry?"

"I mean the girl made an impression on you."

"Yes, of course. I looked at her hard. She was the one most likely to have been infected . . ."

"Now I get you . . ."

"But she was so fat and contented. She didn't look as if she had cancer. It beggars belief that in a hovel like that, with God knows what they ate, the girls could look so beautiful."

"And you took a fancy to her."

"I thought it was a miracle she was so good-looking. They lived between two mounds of shit and a mass of mice. They kept mice in canary cages in the bedroom where they slept, above the same bed where the whole family slept."

"So you also saw the bed..."

"I don't remember..."

"And as her belly was still expanding, you said: 'We must abort her.'"

"I'm sorry?"

"On the contrary! On the contrary! You didn't abort her or do anything! It wasn't you who went on the night of the thirteenth to the fourteenth to their hovel equipped with surgical instruments. You didn't operate on her on top of a wooden board. You didn't trigger a hemorrhage that bled her dry. You didn't make a run for it without informing the police after she died. You didn't hide in a whorehouse. You didn't stay there until we found you. It isn't true the autopsy showed that the operation was carried out with the very same instruments Amador had brought. A man who wasn't known to you, who didn't put you into contact with the family, who didn't assist you in your laboratory. It wasn't you who said despairingly: 'I killed her. I killed her,' when you were questioned for the first time. Do you think I was born yesterday?"

Pedro sensed the truth was evident in that perfect dovetailing of circumstances that coincided like links in a chain of syllogisms. And it was true he should never have attempted to scour her because he'd never been trained to do that. And it was true he should never have attempted an emergency operation, given that there were so many clinicians on duty in the city that night. And it was true he shouldn't have operated, as he didn't belong to the doctors' college and had never been admitted to the profession. And it was true that after ascertaining she was dead, as a doctor, he ought to have informed the relevant authorities. And it was true, for all the above reasons, that he felt under a burden of overwhelming, proven guilt.

"Yes, I did really kill her," he accepted, hanging his head.

"Let's get this over and done with!" said the policeman, addressing the silent, constant witness to the exchange: "Get typing!" *Asked whether he knew the deceased and her family and the house where they lived, he said he did, through the mediation of his laboratory assistant by the name of Amador.* Period. *Asked if he had had any intimate contact with her, he answered that in effect he had checked she hadn't any tumors in her groin that he believed might have developed as a result of fortuitous contact with experimental mice he regularly obtained from that family, the ones he used for his research into cancer.* Period. *Asked if on the day of her death he had gone to the hovel and used his surgical instruments, he answered that . . .*

Pedro heard these words and felt no inner objections. It had happened exactly like that. There was no point in starting to shout no, no, like a child rejecting his punishment. Men must face up to the consequences of their actions. Punishment is the perfect consolation for the guilty, their only possible cure and corollary. Thanks to his punishment, equilibrium would be reestablished in this quite incomprehensible world where he'd been leaping about like a puppet, his head sunk in a morass of deceit.

Certain filthy, smelly, plump individuals, whose bodily crannies accumulate fatty, sticky substances that water never washes away but that are dislodged in the form of scabs when desiccated by time, are made from almost untreated earth; however, a degree of mental activity does persist in their hidden cavities, not in the form of insights or thoughts, but as colored phantoms from a past that slips silently by.

Submerged in the same underground holes as the rest of the arrested, the legitimate wife of Pablo González (nicknamed Snarler years ago by his schoolmates in a distant village near Toledo because of the uncontrollable tics chorea had left him as a memento) filled the dead time in her cell by revisiting scenes from her past.

In the almost raw earth that occupied the hollow space in her skull, she recalled herself crying in front of her daughter, crying in front of her primitive dead mother, dancing before the village Corpus Christi procession, straight-backed though only a young girl, staff in hand and wearing a steepled high bun, surrounded by her girlfriends singing "Nobody's got hair like our Encarna," she saw herself courted by her consumptive husband, smiling like a mouse even at that young age, who abuses her and clambers on top of her on a threshing floor at dusk, when she feels like part of that hot earth, like a loaf of bread under the July sun, so far from any water, and she is the only cool thing on this earth, just what he needs to quench his thirsty body; she was already so fat when she married him, all the village girls laughed at her, and he didn't need to seek leave from the regiment like other boys, because he was a dead loss what with the rheumatic fever that had weakened his heart, his pigeon chest, and the rickets left by childhood illness; then she was giving birth, shouting and kicking; giving birth again elsewhere, when they were on the move along the roads of La Mancha and she had to give birth somewhere or other, worrying the Moors might show up at any moment; seeing how enormous the city was from the outside, from the place where every day she stole seven bricks she heaped up and Rickets told her to build their house; constructing the house herself with hands burned by lime while Rickets drank all afternoon; she saw herself being beaten and battered, night after night, by his hand, his fist, a stick, a long piece of wire, beaten when his snarl accelerated because of his drinking, beaten time and again, but barely feeling it because old food and new food almost like the earth, which she found on dung hills, has been making her roly-poly, swelling that minimal area from her tiny feet to her bun that's not so high now, a dirty hodgepodge under fabrics that stick to her skin, she feels his blows and guesses from their rhythm how soon Rickets will drop to the ground and snore, pain meaning no more to her than the lapse of time separating her from sleep and—*not pain, real pain* as felt by someone who's a human being—but only pain as a sign of how close by her husband is, and that it's nighttime, and he was able to get his hands on money today and that's why he's been drinking and then, if she's in luck and he's not drunk it all away, tomorrow they'll be able to eat, but not a pain that hurts or wounds, a pain that simply indicates how close by he is; in the hungry years she saw her two girls sucking on a plant root she'd pulled out of soil near where the sewers drain away that seemed full of nutritious juices; she saw herself cutting a sweet potato into four and giving slices to the girls and to Rickets who was always famished, and keeping back the peel and cooking it and feeding her whole family in the hungry years and wondering why, while her youngest avidly sucks that stalk and is still alive and she herself doesn't feel hungry because she's lost all capacity to feel, and can only wait, and even so he does manage to bring something home and goes out hunting cats, rats, rabbits, and stray dogs he ties up with a rope, and she feels meekly grateful for the hard work that saves their daughters and keeps them eating for a future she can't imagine but can only feel growing within herself and her daughters, heartbeat by heartbeat, breath by breath, snarl by snarl.

In her dungeon, this earthen being who cannot think, who cannot read, who doesn't know how to treat people, revisits the wretched images of her starving, monotonous existence stretching back through the years, rent by a mechanical moan that fills her cell and spreads down the passageways, her physical despair at the death of the baby she gave birth to, far away, long ago, and had first nurtured on substances from her body, then on substances from the earth, then on her man's cunning, the baby she'd first carried under her shiny, ironed black tunic when she went to church and the priest's blessing seemed almost more directed at the little babe kicking furiously inside her than at her own self that was already so emphatically sunk and damned by a curse she couldn't cast aside because she wasn't one who could change the state of things, or be surprised that the same man who raped her so painfully, then fed her in pain, made her work in pain and prepared her over the years for the pain she'd feel the moment the baby was snatched from her, one she thought the priest's exorcism had saved when he'd made the sign of the cross over her belly.

To be born, to grow, to dance during the village festivities in front of the Corpus Christi procession with her hair steepled high, because she was a good dancer and had decided that, though fated to experience pain and poverty because of where she came from, she *would* dance before the dais on the Corpus procession, when heralding the monstrance brings salvation to every peasant on the plain of Toledo, then sink, slowly sink into the earth, bury her graceful waist (the reason she was selected for the fiesta) in masticated, digested earth, bury herself in poor fat, become roly-poly, roam far and wide surrounded by the roly-poly state fate grants women like herself who have been subjected to a poverty that doesn't kill, fleeing from an army come from God knows where, arriving in a city that's fallen from God knows what star, becoming part of the shifting earth around the city protecting her, molding her, suckling her, destroying her, as she waits and moans.

Knowing nothing. Not knowing that the earth is round. Not knowing that the sun is motionless, though it appears to rise and set. Not knowing that they are three separate Persons. Not knowing what electric light is. Not knowing why stones fall towards the earth. Not knowing how to tell the time. Not knowing that the sperm and the ovum are two distinct cells that fuse their nuclei. Knowing nothing. Not knowing how to treat people, not knowing how to say: "How lovely to see you here," not knowing how to say: "A very good day to you, doctor, sir." And yet to have told him: "You did all you could."

And obstinately repeat: "It wasn't him." Not out of a love of the truth, nor a love of decency, nor because she thought that by saying that she did her duty, nor that, if she said that, she'd rise an inch above the earthen crust where she was still sunk, never being able to speak properly, emitting only grunts and a few words that were more or less comprehensible. "It wasn't him," and faced by an insistent kind of man she'd never thought existed—endowed with such an overbearing presence—though she did sometimes wonder when she gazed at the city from afar under a cloud of black smoke issuing from black holes she'd only become familiar with later, she repeated: "By the time he got there, she was already dead."

"It wasn't him," continuing to mourn the poor girl who'd come out of her belly and through whose own young, opened belly she'd seen with her own eyes a very lovely life depart, the single item of worth she'd passed on to her.

"OK then, it's all done," said the smiling policeman with the gold-green eyes.

"What?"

"Yeah, everything's cleared up. Thanks to the old biddy, you've got her to thank."

"Everything?"

"Yeah. Now we'll return all your belongings and you're a free man."

And reacting to his shocked, incredulous gaze: "Yeah. A free man, a free man . . . Look what I'm going to do with your confession," and before Pedro's eyes he tore the piece of paper he'd signed a few hours ago into two long bits. "Goodbye to all that!"

Then he burst out laughing.

"You intellectuals are always the dumbest. I can never understand why it's always you people, cultured, well-educated folk, who mess up the most. A garden-variety pickpocket, a poor critter, an idiot, the pettiest of petty thieves defends himself better than you do. If it weren't for that woman, I can tell you, you'd have had it rough."

"So . . ."

"Yeah, it's all cleared up."

"That's what I told you: I got the call after the evil deed had been done. I could do nothing."

"Sure, that was your line. But who was ever going to believe that after all the stupid things you did? Who wouldn't think of reporting it? Let alone decide to hide? And where? Where did you hide? Couldn't you think of anywhere better?"

"I was scared."

"Yeah, but that's hardly an excuse. You acted so dumb. I can't understand why. I really can't. The more intelligent you are, the more infantile your behavior. It beggars belief."

"So, can I go now?"

"You still can't believe it, can you?" said the policeman, bursting into laughter again. "You must have had a lousy time down there. You're broken men when you do get out. In a much worse state than any petty thief. You've got no spunk."

"I'll be off then . . ."

"Wait a mo'. Here are your things."

From a big sandpaper envelope he started to extract money, letters, photos... the various items Pedro had been carrying on him and others they must have taken from his room.

"It's all there. Sign the receipt."

Pedro started to put the papers in his pocket. Moving awkwardly and looking myopic, out of it. He ran his hands over his face. They scraped on the stubble. He imagined a sink and a barber. Then he asked: "Have you got the guy who did it?"

"Yeah, he's downstairs. With the girl's father, who's another can of worms. They've had the shock of a lifetime. But please don't answer any more emergency calls of that kind. Don't do anything so stupid again, just work and have a good time. Let the shantytown people alone and they'll solve their own problems."

Pedro got up and went as if to leave. A stream of sickly-looking youths were coming out of the office and along the narrow passageway. Their scant facial hair gave them an unmistakably debilitated air.

He was now walking towards the door at the end of the passageway, through which instinct told him he'd find the street, when the policeman spoke to him again: "Let there be no doubt, if I'd wanted, I could have put you away. There's a criminal case of a cover-up to be made, almost amounting to complicity... but I believed you: I took a shine to you."

"Thanks, thanks very much," Pedro felt duty bound to add.

"No worries. Oh, and by the way, I almost forgot. Someone's waiting for you. In the room next door." He winked at him and held out his hand. "She's very pretty. Congratulations," and he burst out laughing yet again and disappeared down the corridor in the opposite direction.

Dorita and Matías were waiting for him in the pokey waiting room where there was room only for a bench that seated three people. He was stunned by Dorita's beauty as if he were seeing it for the first time. He hadn't thought about her from the moment he'd heard Similiano speak in the brothel. Dorita's large eyes welled with tears. Their lips pressed tight together. He felt possessed by the passion of his forgotten love. "I love you, I love you," Dorita said hoarsely, as their lips parted. An embarrassed Matías looked through the window at the narrow street below. "My love," she said, clasping his neck and leaning her body into him. It was too soon for Pedro to be aware he was holding a woman in his arms. "How are you? Was it horrible?" He couldn't return her caresses. As they kissed, he could only feel the hardness of her teeth that might have drawn blood, but it didn't feel sensual. Sensuality wasn't what mattered. "I love you." She shuddered, she trembled, her whole body shook around him; she hugged him again, cried and laughed. "She loves me," thought Pedro. "It's obvious she loves me."

"Well, this is all for the good. It's fixed," Matías explained. "All fixed." He too seemed to have talked to the police. "No more idiotic behavior. You really put us through it! Do you know? I'd got a lawyer for you, a fantastic lawyer, a friend of mine... but, man, he was so pessimistic. You've been such an idiot. In the end, it's fixed and we didn't have to do a thing."

He also gave Matías a hug. After her outburst, Dorita had gone all quiet and was quietly holding his arm.

"Let's be off! Let's get out of this place!" He suddenly felt anxious. These were the first words he uttered.

They laughed and rushed hell-for-leather down the stairs. When he came out onto the street, he was dazzled by the sun. Cars, cars, and more cars drove by. Horns, claxons, bicycle bells, exhaust pipes blasted away. People, people, and more people walked by, expressionless, as if they'd never thought what a huge gift it was to have that sky above their heads, those small white clouds, apparently still but always shifting, changing slowly, coming from afar, and going far away. A shoeshine walked by holding his black box, and the sight of this everyday fellow, advancing slowly towards a potential customer, brought tears to his eyes. "Shine!" shouted the small man, who'd registered his stare, but Dorita and Matías dragged him towards a passing taxi and took him to the boardinghouse, where mother and grandmother were waiting, looking overjoyed yet reproachful. Matías left him to his ablutions, to a purifying bath, a good bed, clean sheets, and the barely veiled caresses of Dorita.

"I'll come to pick you up tomorrow. You're invited to dinner at our place."

It is surely true that science more than any other human activity has changed the way we live on this earth. Nor does anyone ever question that science is a lever freeing mankind from the infinite alienations that prevent it from adapting its actual existence to its free essence. We conclude it is axiomatic that the glorious protagonists in this boundless field must be seen to be first-class citizens or at least individuals who are neither beneath contempt nor silly, at the most slightly affected, but always worthy and upright.

Starting from these simple baselines we deduce the need to establish within every human anthill a kind of clock in perpetual motion or an indefinitely perfectible mechanism whose workings categorize the efforts of these meritorious males in order to secure maximum output and satisfaction—the outcome desired by one and all: power over the forces of nature, and knowledge of the reasons behind things.

These sublime principles and intentions inform the Institutes, the Councils, the learned Corporations, the venerable Academies devoted to such important endeavors. Thanks to that ensemble of institutions (far too complex to be described here) every groundbreaking youngster or original initiative finds a place in the great march-past of the builders of the future. Like a bellicose army, equipped not with destructive weapons or gleaming bayonets but with microscopes, theodolites, slide rules, and capillary pipettes, the phalanxes of science advance in large, well-organized platoons. A curse on anyone who scorns the drab getup of any of these amazing pioneers! A crumpled suit can hide the fortunate owner of a brain that—ailing yet voluminous—dispenses thoughts hitherto unsuspected by mortal beings, formulas for new elemental particles, antiuniverses, and semielectrons; beneath a seemingly stolid face and narrow forehead may lurk a capable archivist and tireless consumer of palimpsests and microfilms. This studious, research-hungry throng has at its disposal buildings with wide windows, staircases, and corridors built from genuine reinforced concrete. Although their diet is deficient and the cut of their cloth unattractive, although their black leather briefcases conceal a sandwich substitute for the hot dinner they crave, the beadle won't block their way but will respectfully allow them to proceed to premises where a few unpaired rats, or volumes in German, or the incomplete collection of an American journal will provide the necessary tools for them to put their ideas into practice. Comforted by such productive stimuli, why should it seem strange that day after day they surprise us fulsomely with the quality products of their brilliant minds? So many industrial patents arise on our soil only to be quickly snaffled by rapacious foreign industrialists! So many original and effective drugs come every day to improve the fighting power of our massive hospitals! So many theoretical developments in the most abstruse sciences, physics, calculus for vectoral matrixes, the chemistry of macroproteins are made available to the Academies of cultured countries to be studied and admiringly approved! So many brilliant prodigies of applied sciences astonish visitors to any of our Exhibitions of Inventions!

Only a handful of the rather neglected branches of our tree of national wisdom are still housed in old buildings, no longer fit for the purpose. These are modest edifices with a cozy, romantic air, located in shady areas surrounded by ancient parks and paths where local ragamuffin children run and play.

Pedro headed towards one such building when he had rallied his spirits after his deadening subterranean odyssey. Upon reaching the iron gates, he reclaimed the *Don* that he generally left behind after leaving those premises.

"Good morning, Don Pedro." The porter greeted him as if nothing had happened.

"Hello!" said Don Pedro.

In the building's main entrance, where he was greeted by an acrid, doggish stink wafting down from the upper floors, a cleaner was vigorously striving to make the cracked tiles shine.

"Good morning, Don Pedro," she repeated, as if echoing the porter.

Crouched down and bending over, a bucket by her side, she was grasping a gray cloth. She didn't seem to yearn for the advanced machinery—produced elsewhere by the science she so humbly served—that made it possible to carry out the same operation in a vertical position.

"Hello!" said Don Pedro.

And he walked up the broad, expansive staircase. A white-coated lab assistant saw him coming.

"Good morning, Don Pedro."

"Is he about?" he asked, without specifying whom he was referring to.

"He's in there," she said.

Pedro walked to the door and rapped it with his knuckles.

"Just the person I was wanting to speak to," said the Director.

And, giving him a stare, he asked: "So what was *that* all about?"

Pedro searched for a reply that wasn't forthcoming.

"You are insane!" declared the Director without more ado.

"I . . ."

"Completely insane!"

And switching the focus of his commiserations: "You placed me in a very awkward situation."

"I did . . . ?"

"Extremely awkward. You had no right to do that!"

After this solemn exordium and apportioning of blame, the Director paused for a moment before unleashing his inevitable harangue. With both hands he smoothed his gray lion's mane that, in German style—as befits someone who had studied the Meno in Frankfurt—sat limply on his ears, and, a true humanist with a keen sense of his professorial responsibilities, he sighed as he took his seat behind his desk. His large head leaned forward, overwhelmed by genuine grief. Knowledge was visibly amassing beneath his shiny, protruding temples. He wore a white coat that, unlike those of his team's lower ranks, fastened in front, allowing his spartan tie to display a perfect knot, symbolic of his inner need for harmony and beauty. Educated far from the realm of narrow, blinkered Anglo-Saxon positivism, having been imbued in his central European university with a sense of philosophy that gave order to his every act, cognizant that pure scientific data without a rational system coordinating it within the human sciences would remain ineffectual and even pernicious, being *au fait* with every journal in his discipline published in German, English, French, and Italian, authoring books in which masses of information were coupled with an elegant, pleasing turn of phrase, scorning—for good reason—to dirty his hands on the few experimental projects a man can tackle in the course of a lifetime that biological laws ensure is short, lamenting the quantum that in such research depends on chance, on a random observation, preferring to steer clear of such a lottery and operate at a more elevated level and garner the fruit from the world harvest of such propitious serendipity to process and order it behind his splendid temples, the Director could permit himself a penetrating, half-ironic, half-astute smile at the expense of the naiveté of the young men who, recently arrived in his hands, were already asserting they had discovered *something* without taking on board the difficulties that prevent such premature, nay, foolish, discoveries.

"Our profession is a priesthood," he drawled without a hint of anger, "that demands we be worthy of it. I would say it doesn't suffice simply to proclaim that minimal level of integrity, it is necessary for us to *embody* it. There is suspicion that cannot be tolerated. I know you will tell me that you are no longer subject to any accusation. Indeed, you are not subject to any accusation whatsoever, but—let us be clear—you are not above suspicion. Quite the contrary, you are suspicious in the eyes of everyone, and we incur suspicions only when we rashly place ourselves in situations that beget them. There are interactions, behaviors, hasty decisions that offend not only morality but professional ethics, and they are unacceptable. You have behaved badly. On several occasions you have told me—and I believed you—that professional practice didn't appeal to you, that you wanted to devote yourself to research. It was a noble ideal. But you now face me with this situation: the illegal, absurd, and suspect performing of an operation for which you haven't been trained, let alone authorized. How do you expect me to interpret what you did? You cannot ask me to tolerate acts that pertain to the penal code, though they may not be fully covered by it. I am sorry. I am deeply sorrowful. I had come to feel affection for you, as I do for all my students. I thought you possessed a degree of interest, that science interested you. But the truth is that, unfortunately, your research findings have been poor, extremely poor... almost nonexistent (he spread over his desk four or five reports on the autopsies of mice), you have made no progress... However, I clung to the hope that, over time, you would mature. You had scant background in the sciences and were hardly well read. But perhaps a stroke of good fortune or suggestions from your colleagues and teachers would one day have shown you the path to take. It wasn't to be. I am sorry. I don't believe you know what you really want. Take my advice. Give up research. You aren't gifted in this respect. You will achieve nothing. In view of the circumstances, I am duty bound not to extend your grant. Perhaps this will be a boon. You are good with your hands. Go to the provinces. Practice the profession. You could make a decent surgeon. You'll have a quieter life and won't mix with bad company. Take it easy. This isn't for everyone. I think that, in the end, it will benefit you. In a few years you will thank me (standing up and taking his hand). I am sorry our collaboration is at an end (leading him by the shoulder to the door). Go home and prepare for the examinations to enter the public health system. You have a good memory. You will pass without breaking a sweat. I'll put in a word with the examination council. And don't get embroiled again in those goings-on. This will soon be past history: they don't get the Madrid press in the provinces, and even if they do, they won't identify you. You'll have a quiet life. Tell me when you have to put yourself forward and I'll talk to the examination council. You know me, I won't let you down. And read, read and study... I tell you, it's all there, in books."

Amador was so very, very sorry. He knew he was responsible for sending Pedro into the hellish world of a shantytown which infects all those who touch it and which he'd made every effort to avoid after that awful postwar day when his relatives invaded his kitchen with their mattress. Amador had felt scared, but nothing amiss had happened to him. While Snarler and the Wizard with the needle were beginning their unpredictable navigation of cells, prisons, penal courts, supreme courts, and police stations the possible outcome of which was unimaginable for the moment, Amador, smiling blankly, continued to take dogs from their wire cages and look for the vein in the paw where he—of all the assistants—knew how best to inject the substance that in a few seconds would silence their horrendous barking and leave them strapped on a dirty wooden operating table like a black watery canal, all ready to help science advance at the expense of their blood. Amador helped callow young researchers put together their doctoral theses, not only telling them how to operate on dogs, but doing the operations himself, once, after pause for reflection, he'd grasped the gist of the question, that generally varied little within a range of topics that was endlessly repeated: gastric fistulas, saliva fistulas, cross circulations, experimental fractures. When Don Pedro walked down the stairs, slowly, pale faced, without the hint of a smile, the minimal trace of good cheer that came with his release drowned by a fresh bout of melancholy, Amador saw him, and was pleased to see him walk free.

Don Pedro walked very slowly down the steeply inclining street. Deep in his bulky pants pockets, his hands rucked up his jacket. His head bowed, like a boy arriving late to school and not wanting to go in. He kicked a stone and noticed how dusty his shoes were.

"So what did the man say?" Amador gave him a fright as he caught him up. Pedro looked and saw that ever-smiling face, the thick red lips, the big, very separate eyes, the wrinkled forehead and black curly hair.

"Let's go for a drink," Amador insisted. "It's on me!"

They found a seat in a small, dirty, empty dive. An old man wearing a blue apron came over and placed the wine in front of them. They made themselves comfy on the round wooden seats.

"So they fired you, Don Pedro?"

Pedro was grateful Amador gazed at him with such genuine compassion.

"Yes. But I'm not bothered. It's almost better this way. I can now marry and earn money."

"Of course. That makes sense..."

"At the end of the day I wasn't going anywhere here."

"What a waste of time, Don Pedro! I tell you I've seen so many young men wasting their youthful years in this place... And for what, Don Pedro, you tell me, for what? Who was ever going to thank them? They have such outrageous expectations. The only worthwhile thing I saw them do was get to the end of their theses. Then they get a university post. But what else is in it for them? It's stuff and nonsense! Leave! Leave and earn lots of money! That's your way out. I'm stuck here, because it's my trade, and the only one I know, but you people, just tell me what you people get out of it..."

Pedro was suddenly saddened again.

"And for what, I ask you?" he erupted. "I did nothing. You know that I..."

"Enough of that!" Amador ordered him. "Put it all behind you. It was bad luck. That's all it was. Pure bad luck."

"I can't imagine what that fellow can have thought..."

"Enough of that, Don Pedro! Forget it!"

An evil-looking individual walked in. He asked for rotgut. He sported a sparse red beard. His gray-brown corduroy jacket was stained with whitewash. A yellowish dog parked itself in the doorway, stared in, but didn't dare walk in.

Amador lowered his voice to a whisper.

"You must leave this town as soon as possible, Don Pedro. Get out as soon as you can!"

"Sure, I'll be leaving..."

"Go right now!"

"But why?" Pedro didn't understand the rush and was alarmed.

"The guy who got her in that wretched state... an evil character... he thinks you were the one who... you know what I mean."

"That's ridiculous."

"He's an evil character, I'm warning you."

"But what does he know?"

"I told him, Don Pedro, I told him. He drew a knife on me this big. My blood froze. What could I do? I told him everything..."

"Everything?"

"That it was the doctor. I thought you'd be leaving..."

"This is so ridiculous...What can this guy do to me?"

"He's an evil character... I'm just warning you, doing my bit, Don Pedro, because, I'm really sorry, he's an animal, an evil animal."

The family thus honored organized a soirée within their reach or indeed slightly beyond their means. Sensible of their social obligations and of how to proceed if an ingenuous, though pleasant enough, young man is to forget the suffering his wayward behavior has brought upon him. Happy to celebrate simultaneously a betrothal, the release of the captive, and the return of the prodigal, not-yet-but-almost-inevitable son. Content finally to trumpet in the neighborhood the legitimate arrival in their house of a male with a double-barreled surname. Proud of the rarified talents of the chosen one. Warmly moved by the tender loving care emanating from every gesture, every word, every daydreaming stance struck by that svelte body, flesh of their flesh and the family masterpiece: fruit of several generations of blind grafts that had nevertheless led to a consummate conclusion. Aware she was a judicious combination of the eccentric heredity of the colonel and grandmother and the je ne sais quoi of effeminate decadence the darn dancer had introduced in a furtive but fortunate manner, redeeming the aesthetics of a breed which, to that point in time, had always been too thick wristed and long nosed.

It was beyond their pockets to organize a meal served by liveried servants (or at the very least by dinner-jacketed waiters), in which they would have offered a menu of eggs, three entrées, roast, and game, or a supper of consommé, caviar, foie gras, and lobster with iced champagne, because both at lunchtime and dinnertime, the house's dining room was occupied by lodgers. Nor could they organize a cocktail party with exotic beverages and whisky to accompany a wealth of tasty canapés, small cubes of cheese with peppers, warm dwarf olives, and puff pastry on silver platters, because they found these tidbits far from nutritious and quite indigestible. So they offered healthy Spanish fare, with dense, steaming hot chocolate, Arias-buttered slices of toast, churros made by the beautiful girl's mother (dim-witted but gifted in the culinary arts), genuine sponge cakes from Astorga acquired at a secret address where truck drivers from that distant, foggy city made a stop, and honey or jam fritters.

At this mid-afternoon hour, the house assumed an air of mystery, different from the mystery of early morning, and helped by the presence-absence of lodgers. While some—the minority—went out to work, others—the majority—stayed in their rooms, engaged in unknown occupations and pretending not to notice what was undoubtedly happening. These long hours would perhaps be filled by reading, prolonged, sticky siestas, stealthy spying through inside windows or outside balconies, games of solitaire in which cards lay in four grimy columns crowned by an ace, or melancholy reveries rehearsed hundredfold in which the dreams of youth appear, haloed in despair, dreams life has always frustrated. But they broke off these clandestine activities on that afternoon when the noble ladies celebrated the return of the swain.

The ladies (as they too labored away in the house that gave them shelter) felt a degree of discomfort that derived from their coexistence with lodgers. They tried to sidestep it by erecting ramparts of feigned indifference. Thus—during the party—they acted as if they didn't know that the lodgers they'd not invited were training their vigilant antennae their way hoping to capture whatever joy or sorrow might move their weary hearts.

To add insult to injury, the ladies exacerbated the willful ignoring of the decent feelings of long-standing lodgers—in total disregard of their rights—by inviting friends who lived outside the guesthouse. Thus one saw the stout mother (in a black dress topped by silk crepe filigree) of Dorita's best friend wander through the dining room in the steamy haze from the delicious hot chocolate, and her daughter mentally reviewed the far from splendid roster of her present, past, and potential suitors in paroxysms of envy and jealousy, and didn't eat a bite, unlike her gluttonous progenitor. Similarly, an elderly, quite lecherous gentleman was to be seen all afternoon at the mother's side, perpetually smiling, also dressed in black and clasping a walking stick, a loan merchant who in hard times had helped keep the sinking ship of the boardinghouse afloat by means of unspecified favors upon which we shall not dwell. The stern grandmother's generation was represented by a widow with a battle-hardened mustache, a good-looker in her prime, who'd come with high hopes and not a little curiosity, and who now hinted at how many cross looks she might have endured when she was a source of scandal at her height and the reason for her little husband's request for early retirement, after which he became immediately consumed by a sadness his spouse's attentions sporadically attenuated. These individuals, products of a contemptible but real slice of history, existed despite their wraithlike appearance, and consumed great quantities of fritters and sponge cake, the likes of which they'd not seen in a long time. For that reason the conversation wasn't particularly sparkling, but gratified and glowing gazes were enough to create an atmosphere of good humor and jollity only marred by Dorita's resentful friend and her stubborn lack of appetite.

"Eat, daughter!" her mother insisted. "It's delicious. If you don't eat, you'll always be a beanpole."

Her daughter preferred to stare at Dorita brazenly holding one of her crestfallen gallant's hands.

"When's the wedding?" she inquired caustically.

Pedro and Dorita looked at her, taken aback, and then at each other without responding. Dorita was simply too gorgeous. What light shone from her large eyes! How delicately shaped her nose beneath a spotless forehead! How tender and juicy the tissues beneath her temples, where time likes to draw its first furrow!

"My first establishment was on the Calle del Pez," explained the elderly gentleman. "I lived in the garret and my little shop was down below in the entrance. What times they were! Five pesetas was a fortune. Not like now when we don't know what the world is coming to. At times I'm tempted to give up and retire. Everything is so appalling. You can trust no one and nobody has manners anymore."

Dora, the mother, who knew she had to curry favor with the loan merchant and keep on his right side with a view to the extra expenses the imminent wedding would entail, blurted nonsensically: "You'll never change, Don Eulogio! One never knows when you're being serious. You're terrible. Naturally, that's of no matter to those of us who know you well. You're a good-hearted man."

"True enough," Don Eulogio allowed.

And turning towards Pedro: "And you, young man, where are you hoping to settle down?"

The dowager hovered over the whole party, keeping a sharp eye on the young man's ever more downbeat mood, the droop on his lips, and the way he was lapping up her granddaughter's beauty. She didn't draw any hasty conclusions from her mediocre social circle or the suppressed hatred surging from the surrounding bedrooms, but could already envision a well-appointed consultancy in which an attractive nurse, though not as beautiful as the wife, ushered in large numbers of provincial clients who were good payers, if not the filthy rich.

"You should pay me a visit, Don Eulogio," the military widow suggested.

"Delighted to, milady."

"Why don't you come to the café? There's a group of us widows and widowers who meet for a chat. All old fogies," she quipped to much laughter.

"Let him be. Don't stir him up," protested Dora, single-mindedly.

"Have you known each other for long?" the resentful friend's mother asked, after she'd eaten her fill.

"Not so long, madam. We aren't that long in the tooth."

"Twenty-five years. A trifle."

"Why do you say that if it's not true? You know only too well you're a spring chicken."

"Yes, a spring chicken who likes a bit of spice."

"Do you remember that charity bash in Lugo?"

"How could I forget it! What times they were! It was when you asked for early retirement."

"It was a difficult time . . . poor thing. He was intimidated."

"And did you know my husband by any chance?"

"I don't know... Perhaps he was a client of mine?"

"Shush, Don Eulogio! You'll never change! Why would he have been a client of yours?"

"Have you seen what's on at the Callao?"

"We haven't, have you?"

"No, I'm going tomorrow with a boy."

"It looks good."

"Yes, I think it *is* very good."

"But you've always been one for the ladies."

"Can't be helped, madam! One isn't made of stone. If it weren't for you lady folk, life wouldn't be..."

"You *must* come to our café chitchats. As I said, we're all old fogies. You'll be the spring chicken."

"I told you not to get him worked up."

"Don't you worry, Dora, you can come too."

"Me? I go from home to church and back again. You won't change my routine. I'm not one for café tittle-tattle."

"What can we gossipers say?"

The doorbell rang and rang; the flustered maid ushered Matías into the party unannounced, where he was greeted by the stench of cold oil from the leftover churros in a white porcelain dish in the middle of the table.

Pedro looked up and felt himself blushing a bright red. He waved, after disentangling his hand from Dorita's. The entire illustrious gathering turned their eyes towards Matías.

"Come in! Come in! What would you like?" asked the grandmother, not flickering an eyebrow.

"Most kind," said Matías. "I only came to get Pedro."

"I don't know if you know..." began Pedro, and then he shut up, while Matías embarked on a round of waves to the whole room.

"He's a good friend of Pedro's," Dorita explained.

"I see you are very busy," Matías apologized.

"Quite the contrary, let's go right away," Pedro rejoined.

"Pedro!" Dorita protested. "You said you would take Mama and me to that variety show."

"I'd completely forgotten. Matías—"

"Don't worry! It's all good. I'll be off. We can go out some other day."

"No, wait, Matías. Wait. I do want to go with you."

"Pedro, you can't do this to me! Today of all days!"

"You *said* you would take us!" interrupted a breathless Dora, forgetting about Don Eulogio at her side. "Don't be so rude..."

"Be quiet, Dora!"

"I'm sorry, next time," Matías said. "I'll be off now. It's completely fine."

"I've already reserved tickets," Dora explained. "It's what you have to do because if you don't, the front rows..."

Pedro stood in the middle of the dining room, surrounded by guests gorged to the gills, and saw Matías's head moving way, saw him wave again, trying not to stare at him, bowing, apologizing, laughing faintly, and finally disappearing. He slumped down in his chair. Dorita was by his side. He held out his hand, which Dorita, in a slow, self-assured movement, took back, then she leaned her divine, warm body into his, whispering in his ear: "Thank you, thank you... You know, Mama was so looking forward..."

What a surprising-lame-devil-raising-the-roof-off-a-surprised-bared-for-all-to-see space![34] What refractions of an unlikely kind diminish distances and bring fantasies closer, the mescaline trip, the collective unconscious, the houris the Prophet promised believers seventy times seven with their nightly renewed virginity wrapped in transparent peplum, the archetype of what we desire as thirteen-year-olds in our lonely beds, the calves we've started to notice as we walk down the street, cavorting before us like glossy-coated animals, the opacity of flesh, eternity simulated in weightless form, which jumps, flies, and rises through the air, which descends not because of the nature of weightiness, but to musical rhythms that must be scanned in some way, and prosaically elects to go into free fall, no wrinkles, no spots, no black shins, plump proportions, flabby skin that seems, from the third row, to the partially myopic, as smooth as marble! Faces contorted in gelid smiles, they barely open their mouths when singing, barely half close their eyes when winking, barely moved by thought when robotically provoking, faces that don't correspond to the women lurking behind them but to other, more basic organisms that exist not in their gracefully swaying bodies but in the greedy souls of those who read them like written symbols easily comprehended by the species—before any of those individuals was born!

Swimming in such glorification and cascades of colorful light, turning a blind eye to leotards darned with different threads, their resplendent beauty erasing the yellows, ochers, crimsons of the cardboard scenery, nightly accumulating an extra layer of filth in the sweat-stained armpits of their folkloric garb (sizes interchangeable in case a houri catches a cold), hoping the deficiencies in choreography or choruses will be forgiven, even go unnoticed by all who come to marvel at the spectacle (no less needy—given the lack of a decent minimum wage—of constant euphoria to compensate their poor diets), drunk on folliculin, gleaming white thighs licked by the flames of perfectly synced instincts, two lines of chorus girls converge on the stage, swaying their necks towards the black hole where the audience is steaming up, shifting their limbs more exuberantly on that side than the other, taking one little step forward, a shorter one back, repeating the routine and—as in a children's game—approaching center stage, where, before any catastrophe or collision or coming together of a welter of bodies drowns everything, the superstar, screaming, surging from another (surprising, though not unexpected) angle, raising her arms as if to fly or swim into the void, sealed in silver foil or fish scales, draws all the beams of light that were shining languidly on the chaotic stage and is now the focus of all that brightness, her glowing splendor dazzling the eyes of all those in the front rows attempting to see her as she is.

"How lovely!" says the mother, pressing her elbow into the side of the fiancé, who tightens his grip on the arm of her most beautiful daughter, for the moment bereft of seductive wiles, of public praise, brilliance, of nudity in its starkest form, who presses her shoulder against that of her fiancé, who bought the tickets, who smells his fiancée, takes her arm, touches it, and feels the mother's elbow dig in when she says "How lovely," and she, the mother, also projects herself on the stage, as if she were the one casting off the dingy garb of daily life and audaciously calling out to lascivious males, "Desire me," the one who succeeds, once fulfilled, in achieving the unattainable goal for which the female body was made, towards which it endlessly aspires, despite all the obstacles and opposition woven around it by a tottering edifice of culture that's been so often fractured and tarted up.

"Don't look at her like that!" Dorita says, placing a cold hand on the neck of her fiancé, whom a maternal elbow jabs from the other side and who tries to look at his fiancée and can't conceive why she's so upset when she says "Don't look at her," when all he sees on stage is a fat woman with massive hips whose only virtue, apart from approximating a perfect sphere, is the fair effort she makes at contorting her body, shaking so her hips which seem not part of a live, elastic body, but more a metal item inserted into a device invented to demonstrate the basic laws of physics, while all he can see in his fiancée's eyes is a glow reflected from the wretched lights of the stage, where florid women now form rosettes and jump this way and that, when someone cracks a joke and everyone guffaws and the maternal body's fidgets irritate him as does the laughter of his fiancée, who has rapidly forgotten her chaste, jealous, puritanical, or simply mocking "Don't look" because laughter is sane rather than sinful.

If the honest people—jam-packed, sweating, oppressing and oppressed, eating peanuts and almonds, crackling their crushed toffee or potato chip packet paper (a sound to puncture the bliss of sentimental spinsters in local fleapits, though here it blends harmoniously with the sound of brass and strings surging from the pit summoned by an equally sweaty maestro towards whose pink pate the superstar smiles her finest)—want the triumphant coronation of the polychrome image of the woman (one of *them*, practically one of *them*), with her fleshy pink thighs and pale yellow legs, swaying to syncopated music written by composers so adroit at interpreting the collective soul of the masses, consumed by memories of a famous feudal fable of rabble-rousing infantas fanning themselves and naked duchesses posing for the palettes of plebeian painters, it's so slavering gents (in proscenium boxes, stalls, and private rooms in nearby taverns) worship her and decide she is indeed the very same female so lustfully hunted down and abducted by a brawny Manolo from a candlelit dance floor, then dragged to palace stables for the delectation of kings playing cards with their journeymen, so the honest people may forget their alienations and, fired in the innermost fibers of their proud yet deferential souls, confess quietly—though utterly sincerely—"Long live our chains!"[35]

The people's love, for those who love and understand it, is love that's not bought, not traded, but simply rapture as befits love that is the genuine item: it isn't prostituted love but matrimonial love, backed by the most ancient institutions, blessed by the requisite number of tonsured males, and displayed as an example of coexistence and decorum, of balance and unmitigated peace. Why attempt to find a needle in a Madrid haystack if the lucid lyrics from the superstar's red lips spill out grandiose yarns (rumbala, rumbala), as she shimmies her fish scales: "Eugenia de Montijo, make me happy with your love, I for my part will make you empress of France," and nobody can ever think to treat as purchase, deal, or barter a transaction conducted in such an elevated poetic tone, so hopefully copulative, such a blissful birthing of Suez canals and dividends paying 318 percent?[36] That this is the image of the woman who used the same arts that any woman of the people could deploy if she were given the opportunity to triumph over the descendant of the eagle of war and destroyer of all the libraries that the venal ministers of Carlos III had distributed across the hide of the bull, comforting, entertaining, and avenging a defeated people painted by the deaf man by the light of a street lamp, a people who, amid Mamluk after Mamluk, spat bright red blood on the same squares above which small white clouds scurry today,[37] is cause for consolation and a sacred sign of the establishment of Civitas Dei over Felipe's barren heath.

That's why the jolly duty policeman can laugh with the people at a lewd joke to make a highborn soul laugh who refuses to be fired up by stories that are past history: that's why the secret policeman also splits his sides, conscience clear, knowing full well that when he laughs, criminals, police, and even judges (if the stiff stays of their corsets allow them to stoop in the difficult maneuver required to sit in these would-be stalls) are simply Christlike bearers of human joy who hate no one and refuse to dwell on the awkward gestures and howls of the ham-fisted dancer, clinging instead to what the dancer represents and proclaims, a message of peace, happiness, and harmony across the ages; that's why the ruthless censor does nothing, nor did he ever intend to, against such explosions of popular, triumphant joy and is of the opinion that the motley audience is quite educated enough to know that illegitimate children exist, that these misfortunes happen in a way that's common knowledge, that children don't arrive from Paris and that, at the end of the day, the uncle of the rascal responsible will bequeath an inheritance to the blessed offspring, so the shameless father of the daughter, all the more delightful for having been raped, can loll back in armchairs to which the people—and why not shout this from the rooftops?—sometimes has access along with cigars that originally, according to the blind but divine laws behind the distribution of earthly wealth, were the preserve of the seducer, his friends and quite possibly his chauffeur or trusted servant.

"He's such fun!" said the mother breathlessly. "This fellow is driving me mad," referring to an elderly species of wire doll, who jumped in the air, fell and jumped again, grimaced, looked vacant, and finally gestured obscenely as if to say anything goes, as long as he could grab, if only for a second, the monuments of flesh that, dressed like well-to-do young ladies, were perambulating across the boards, he'd put up with the sneers, the slaps, the laughter, and the humiliating kick from the pointy black shoe of the aristocrat who owned all the items traced on butts bony from so much past hunger. Because *he* was clever and knew how to play the game, knowing what was strength and what was weakness, knowing which side you needed to be on, and had forgotten long, long ago—or had never known—the perils that came with hindering or being a drag on this happy process of adaptation. If the most violent laughter, if the most genuine guffaws (uniting men and women, police and pickpockets, members of the honorable claque and well-heeled shopkeepers, university students and electricians working for Standard, honest married couples and mistresses on their night off) exploded at the precise moment the truth of this way of thinking and the wisdom of that wily scarecrow were demonstrated, it's maybe because the ingenious inventors of this type of show had discovered that female licentiousness glitters most against a backdrop of male malevolence. Or else because it's only in the malevolence of one man, against a scenario of sequin-covered flesh, that can one can identify and greet like an old female friend the malevolence of an entire people.

Pedro too, yes, Pedro too, pressed by the mother's elbow, squeezed against his fiancée's arm (so firm, so smooth, the softest hassock whereon to rest your head), surrounded by the people in front, behind, over, beneath, facing the people mesmerized by the spectacle, under the people ululating to the distant gods, in front of the shameless people in the back rows who don't pay but shout, laugh, and clap, smelling the sweat filling the theater like a single cloud, laughing and hearing his own guffaws both along the external, aerial route, where they were drowned out by the communal, collective guffaw, and through his own bones, his hard skull and his encephalic mass curdled by studious neurons, and hearing his own slower, gruffer guffaw, laughter that wearied the moment it began.

As old Dora had insisted he take them—although he didn't feel like it at all—he had to knuckle down and escort them to the fair. As if *he* were in the mood for a fair. But there was no way out. She'd insisted they simply *must* go, because she never left the house, let alone at night; she said he should act graciously towards his womenfolk, and he did. It was a cool night and Dora was very anxious or acting as if she was, feeling squeamish about the pretty little flower of a daughter that barbarian in white would take from her one of these days, and then never again would she accompany the mother who'd suckled her on her tit and loved her more than the apple of her eyes, if one might employ such a term. But that's what children are, uncaring ingrates, though she hadn't been, she'd sacrificed her future and wealthy suitors galore who'd wanted to carry her off when she was a budding beauty, blossoming and gloriously bursting forth, desired and pursued by the dogs of men who trailed after her, their tongues hanging out, but, come what may, through thick and thin, against wind and tide, she had struggled to keep herself intact for her beloved daughter, whom she hadn't loved any the less for being the fruit of a silly slip, because we all know how tender is the fruit of forbidden love. She refused to dwell on that demon dancer or the time she kicked over the traces and Rhum Negrita had led to such a lunatic veering off the rails. They heard the pleasant buzz from the fair and saw groups heading frantically in that direction on a coolish night kept at bay by white silk scarves, tightish jackets, and peaked caps pulled down hard. Some women were fat and big butted, sleeves rolled up, absolutely up for it, draping silk-flecked Manila shawls over their shoulders, the sight of which saddened her even more because she'd not worn hers, the one the deceased colonel had brought from islands that were so rightfully ours, the one adorned with birds of paradise. Those shawls hung in the glass cabinet in the reception room and were so delicate they could easily rip, but if she'd donned one carefully, taking every care, everyone would have thought how awfully, awfully well it suited her. Dorita, the happy bride-to-be, clung to her fiancé, and he thought it was a joy to be with her like that, glancing now and then, as they walked under streetlamps, at her little face one could have mistaken for a Virgin from Seville or any of those holy images molded by the fingers of long-departed sculptors who knew what they were doing when they fashioned life-size, soft-tinted angels with glinting, waxlike faces, because lovely Dorita was so virginal in that manner, though a tad soiled, her waist swaying by his elbow, brushing against it, and making him dream of those evenings when he had watched her rocking on her chair after dinner, her svelte legs peeping out from under her skirt. He'd been in no mood to take them to the fair, but her mother had insisted, so what else could he do but escort them to that fenced-off precinct where happiness is permitted by municipal regulations, pay the entrance fee, look towards the lighted area for vacant chairs by an open-air café and buy a slice of coconut for Dorita, who fancied one. He stood and stared at her as her healthy, strong, gleaming white teeth chomped on the coconut her juice-dribbling mouth was chewing. She smiled as she savored the rare pleasure of endless mastication till the coconut slipped down her throat, inside her long swan's neck, a long, beautiful neck he had kissed. The mother asked the waiter for horchata, as if it were summer, and the young man said no way, there was no horchata because it wasn't summer, it was too cold for horchata, why didn't she order a Mahou with dressed black olives or even the prawns, which weren't past it, but as there was no horchata, she ignored him and said it had to be soda pop. For she could clearly remember, and had no reason to dismiss the memory, what had happened to her when, as a result of a mindless mother's negligence—a mother who, unlike her, was far from irreproachable—she had consumed immoderate quantities of alcohol dangerously laden with whatever some devil had put in her Rhum Negrita. The poor musicians, who with union permission would sometimes perform on the stage in that fair and next morning would turn up late at the office, a detail humanely ignored by their bosses, and enjoy a restorative morning nap that's always pleasing to birds of the night, struck up mambo music, out-of-fashion boleros, and rumbas unrecognizable beneath the Iberian riffs that are endemic to small-town combos that play on summer nights on threshing floors, the flattest surfaces to be found in Castilian municipalities, which, smelling of trampled straw and squashed meadow saffron, shape the gamboling of couples and lull the contingent of daydreaming civil guards in attendance to ensure the partying is peaceful. But here one noted a higher quality of dance; the citizenry's well-shod feet tripped the light fantastic not over a threshing floor but over firm flagstones. It was then that Dynamite, the man in black, walked through the door and surveyed the scene without espying worthwhile prey until his eyes came to rest on the woman he was after, one he must have already known by sight, for, if not, it was hard to account for his wary attitude. When her mother said, Go dance, my children, Dorita felt exhilarated in the chill of a night where she'd been sitting at a table quaffing soda pop with a fiancé who didn't say a peep. He was the type who could barely dance and worse still, if he had done, it wasn't over uneven flagstones, but sporadically, ages ago, when as a student he'd danced in underground hops where men gained entrance and a drink for five pesetas and girls got in for nothing and no drink. Let's give it a try, he told himself, in any case, I don't have much choice and it will warm me up. Dorita's mouth still tasted of coconut and she wafted a whiff of coconut in his direction, thrilled that she'd finally landed this handsome fiancé. Because if her mother had managed to give her only a father, she had taken one step further, maybe because she was more virtuous, or maybe it was a concession granted by a destiny that guides the paths of illegitimate daughters of dubious descent whose pockets were empty and whose pretty bodies ensured they could forgo an inevitable decline. And they danced, unaware of their bodies' relation to the other whirling dancers, locked in a single capsule that spun and spun as they moved around the orchestra like a couple of conjoined planets or twin satellites, mutually intertwining, eyes only for each other. He placed his hand around her waist, felt her malleable, quasi-vegetable, but most human midriff, while she placed a hand on his hot, manly neck in that zone where a barber's skills reveal a degree of naked bone and muscle that speaks to the intellect and strength of the male who's been hooked, which is why women like to put a hand there and feel the virile sap seep down the conduit where the image of herself gives man his potency and where the nutritious juices ascend that allow him to obsess about her and desire her. Thus infatuated, they were convinced the phenomenon was their purely private pleasure and could never be experienced as intensely by any of the other couples, a passion surging from desire they shared body and soul. However, that wasn't the case, because the blessed people were sweating, gripped tight, huddled, fighting the imminence of a death that threatens us all, only too conscious of the relentless nature of the worm endlessly drilling our flesh as we pretend not to hear it.

It's *schottische*, a *schottische*, she said, singing in his ear words from her lips that smelled of coconut and the heat of desire, *Madrid, Madrid, Madrid, en México se piensa mucho en ti*, which he thought meant I love you, I adore you, you're the center of my life and for me you are the one and only and I cling to you here, yours forever and ever. While the poor musicians, those humble clerks, played, never daring to perform as top-dollar musicians do, laughing, jumping, and swaying their hips so entertainingly, no, they played solemn-faced like musicians at a funeral, as impecunious musicians should, and not even the man with the maracas, or whatever you call that rattle-like item, not even he, and this is amazing, dared to smile even though his instruments were clamoring that he should, but he too was po-faced and grave, respectful and mournful, shaking his spherical instruments and looking for all the world like a gentleman at the burial of the count of Orgaz.[38] The honest people for once were permitted to enjoy themselves, and held on to those whom luck had sent their way, a small crumb of comfort to help them find solace from their labors and days that inexorably ground them down, trying the best they could to act as if they were having a ball and could forget the beady-eyed matrons watching their daughters swirl with a cheek-to-cheek togetherness that mutual solace demanded. And motionless in their midst, lost in thought, the man in black looked on, keenly, yet self-absorbed, a cigarette hanging from his lower lip. Shooting ranges had also been installed in imaginative vein by the local authorities to bring a little relief to the lower classes, so nobody could say the honorable town hall wasn't aware how essential it was to keep the masses amused, because they too have feelings and, for Christ's sake, ought to be allowed to let their hair down from time to time. So now their moment of ecstasy was at an end, Pedro and Dorita made their way to the shooting range, leaving her mother to enjoy her soda pop and wallow in nostalgia for her genuine Manila shawl, and Pedro asked Dorita if she wanted to shoot and she said she didn't, that he should, and he said he didn't have a clue how, and she said so what, he should try his hand, because shooting at close targets fulfils, at a lower level, the same erotic-sexual function as hunting antelopes in darkest Africa, so an absent-present female, lightly clothed or lightheaded, can admire the trophy one day, sipping a glass of champagne, supine on the bearskin rug in the drawing room where his trophies aim their countless horns upwards, showing us the true way to heaven. Her fiancé grabbed the air gun that fired fat lead pellets from a very short range at big, slow-moving wooden balls, and it was inevitable he would hit the odd one, to the jubilant delight of the female beside him who gazed awestruck at the virile powers of her male whose fire stick takes out frightful enemies in defense of a distant, coveted cradle and the pink, moist lump she'll put there when the time comes, a lump that pees, screams, and consumes milk from its victim's body. Dorita wondered at the splendid marksmanship of the fiancé she'd landed, stodgy one minute, full of prowess the next, and at the fantastic time she was having, she'd thought she'd be bored stiff because going to a fair with your mother as a third wheel is something nobody did nowadays, you know, it was completely démodé. So irritating too. And then they came to the heaviest hammer, which you had to bang down to make a metal wedge shoot up a pole, and if it hit the very, very top, it clinked and a light flashed, and the perpetrator would flush with pride, considering how high, how very high up the little red light was. Whack it, whack it, said Dorita, whack it hard. I'm not strong enough, said he, thinking for a moment he should leave it because something told him he could never whack it hard enough, and he ought not leave her completely alone in order to grab the mallet in both hands, amid a crowd of sinister folk who weren't like him, to whom she didn't belong, who weren't part of her as they were of him, but she said, Come on, don't be chicken, and he just had to take heed, while the man in black, a man of the people, stationed himself by her side, though not touching her, a dead butt stuck on his lip, looking at him, not at her, smelling the sweat she'd worked up while dancing, a mixture of scents that drowned out the coconut on her breath, and watching the gleaming white teeth her ever-present smile displayed to the outside world. A pity there are no merry-go-rounds, don't you agree? she said, after he'd struck the device futilely with all his nonexistent might, achieving a derisory result, whilst a moment later, that sinister little man, using only his left hand, rapidly twisting his agile body, lit up the red light, as if he were sending an alarm signal out over the poverty-stricken antics in that fairground swarming with ant-like humans, less drunk than they needed to be to attain the threshold of the only happiness within their reach. And they continued their nighttime meandering past a daydreaming mother they'd practically forgotten, happy finally to be together, pointlessly drifting this way and that. They came to the wafer seller. And bought wafers after spinning the wheel, where 13 or some other number came up. And then came to a strange hut where a man was making candy floss on a machine that spun round and Dorita said, I want some, I want some, so he bought some and said, Here you are. And they reached a spot where a little old woman with the tiniest of carts was—yet again—selling coconut and Dorita wanted another slice and he bought one and gave it to her and Dorita nibbled that tropical substance. It will make you sick, said the man in black, snatching the slice from her hand. Her fiancé was looking in the other direction and didn't notice and she nudged closer to him, but said nothing and stared at the man in black who'd snatched her slice of coconut. Look, they've got churros over there, he said, frantic to bring her more gifts, I'll go get you some. Because a big crowd stood between him and the frying pan on the only proper stand, a real success whose products were being eagerly consumed. Young girls walked past with churros they'd finally managed to buy, strutting their stuff and raising a churro to their pink lips now and then. Other laboring men and women, cheek by jowl with stout local matrons, were also trying to collar the in-demand product, holding their hands out to the man in white who was scattering white powder from a big sugar pot into paper cones laden with pleasure for humble mortals. Let me go and see if I can get some, he said, starting to make inroads into the throng, but despite his every effort he was still a distance away and couldn't even raise a coin-clasping hand in a silent expression of his consumerist passion. Then Dynamite grabbed Dorita's hand and pulled her away, saying, Let's dance, my lovely. Dorita shouted but nobody noticed because, quite frankly, a whole lot of shouting was going on at that time of night in the fenced-off municipal precinct. Who are you? asked Dorita and Dynamite replied, Shut up, shut your mouth, sticking a bare blade into her side, a sure thrust he'd tried more than once, and while Dorita fell to the ground and was gradually surrounded by a pool of bubbling blood that looked black in the night, he made his exit, not waiting to see the expression on Pedro's face when he came back with his big cone of churros to discover that revenge had been exacted, that all pledges must be honored, that no debt goes unpaid.

No, no, no, it's not like this. Life isn't like this, it doesn't happen like this in real life. He who does the deed doesn't pay the price. He who dies by the sword doesn't kill by the sword. He who makes the first move doesn't make the second. An eye for an eye. A glass eye for an empty red socket. A tooth for a tooth. Gold and celluloid fillings for a toothless loser. The fury of the avenging gods. The poisoned darts of their wrath. Not seven but seventy times seven. Cava's sin also had to be paid for.[39] The braggart river Tagus spelled out the words *mene, mene, tekel* on the wall for the king to see. A man by the name of Goethe zealously studied the motives behind the sacrifice of Iphigenia, and once he'd perfectly understood them, he strenuously worked them into a tragedy. He who does the deed pays the price. Not always he who does it: he who thinks he did it or the one who it is rumored did it or the one who succeeded in persuading those around him that he did it when he wrapped himself in a traitor's black cloak, pale face, sallow gaze, baleful smile. Man or wolf? Werewolf? The wolf who was a man on nights with a full moon? The savage wolf whose maw is four times broader than a man's? Werewolf for a man? The fight against dangerous predators who descend on valleys and ravage flocks. Man is the measure of all things: measure a wolf's mouth against a man's and you'll find it's four times larger, and the palate so soft and pink in a man's (and woman's) mouth, the back of which is especially tender and is usually called velum in both sexes because it is so soft and likes to hide whereas in wolves it is menacingly black. "In this I shall imitate the sun that allows vile poisonous clouds to hide its beauty from the world in order (when it's happy to be itself once again) to make itself all the more admired by forging a path through the filthy clouds that seemed to choke it. Thus, when I leave this life and pay my debts, I will exceed the hopes that might have been placed in me." But it beggars belief that things should have happened like that, so soon, tonight, so abruptly.

If I don't find a taxi, I'll be late. Who might the Príncipe Pío be?[40] Prince, prince, in principle, it's the beginning of the end, the beginning of evil. In principle, I'm at the beginning, it's all over, I'm finished and I'm leaving. I'm going to begin all over again. I can't finish what I began. Taxi! So what? Let him see me in this state. I mean, what do I care? Matías, Matías, or whoever. How will I find a taxi? There are no true friends. Goodbye friends. Taxi! At last. To Príncipe Pío. That's also where I began. I arrived in Príncipe Pío, I'm leaving from Príncipe Pío. I arrived alone, I leave alone. I arrived without a cent, I'm leaving without a . . . What a lovely day, what a beautiful sky! It's still not cold. That woman! I thought it might have worked for a moment, I can't get her out of my head. Of course, she's the same as the other one. Why so, why is it I can't tell one from the other now they're dead, buried on top of each other in the same hole: in this autopsy too. What do they hope to find out? So many autopsies; what's the point, if they find nothing? They don't know why they open them up: myth, superstition, a congregation of corpses, in the belief that virtue resides within, animists, they're looking for a secret and yet they won't let those of us who might find something take a look, but so what, what's the point, he already told me I wasn't gifted and he's probably right, I'm not. The impression she made on me. Always thinking about women. All down to women. If only I'd devoted myself to rats. But what was I ever going to achieve? If that's how things are ordained. There's nothing you can change. We know what we must learn, we must learn to prescribe sulfates. Pleurisy, pericarditis, pancreatitis, pruritus of the anus. Let's see what life's like there. You can hunt. Hunting is healthy. You can take a double-barreled gun like old Miguel, the man with the scarf, and bang-bang, dead. There are lots of hares because so little land is cultivated. Game abounds in the wild. I'll go hunting, whenever there's a national holiday and on summer afternoons, when the sun goes down between the stubble and the rockroses, I'll hunt hares. Partridges in stubble fields, plump as a woman, after the harvest; dropping onto the stubble, hunted on horseback. Partridges that can't run because they're stuffed with grain, and old Miguel catches them with his hand when they're out of breath. Tasty partridge in partridge sauce that's thick, hot, and brown, and peppered with herbs And frogs' legs; no need for bait to catch frogs, just a red rag on a length of thread, they flick out their retractable tongues, put it in their mouth with the rag and it's a done deed; frogs' legs like chicken breast. Delicious! Little round white legs; over the last ten years I've only seen frogs to study mesenteric circulation live, red corpuscles pale as black-eyed peas in the capillary mesh and the animal stripped naked, no skin, no hair, no feathers, gutted before you get there, a real San Martín's slaughter,[41] a naked animal looking like a dead person before it's killed, only the black lentils circulating through the venous mesh of the mesentery, vivisection. That's what it is, vivisection, English suffragettes protesting, exactly the same, exactly as if that's what vivisection was. They reckon they'd be just like frogs if they were stripped naked; Florita, on the other hand, the naked little flower in the hovel, the tiny flower, the tiny bloom the old woman called her, the second little flower that... ugh! I'm off, I'll have a ball. Diagnosing pleurisy, peritonitis, heart murmurs, colic, gastric fever, and one day the spinster schoolmistress's barbiturate suicide. Girls on fiesta days walking in front of the procession, behind the pallium, flushed and chubby cheeked, looking out of the corner of their eyes to where I am, disgusted to watch them walk by, looking at their legs, sitting in the casino with two, five, seven, fourteen gentlemen who are playing chess and who hold a high opinion of me because of my superior intellect and top mental caliber. We're here, Príncipe Pío. Yes, upstairs. Then you go down in a gratis elevator powered from underneath by a winch someone seems to be turning... Buy a Maigret for the train, I've not read a thriller for a while, fancy, me reading a thriller! Why are all the porters from Galicia, what might a porter earn, where does he find all his strength? They simply have to employ Galicians or Asturians because Andalusians or Manchegans wouldn't have the muscle. You need strength. They are level-headed, smiling, unctuous, humble, they know they are fated to be porters, know it only too well, and don't pretend to be anything else but porters inside or outside the station, and carry as many items as they can. All they need do is count one, two, three, four, five, six items and this bag madam will carry herself because it contains the crown jewels, the royal crown of the king of spades, why do I come out with such nonsense? I should despair more. The crown of laurel and myrtle, glorious symbol of the Olympic Games, on the podium and raising an arm in the Roman salute that was later resurrected. Receiving the congratulations from the king of Sweden, so white, so pale, so tall, who's never felt the real sun, who doesn't care one jot about science, but that's why it's his job to be king. But why don't I despair more? The long hands of the king of Sweden, his crown of myrtle correctly braided and given a permanent wave. The fat buttocks of the porter who never washes, who sits on a bench, drops by a tavern, and washes down one glass of red after another, like Amador with those hugely eloquent thick lips of his, the man of destiny, Amador, another Galician, the vivisection porter, Amador-Cassandra, ears born not to hear, slow-witted brains created to curse those who carry you. Amador, Amador, your name's ill fated. Am I going to laugh at myself? The man who's been destroyed, the man not allowed to do what he should be doing, who in the name of destiny was told: "Enough is enough!" and dispatched to Príncipe Pío with references, a stethoscope, and a manual for diagnosing the anal pruritus of village maidens. Scatological, pornographic, always thinking of dirty filth. Stupid, stupid, the buttocks of the porter who effortlessly carries one, two, three, four, five, six items to my compartment and places them in the rack. Why a rack? And I, without a hint of despair, because I'm a hollow man, because they have wiped me with chammy and cleaned out my insides, given me a good soak and left me to ferment, hanging by a thread in a kind of anatomical museum of the living in order to showcase the hygienic and empyreumatic, sterilizing and dissecting, righteous and wrathful qualities of the man of the mesa, of that manner of man of the mesa who made history, who built a world, who, starting from the plains of La Bureba,[42] began to pronounce Latin with Basque phonetics and later added aspirate aitches transformed into *j* under the Moors, who constituted a battering ram that traveled the world, rocking this way and that, and now, withered and worm-eaten, the man of the mesa becomes jerky, put out to dry like me to become jerky in the fair winds of Castile, where the idea of what the future might be disappeared three and a half centuries ago and the future is now only the worm-eaten carcass the body of an ox becomes when it's put out to dry and its flesh becomes jerky and I like jerky and there are men like me who gradually get used to eating jerky with a glass of wine and prefer it to caviar and herrings and the foie gras that comes from the Landes. Woe betide those of us not equipped for blissful ecstasy! Who will help us? How will we fix it to enter those innermost, recondite, deep Mansions where we must live?[43] I will look at Castilian girls, plump in the leg, like corn-fattened partridges, girls that, like partridges, you can savor with your teeth and mouth or else strike to the ground where they lie still and don't squirm like obscene worms, but stay catatonic, *sich tot stellen*, their reflexes immobilized, across the whole range of the animal world, insects, toads, gazelles, hemolytic entamoeba, motionless, festering virgins, awaiting. But why don't I despair more? Why do I let myself be gelded? The phallic man in the red cap with its red-pointed top, endlessly fertile when it comes to moving in straight lines, promenading proudly with his large red-cephalic foreskin, cock in hand, with his standard furled, endowed with manifold attributes that unleash the giant erect organ that will drill into the womb of mountains, while I let myself be gelded. Something does explain why I let myself be gelded and why I don't even scream when they do it. It's common knowledge that when the Turks castrated their slaves on the beaches of Anatolia in order to create eunuchs for their harems, they buried them in the sand, and their cries of pain, protest, or farewell to their virility were heard miles away, night and day, by sailors on the high seas. It was an effective method to ensure asepsis, burying them waist deep in the sand, a clean, absorbent substance that eliminated secretions and putrefaction thanks to iodine and other carminative sea salts. Much better is present practice, as a result of which not only is there no screaming, but there's no pain and consequently it is no longer any use to unwary mariners as an acoustic lighthouse. Not so now, we live in the age of anesthesia, we live in an age when things are almost noiseless. The bomb doesn't kill through noise but through alpha radiation that is in itself silent, or with deuton rays, gamma rays, or cosmic rays, all more silent than a garotte. They also castrate like X-rays. As for me, in the end, what *is* the point? It is a time of silence. The best, most efficient machine is the one that makes no noise. This train makes a noise. It goes trickety-track, and is no supersonic airplane, of the sort that travel through the stratosphere, where you can build a house of cards at a height of sixty-five thousand feet—not a single vibration. Down here we crawl along and eventually make it to the place where we must stand and wait in silence for the years to pass and then go silently to the place where all the little flowers of this world go. But I feel I don't despair enough, I feel a coiled spring of pleasure in this archaic device that gallops and gallops and gallops like an animal, its hypnotic trickety-track in sync with the rhythm of an electric encephalogram, harmonizing like tribes in Africa, dancing and dancing to the festive nighttime beat of their tom-toms, those lucky people enter a state of ecstasy we don't come near, even in our dreams. If only I could enter a trance, if only I could fall to the ground and kick my feet before the itinerant priest I could be converted, engage with the necessary brainwash and turn into a hunter of plump partridges and submissive village girls. But we aren't blacks, we aren't blacks, blacks jump, laugh, shout, and vote to elect their representatives to the UN. We aren't blacks or Indians or people from underdeveloped countries. We are strips of jerky hung out to dry on rusty wire in the pure, pure air of the mesa, till they have their silent moment of ecstasy. Tricketytracktricketytracktricketytracktricketytrack: you can make rhythm, it's only a matter of giving it a form, a gestalt structure, you can get different rhythms depending on how you lounge back to listen, a rhythm every two, every three, or every four and then repeat it, or another rhythm you might see in the optic figures in a wineglass or the profile of a face. Morbid rationalism, what do I care about rhythms, figures, and gestalt if they're gelding me alive? And why don't I despair? It's a relief to be a eunuch, it's soothing to be devoid of testicles, it's a pleasure despite being castrated to breathe the fresh air and feel the sun while silently turning into jerky. Why despair if you are quietly turning into jerky while roses are . . . still roses . . . ugh. You can hunt partridges, you can hunt the fattest of partridges when it's the harvest . . . you can play chess in the casino. You've always liked chess. If you haven't played chess more often, it's because you've never had time. Remember how you would employ the Philidor defense. Chess is a joy, besides, if you're not despairing, it will be so easy to get back into the habit now you're not. It will be so easy, you just have to take it easy at the start because, if you get stressed, you might reopen the wound. Take it easy. Then a woman will come, a pretty woman will come to your consultancy and she'll say she's suffering from pruritus of the anus. You'll give her a diagnosis, and prescribe what she needs. She'll say the new guy is so nice. You may have to wait for that woman to come, but it will soon seem like no time at all. You'll get over it. Then they'll say, He's better than the last guy. This new guy's better. There will be some who won't, who won't, who'll continue to think the old guy was better or feel embarrassed about leaving him. All to the good, or you'd have no time to hunt partridges. So you stay like that for a while, say nothing, bad-mouth nobody. It's all about keeping calm. Not letting on. Soon everybody will see how generous, clean, and knowledgeable you are. There is this barren heath, a barren heath like skin stretched over a skeleton. At this time of year, there are the gold-red trees of autumn, there is only dry soil, a masculine landscape that's never been castrated, from which who knows what new stones can be found if the earth is disturbed. Round granite, caressed so long by the breeze it's become smooth and round, and gold stones, black stones, red stones. There'll be lizards. No, not yet. They sleep in the autumn. Blue mountains are approaching, soon to be drilled by the train, mountains that seem to hide a secret. It's there, it's better than nothing. There's hope. The Moors are still on the other side. One raid and we'll throw them out, another and they'll go to the next mountains, repopulating, repopulating, burdening the earth with children, with men, with women who give birth, swamping it until they're all skin and bones and are so hungry they look like strips of jerky, deport them and then you'll see, then you'll see what they do. But if there's nowhere to deport them to, what *do* we do. I'm here. I don't know why I think. I could fall asleep. I'm a laughingstock. I despair because I don't despair. But I could also not be despairing because I'm despairing because I don't despair. What's the point of that tongue twister now? I reckon I'd like to say it to someone. They'd think I'm smart and wouldn't have to ask me how I came to be so smart, because why would they... And why the hell would anyone care if I'm smart or not, or if the whore who gave birth to me was smart. Idiot! Once again I'm thinking and I enjoy thinking, as if I feel proud to think what I'm thinking is brilliant... ugh. The sun is coming as peacefully as ever into my compartment and I see the outline of the monastery.[44] Its five towers pointing upwards that couldn't give a fig. It doesn't move. Its stones are lit up by the sun or beaten by the snow and they couldn't give a fig. There it stands, pinched, squat, imitating the griddle where they say that san lorenzo of our sins was vivisected, that sanlorencenzaccio you know so well, it's me, *that* lorenzo, the lorenzo you turn over because I'm already done on one side, like a sardine, lorenzo, like a poor, humble sardine, I've been toasted, the sun toasts, keeps toasting me dry, making jerky of me, sanlorenzo was a macho, he didn't scream, he didn't scream, he stayed silent while pagan Torquemadas toasted him, he stayed silent and all he said—history only remembers what he said, I'm done on this side, turn me over... and his executioner turned him over out of a simple desire for symmetry.

NOTES

1. Santiago Ramón y Cajal (1852–1934), the man in the photo, was the first Spaniard to be awarded the Nobel Prize in Physiology or Medicine, in recognition of his work on the structure of the brain. In 1922 he founded the Institute for Biological Research in Madrid. His hundreds of drawings of brain cells influenced the surrealist painters, and a selection of his illustrations toured the United States in 2017 in the exhibition "The Beautiful Brain."
2. This reflects one of the most famous lines in Spanish literature, from the opening of Jorge Manrique's *Stanzas on the Death of His Father*, which he wrote as the funeral eulogy to his father in 1476: "Our lives are the rivers that flow into the sea which is death."
3. A German word meaning "cheated" or "deceived."
4. Allusion to a line in Lorca's *Libro de poemas*: "Robust, graceful / like a young peasant / leaping across / the river."
5. The equestrian statue of Philip III in the Plaza Mayor, the square in the center of Hapsburg Madrid.
6. The years after the end of the Spanish Civil War when the economy suffered from Franco's policy of economic autarchy.
7. The war between Spain and the United States in 1898 when Spain lost Cuba, the Philippine Islands, and Puerto Rico, interpreted at the time by many as the final disaster in Spain's loss of empire, and the nadir in the nation's decline.
8. Spain's war in the Rif Valley against the forces of Abd-el-Krim, 1921–26. Spain's defeat in the 1921 Battle of Annual was seen as its biggest military defeat, and its "second" disaster.
9. Atlético de Madrid played in the stadium that was built in the Tetuán area in 1923.
10. Migrants from Murcia, Almería, and Andalusia were referred to as *coreanos* (Koreans), for a period after the Korean War started in 1950.

11. Café Gijón and Café Gambrinus were popular places for writers and writers to meet in central Madrid to discuss literature and philosophy. Martín-Santos and younger, more progressive writers like Carmen Maria Gaite and Juan Benet favored the Gambrinus, as they preferred Camus, Sartre and the existentialists to Ortega y Gasset.
12. The beach in San Sebastián popular with the smart set.
13. Garcilaso de la Vega was a leading Renaissance poet, but the specific reference is to a literary magazine, *Garcilaso*, published between 1943 and 1946, that propounded a return to classical forms that were out of touch with the grim realities of life under the dictatorship.
14. Ultraísmo was a school of writing that rejected the modernism of poets like Rubén Darío and advocated, in the style of Italian futurism, the use of metaphors in lines that did without usual punctuation, drew on scientific and technological innovation, and rejected long-winded rhetoric. The movement began in Madrid in the Café Colonial and was taken to Argentina by Borges.
15. Ramón Gómez de la Serna (1888–1963) was an avant-garde writer active in Madrid's literary cafés in the 1920s and '30s. He developed a style of writing called "greguerías," enigmatic sentences larded with metaphors and allusions. He was championed by Valery Larbaud in France. He sided with Franco but went to live in Argentina in 1933.
16. An allusion to a well-known poem by Juan Ramón Jiménez: "Touch it no more, such is the rose" (*Piedra y cielo*, 1918).
17. José Vidal Beneyto (1927–2010), known as Pepín Vidal, was a Spanish philosopher and sociologist, an anti-Francoist, and a founder of the daily newspaper *El País*. As a young man he joined the Opus Dei, a pro-Franco repressive Catholic organization, but he left it in 1947 and joined Martín-Santos and other radical left-wing intellectuals in organizing events and congresses against the dictatorship. Perhaps "from Egypt" refers to his freedom after being in the Opus, likening it to the Israelites escaping slavery in Egypt.
18. A slurred version of "Ainsi soit-il," French for "amen"; literally, "so be it."
19. Hegel or Heidegger.
20. A reference to a line from a sonnet by Lupercio Leonardo de Argensola (1559–1613), Spanish poet and dramatist: "Terrifying image of death / cruel dream, disturb my breast no more."
21. A saint who symbolizes the purity of youth. Born into an Italian aristocratic family, he became an ascetic and Jesuit and died in 1598 at the age of twenty-three while caring for victims of the plague in Rome.

22. A verse from an ode by Horace: "Postumus, Postumus, the years are passing!"
23. The viaduct over the Calle de Segovia, a frequent site of death by suicide, in Madrid, city without cathedrals, lit up by the Royal Palace.
24. Women who practice fellatio or cunnilingus. *Auparishtaka* is a Sanskrit word, and chapter 9 of the *Kama Sutra*, written by Vatsyayana, is devoted to what Sir Richard Burton translates as "mouth congress."
25. The cinema where philosopher José Ortega y Gasset gave a series of twelve weekly lectures beginning on 23 November 1949, which Martín-Santos attended. The novelist parodies Ortega y Gasset's perspectivist philosophy and view of Spanish history, as well as depicting him as a fourth-rate imitation of his German masters. The later reference is to his opus, *The Rebellion of the Masses*, 1930, in which he argued for strongman leadership.
26. Two singers who performed at La Bohemia cabaret in Barcelona after the war and were a hit with their repertory of belle epoque–style songs.
27. A reference to the ceding of the Islas Carolinas to Germany by Spain in 1899, and symbolizing the way Ortega capitulates to German philosophy, itself prefiguring what Franco did in the civil war.
28. Ortega described himself as such a youth to indicate he didn't like to pontificate.
29. A neologism created by Martín-Santos, bringing together the names of Ormuzd and Ahriman, the two opposing deities of light and dark in Zoroastrianism.
30. Robert Brown, a Scottish botanist (1773–1858), best known for his descriptions of cell nuclei and discovery of the continuous motion of minute particles in solution, the Brownian motion.
31. Frederick W. Taylor (1856–1915) was an American engineer who developed theories centered on the timing of minute movements of workers in order to eliminate wasteful actions. His ideas were ruthlessly put into practice by Henry Ford and industrialists throughout the world and were refined by Charles Bedaux. Bedaux was arrested on suspicion of treason for his collaboration with the Nazis, and he committed suicide in US custody.
32. Huts in the Second Republic where shows were put on by singers and dancers for all-male audiences.
33. See note 25.
34. A reference to the novel *El Diablo cojuelo*, written by Luis Vélez

de Guevara and published in 1641, in which a student liberates a devil who then gives him a tour of Madrid, lifting the roofs of houses.

35. Crowds throughout Spain greeted the fall of the liberal government and the restoration to the throne of Fernando VII in 1823 with this cry, which became the emblematic slogan of the populace, stirred up by clerics and absolutists.
36. Eugenia de Montijo was a noblewoman of Spanish and Scottish descent who married Napoleon III and became empress of France. She embraced ultra-Catholic and absolutist ideas and hence opposed the liberal reforms that Carlos III had introduced, though she also campaigned to get the Académie Française to accept George Sand as a member and to establish equality of education for women. She went to Egypt to inaugurate the Suez Canal. This line comes from a popular song of the time. The Spanish considered her marriage to be revenge for Napoleon I's devastation of Spain.
37. An allusion to Goya's painting *El Dos de mayo, 1808*, which depicts the day when the people of Madrid rose up against the French occupiers and their Mamluk cavalry.
38. El Greco painted *El Entierro del conde Orgaz* in the Church of Santo Tomé in Toledo between 1586 and 1588. It is still exhibited in that church.
39. As the story goes, La Cava was the daughter of Count Julián, who sent her to the court of King Rodrigo, who raped her. In revenge Julián allowed the Muslim forces to enter Spain from Morocco in 708, after which they rapidly occupied most of the country.
40. The Estación del Norte was once the main station for trains arriving in Madrid from the north and the French frontier. It was popularly called Príncipe Pío, after a nearby hill named for an Italian noble, Francesco Pio di Savoia (1672–1723). His mother was Spanish and he became a leading political and military figure in Spain. He and his wife were drowned when storm waters swept their carriage into the river Manzanares.
41. November 11 is the day of San Martín, the traditional day for the slaughter of the family pig. The Spanish proverb "Every pig gets its San Martín" implies that you will always get what's coming to you.
42. An area in the northwest of the province of Burgos, near the Atapuerca Mountains, and famed to be the place where the purest Castilian emerged and was spoken. Martín-Santos reminds us how Spanish was always influenced by other languages, including Basque and Arabic.

43. *The Inner Castle* written in 1577 by Santa Teresa de Ávila, describes the seven stages through which the soul must pass in order to reach God in mystical ecstasy.
44. The Royal Monastery of San Lorenzo in El Escorial, constructed between 1563 and 1584. Philip II commissioned the architect Juan Bautista de Toledo to build this grandiose complex to be, amongst other things, a burial place for Spanish monarchs. It was laid out like a griddle to reflect the grill on which its patron, San Lorenzo, was said to have been martyred in the third century for having given the wealth of the church to the poor in Rome rather than to the Roman emperor, and Martín-Santos gives us his final words, which have made him the patron saint of chefs and comedians. The story was almost certainly given this apocryphal twist by an inventive translator of the original Latin.

OTHER NEW YORK REVIEW CLASSICS

For a complete list of titles, visit www.nyrb.com.

DANTE ALIGHIERI Purgatorio; translated by D. M. Black
CLAUDE ANET Ariane, A Russian Girl
HANNAH ARENDT Rahel Varnhagen: The Life of a Jewish Woman
OĞUZ ATAY Waiting for the Fear
DIANA ATHILL Don't Look at Me Like That
DIANA ATHILL Instead of a Letter
HONORÉ DE BALZAC The Lily in the Valley
POLINA BARSKOVA Living Pictures
ROSALIND BELBEN The Limit
HENRI BOSCO The Child and the River
ANDRÉ BRETON Nadja
DINO BUZZATI The Betwitched Bourgeois: Fifty Stories
DINO BUZZATI A Love Affair
DINO BUZZATI The Singularity
DINO BUZZATI The Stronghold
CRISTINA CAMPO The Unforgivable and Other Writings
CAMILO JOSÉ CELA The Hive
EILEEN CHANG Time Tunnel: Stories and Essays
EILEEN CHANG Written on Water
FRANÇOIS-RENÉ DE CHATEAUBRIAND Memoirs from Beyond the Grave, 1800–1815
AMIT CHAUDHURI Afternoon Raag
AMIT CHAUDHURI Freedom Song
AMIT CHAUDHURI A Strange and Sublime Address
LUCILLE CLIFTON Generations: A Memoir
RACHEL COHEN A Chance Meeting: American Encounters
COLETTE Chéri *and* The End of Chéri
E. E. CUMMINGS The Enormous Room
JÓZEF CZAPSKI Memories of Starobielsk: Essays Between Art and History
ANTONIO DI BENEDETTO The Silentiary
ANTONIO DI BENEDETTO The Suicides
HEIMITO VON DODERER The Strudlhof Steps
PIERRE DRIEU LA ROCHELLE The Fire Within
JEAN ECHENOZ Command Performance
FERIT EDGÜ The Wounded Age *and* Eastern Tales
MICHAEL EDWARDS The Bible and Poetry
ROSS FELD Guston in Time: Remembering Philip Guston
BEPPE FENOGLIO A Private Affair
GUSTAVE FLAUBERT The Letters of Gustave Flaubert
WILLIAM GADDIS The Letters of William Gaddis
BENITO PÉREZ GÁLDOS Miaow
MAVIS GALLANT The Uncollected Stories of Mavis Gallant
NATALIA GINZBURG Family *and* Borghesia
JEAN GIONO The Open Road
WILLIAM LINDSAY GRESHAM Nightmare Alley
VASILY GROSSMAN The People Immortal
MARTIN A. HANSEN The Liar
ELIZABETH HARDWICK The Uncollected Essays of Elizabeth Hardwick
GERT HOFMANN Our Philosopher
HENRY JAMES On Writers and Writing
TOVE JANSSON Sun City
ERNST JÜNGER On the Marble Cliffs

MOLLY KEANE Good Behaviour
WALTER KEMPOWSKI An Ordinary Youth
PAUL LAFARGUE The Right to Be Lazy
JEAN-PATRICK MANCHETTE The N'Gustro Affair
JEAN-PATRICK MANCHETTE Skeletons in the Closet
THOMAS MANN Reflections of a Nonpolitical Man
JOHN McGAHERN The Pornographer
EUGENIO MONTALE Butterfly of Dinard
AUGUSTO MONTERROSO The Rest is Silence
ELSA MORANTE Lies and Sorcery
MANUEL MUJICA LÁINEZ Bomarzo
MAXIM OSIPOV Kilometer 101
PIER PAOLO PASOLINI Boys Alive
PIER PAOLO PASOLINI Theorem
KONSTANTIN PAUSTOVSKY The Story of a Life
DOUGLAS J. PENICK The Oceans of Cruelty: Twenty-Five Tales of a Corpse-Spirit, a Retelling
HENRIK PONTOPPIDAN A Fortunate Man
HENRIK PONTOPPIDAN The White Bear *and* The Rearguard
MARCEL PROUST Swann's Way
ALEXANDER PUSHKIN Peter the Great's African: Experiments in Prose
RAYMOND QUENEAU The Skin of Dreams
RUMI Gold; translated by Haleh Liza Gafori
RUMI Water; translated by Haleh Liza Gafori
JOAN SALES Winds of the Night
FELIX SALTEN Bambi; or, Life in the Forest
JONATHAN SCHELL The Village of Ben Suc
ANNA SEGHERS The Dead Girls' Class Trip
VICTOR SERGE Last Times
ELIZABETH SEWELL The Orphic Voice
ANTON SHAMMAS Arabesques
CLAUDE SIMON The Flanders Road
WILLIAM GARDNER SMITH The Stone Face
VLADIMIR SOROKIN Blue Lard
VLADIMIR SOROKIN Red Pyramid: Selected Stories
VLADIMIR SOROKIN Telluria
JEAN STAFFORD Boston Adventure
GEORGE R. STEWART Fire
GEORGE R. STEWART Storm
ADALBERT STIFTER Motley Stones
ITALO SVEVO A Very Old Man
MAGDA SZABÓ The Fawn
ELIZABETH TAYLOR Mrs Palfrey at the Claremont
SUSAN TAUBES Lament for Julia
TEFFI Other Worlds: Peasants, Pilgrims, Spirits, Saints
YŪKO TSUSHIMA Woman Running in the Mountains
LISA TUTTLE My Death
IVAN TURGENEV Fathers and Children
KONSTANTIN VAGINOV Goat Song
PAUL VALÉRY Monsieur Teste
ROBERT WALSER Little Snow Landscape
MARKUS WERNER The Frog in the Throat
EDITH WHARTON Ghosts: Selected and with a Preface by the Author
XI XI Mourning a Breast